1986

LUCREZIA FLORIANI

Lucrezia Floriani

by

George Sand

Translated by Julius Eker

Preface and Foreword
Translated by Betsy Wing

Academy
Chicago
Publishers

Published in 1985 by

Academy Chicago Publishers
425 North Michigan Avenue
Chicago, IL 60611

Printed and bound in the USA

Library of Congress Cataloging in Publication Data

Sand, George, 1804-1876.
   Lucrezia Floriani.

   I. Title.
PQ2407.L913   1985   843'.7   85-3876
ISBN 0-89733-143-5

Introduction

In the spring of 1846, when George Sand was forty-two years old, she had been legally separated for ten years from her husband, Casimir Dudevant, and was living at Nohant, the country estate she had inherited from her grandmother, with her two children, Maurice, then twenty-two years old, and her daughter Solange, eighteen. Frederic Chopin, the Polish composer, lived at Nohant as well: he was then thirty-six years old, and suffering from the disease which was to kill him in three years. He had been Madame Dudevant's guest since they had spent the winter together, with the children, in Majorca in 1838.

By 1846 George Sand's relationship with Chopin had deteriorated badly, and it was in the spring of that year that she began to write *Lucrezia Floriani*. Consequently the novel created a minor scandal: word had gotten out well before publication that the neurotic Prince Karol was obviously Chopin, and that Lucrezia herself was the author, thinly disguised. Chopin had not seemed to recognize himself in parts of the novel which were read aloud to guests at Nohant, and the author stoutly denied that the book was anything but a fabrication. Nevertheless the protagonists were clearly recognizable, and in fact Chopin left Nohant in 1846 because of a quarrel with Maurice, and was never to return.

The appearance of *Lucrezia Floriani* was deplored by George Sand's friends and added fuel to the fires of her enemies, who were legion. Madame Dudevant was, after all, an avowed socialist, a woman who used a man's name, had worn men's clothing, smoked cigars, was separated from her husband, and had had frequent passionate love affairs. She was much admired as a writer, but her life and much of her writing were considered outrageous by the moral and religious standards of the time.

If George Sand's work and personal life upset the French, one can imagine the reaction to both in the England of Victoria and Albert. She was however read in the original by most Victorian writers and especially admired by the Brownings, Charlotte Brontë, George Eliot, Matthew Arnold, John Stuart Mill and Jane Carlyle, although Thomas Carlyle disliked her work intensely, as did John Ruskin. Despite the obviously controversial nature of her work, the first English translation of it appeared in 1842: *Spiridion*, a novel concerned with religion, which had been published in France three years earlier. Thereafter, through the decades, Sand translations appeared of those works, at least, which would not offend the eyes of clergymen and other protectors of the innocent. *Indiana*, published in French in 1832, and concerned with flaming passion outside a loveless marriage, appeared first in English in 1850, not in England but in America.

Despite this rather tepid spate of translations, influential journals thundered from the right against the French writer. Thackeray wrote an article deploring her attitudes toward marriage. It was not until 1902 that many of the novels which scandalized the Victorians (*Indiana, Valentine, Leone Leoni, She and He,* etc.) were finally published in good English translations. And *Lucrezia Floriani,* obviously, was not among them.

And indeed, even in 1902 *Lucrezia* would be a shocking book. An actress, never married, with a family of children with different fathers... a woman from the lower rung of society, whose father lives on her estate... a woman who has a love affair with a nobleman several years her junior... and for whom, despite all this, we must feel respect, sympathy and affection. It was too much. And through all this, the sharp intelligence which watches everyone, and especially Prince Karol, and notes reactions and attitudes with a psychological insight which appears no less admirable today than the day it came first to public notice. A remarkable, and in some ways, a pitiless book.

When society had changed sufficiently so that Madame Dudevant no longer shocked and upset the bourgeoisie, she had come to appear old-fashioned and even unimportant. In the male-oriented establishment of English letters, her obvious influence on some of the greatest English writers was ignored or unknown. It was not until an excellent British television series based on her life was broadcast in the early seventies that people began to hunt her up in libraries (where for the most part she could not be found in English), that feminists rediscovered her, and work was begun to give her her proper place in the history of literature.

Anita Miller

Preface

There is no need for me to state here the literary ideas that influenced me in writing this novel, because it has a foreword summarizing my opinions at the time, and because these opinions have not changed. But I am anxious to be explicit about something I only mentioned in that foreword in regard to contemporary productions whose form I criticized and example I rejected.

It is not false modesty, even less a faint-hearted nature, that makes me say I like romantic events very much in a novel — the unforeseen, intrigue, *action*. For the novel, as for the theatre, I should like someone to find a way to unite dramatic movement with real analysis of characters and human sentiments. Without wishing now either to criticize or praise anyone, it is my opinion that this problem has usually not been completely resolved either for the novel, or for the theatre. For twenty years we have been hesitating between the two extremes, and I have, for my part, liking strong emotions in fiction, nonetheless gone to the other extreme, less through inclination than consciously, because I saw this direction was neglected and abandoned by the current fashion. I tried my hardest, without exaggerating either the weakness or importance of my efforts, to keep the literature of my time on a practicable path between the peaceful lake and the wild torrent. My instinct would have sent me towards abysses. I still sense this in the interest and impetuous eagerness with which my eyes and ears seek out drama; but when I am back once again with my thoughts assuaged and satisfied, I do as all readers and spectators do; I reconsider what I have seen and heard, and ask myself why and how the action moved me and carried me along. Then I notice things that are suddenly implausible or inadequate causes for events driven along before the torrent of imagination, regardless of any obstacle of reason or moral truth. That is the moment an impulse drives me backwards, like many others, back towards the calm, monotonous lake of analysis.

However, I should not like to see my generation forget itself for too long on these still waters and be unaware of the progress that ceaselessly calls it towards new horizons. *Lucrezia Floriani*, this book that is all analysis and meditation, is no more than a relative protest, therefore, against the abuse of forms fashionable at that time, those veritable surprise machines, whose qualities and flaws it seemed to me were confused with each other by a public that used little judgment.

Shall I now say a word about my own work, not about its form, which has all the flaws (admitted in advance) that my plan entailed, but about its content, that inalienable question of intellectual freedom that every reader has always claimed and always will claim the right to dispute? That is exactly what I want to do. Victor Hugo, in the preface to *Orientales*, denying that the public had a right to address its insolent *why* to the poet, and declaring that as regards the choice of subject the author answered only to himself, would certainly be right in the eyes of that superhuman power who sends the poet inspiration without consulting the taste, the customs or the opinions of the century. But the public does not bow to such lofty considerations; he keeps on saying to both great and small: Why are you serving us this dish? What is it made of? Where did you get it? What did you season it with? etc. etc.

Questions like that are pointless, and they are especially awkward; because the instinct that brings a writer to choose some subject or other today that might not have struck him yesterday, is elusive by nature. And if one gave a simple answer, would the public have gotten much farther?

If, for example, I told you what a very great poet told me one day, unaffectedly and even with a playful innocence: all the time there are thousands of subjects surfacing one after the other in my brain: all of them please me for a moment, but I don't stop, knowing that one I am able to treat *will grab hold of me* in a very special way and make me feel the authority it has over my will by indisputable signs.

"What are they?" I asked him with great interest.

"A sort of dizzy spell," he answered, "and my heart's beating as if I were going to faint. When a thought, an image, any old fact, passes through my mind in a way that stirs my physical being, no matter how vaguely, it is this sort of vertigo that lets me know I have to stop there to seek my poem."

So, what would you have to say to this poet? Would he have done better to consult you than to listen to this inner voice that summoned him to obey it?

On a less elevated level of ideas and productions, there is a mysterious attraction that I shall not have the arrogance to call *inspiration*, as it concerns myself, but to which I surrender without wanting to fight when it comes. People who do not create works of imagination believe that they are only made out of memories, and always ask you: "Whom did you mean to portray?" They are very much mistaken if they believe it is possible to make a real person into a character in a novel, even in such an unromantic novel as *Lucrezia Floriani*. One would have to add so much to what is real, in order to make this person logical and defensible in a fictional event, even if it were only for twenty pages, that by the twenty-first one would have stepped out of the resemblance and by the thirtieth, the character you might have claimed to copy would have completely disappeared. What is impossible to accomplish is the analysis of a sentiment. In order for it to make sense to the intelligence, therefore, while passing through the prism of imagination, one must create characters for the sentiment one wishes to describe and not create the sentiment for the characters.

At least that is my procedure, and I have never been able to find any other. A hundred times *subjects* have been proposed for me to treat. Someone would tell me an interesting story, describe the heroes, even show them to me. Yet never has it been possible for me to make use of these precious materials. I was immediately struck by something that all of you must have observed more than once. Which is that there is an obvious, unexplainable, but utterly complete divergence between the behavior of people on the fabulous occasions of life, and the character, the habits, and appearance of these very people. Hence our first reaction, at the sight of someone whose works or deeds have made an impression on us, is to say: I didn't think he looked like that!

Where does that come from? I don't know, nor do you, my friendly readers. But that is how it is, and when we have time we can look for the answer together. As for now, to cut short a preface that is already too long, I only have one word in answer to your usual questions. Examine whether or not the portrait of the passion, which is the subject of this book, has some truth, some depth, I won't say something to teach; it is up to you to find the conclusions, and the writer's only job is to make you reflect. As for the two characters who are sacrificed (both of them) to this terrible passion, make them over again better within yourself, if the author's imagination has badly suited them to the example they ought to provide.

George Sand
Nohant, January 16, 1853

Foreword

My dear reader (an old phrase and the only good one), I am bringing you my new attempt whose form is borrowed from the Greeks at the very least, and which you may not particularly like. Gone are the days when "... kneeling in a humble preface, the author begs the public's pardon." We have definitely cured ourselves of this false modesty since the time when Boileau reported it with no regard for the great men. Today, we are quite cavalier, and if one makes a preface, it is to prove to the dismayed reader that he should respectfully remove his hat to read, admire and keep quiet.

We did well to act like that with you, kind reader, since it worked. You are just as pleased, because you know very well that the author is not so headstrong as he would like to appear, that it is a manner, a style, a way of dressing himself for the role, and that, basically, he is going to give you his best and serve you according to your taste.

Now, you often have extremely bad taste, my good reader. Ever since you have stopped being French, you like everything that is contrary to the French spirit, to French logic, to the old customs of the language, and to events and characters that are clearly and simply inferred. To please you, an author has to be simultaneously as dramatic as Shakespeare, as romantic as Byron, as fantastic as Hoffmann, as frightening as Lewis and Anne Radcliffe, as heroic as Calderon and all of Spanish theatre; and if he contents himself with imitating only one of these models, you think it is pretty colorless.

The result of your reckless appetites is that the school of the novel has rushed headlong into a web of horrors, of murders, betrayals, surprises, terrors, bizarre passions, astounding events; in short, into movement dizzying to good folk who are not sure-footed enough or quick enough at seeing to keep up.

That is what we have done to please you, and if you were given a few slaps as a matter of form, it was a way of holding your attention, in order to gratify you later with the satisfactions you hope for. So never, I say, has any public been more caressed, more flattered, more spoilt than you nowadays, showered by works.

You have forgiven so many impertinences that you will let me get away with one little one; that is to tell you that you are ruining your stomach eating so much spice, that you are wearing out your emotions and exhausting your novelists. You force them to overtax their means and push them to an exhaustion of imagination after which nothing will be possible any more, unless we invent a new language and discover a new race of men. You no longer allow talent to apportion itself and it spares no efforts. One of these mornings, it will have said everything and be forced to repeat. That will bore you, and ungrateful towards your friends as you have always been and will always be, you will forget the marvels of richness and imagination they have made for you and the pleasures they have provided.

Since that's how it is, run for your life! Tomorrow a movement backwards will begin, reaction will set in. My colleagues are dog-tired, I bet, and are going to join forces to demand another sort of work, and salaries less painfully paid for. I feel the storm coming in the air that grows leaden and heavy, and, cautiously, I begin by turning my back on the frenzied stir of rapid change you liked to have mark your literature. I sit by the roadside and watch them all go by: brigands, traitors, gravediggers, stranglers, extortionists, poisoners, cavaliers armed to the teeth, dishevelled women, the whole enraged and bloody troupe of modern drama. I see them, wearing their daggers, their crowns, their beggars' rags, their scarlet cloaks, flinging curses at you and looking for some job in the world other than racing like a horse.

But how shall I start, poor devil that I am, who never attempted or managed to make any innovation in form; so that I won't be swept away in this whirlwind, and yet so I won't find myself too far behind when the new style, still unknown but imminent, lifts its head.

First I'm going to rest and make a quiet little life work, after that we'll see what we see! If the new style is a good one, we shall follow it. But today's is too fantastic, too rich; I am too old to apply myself to it and my means do not allow me to. I shall keep on wearing my grandfather's clothes; they are comfortable, simple and solid.

So, reader, in order to do it the French way like our good ancestors, let me warn you that I am going to cut the main ingredient out of the story I shall have the honor of offering you — the strongest spice around in current use: that is to say, the unforeseen, the surprise. Instead of leading you from one astonishment to the next, instead of making you fall every chapter from fever into sickly heat, I shall lead you step by step down a straight little road, making you look in front, behind, right and left at the bushes in the ditch, the clouds on the horizon, everything that comes into view in the peaceful plains we shall have to travel. If, by chance, there is a ravine, I shall tell you, "Watch out, there's a ravine here"; if there's a torrent, I shall help you get over it, I won't push you into it headfirst for the pleasure of telling others: "That reader certainly got taken in," or the pleasure of hearing you exclaim: "Ouf! I've come a cropper here, I didn't expect that in the least; our author played a good trick on me."

In short, I won't look down on you; I think it would be impossible to do better than that ... And yet, it is highly likely that you will accuse me of being the most insolent and the most presumptuous novelist of all, that you will get angry halfway along, and that you will refuse to follow me.

However you like! Go where you feel like going. I am not annoyed with those who enthrall you by doing the opposite of what I want to do. I don't hate the fashion. Any fashion is good as long as it lasts and suits; it is not possible to judge it until its reign has ended. Divine right is on its side; it is the daugher of the genius of the times: but the world is so large that there is room for all, and the freedoms we enjoy extend even to allowing us to write a bad novel.

GEORGE SAND: CHRONOLOGY

1804
July 1 Birth at 15 Rue de la Meslay, Paris. Daughter of Maurice Dupin and Sophie Delaborde. Christened Amandine Aurore Lucie Dupin.
Family moves to Rue de la Grange-Batelière, Paris.

1808
Aurore travels to Spain with her mother. They join her father at Palace de Goday in Madrid, where he is serving in Napoleon's army under General Murat.

1809
The family goes to Nohant in France, the home of Maurice Dupin's mother, born Marie-Aurore de Saxe, Comtesse de Horn, the daughter of the illegitimate son of King Frederic-Augustus II of Poland. Death of Maurice Dupin in a fall from a horse.

1810
Sophie Dupin gives custody of Aurore to Madame Dupin in return for a pension.

1810-1814
Winters in Paris at Rue Neuve-des-Mathurins with her grandmother and visits from Sophie. Summers at Nohant.

1817-1820
Educated at the English Convent des Augustines in Paris.

1820
Returns to Nohant. Studies with her father's tutor Deschartres.

1821
Death of Madame Dupin. Aurore inherits some money, a house in Paris and the house at Nohant.
Moves in with her mother at 80 Rue St.-Lazare, Paris.

1822
Meets Casimir Dudevant on a visit to the Duplessis family.
September 10 Marries Dudevant, son of Baron Dudevant. They move to Nohant.

1823
June 30 Maurice is born at Hotel de Florence, 56 Rue Neuve-des-Mathurins, Paris.

1824
Spring and summer at the Duplessis' at Plessis-Picard near Melun; autumn at a Parisian suburb, Ormesson; winter in an apartment at Rue du Faubourg-Saint-Honoré.

1825
Spring at Nohant. Aurore is ill in the summer. Dudevants travel to his family home in Gascony. She meets Aurélian de Sèze, and recovers her health.
November 5 Writes long confession to Casimir about de Sèze. She gives him up.
Winter in Gascony.

1826
Moves to Nohant. Casimir travels, Aurore manages the estate and writes to de Sèze.

1827
Illness again. The water cure at Clermont-Ferraud, where she writes *Voyage En Auvergne,* autobiographical sketch.

1827-1829
Winter at Le Châtre. Summer at Nohant.

1828
September 13 Birth of Solange.

1830
Visit to Bordeaux to Aurélian de Sèze. Their correspondence ceases. She writes a novel *Aimée*.
December Discovery of Casimir's will, filled with antipathy to her.

1831
January 4 Moves to Paris to 31 Rue de Seine.
Joins staff of *Le Figaro*. Writes three short stories: *La Molinara* (in *Figaro*); *La Prima Donna* (in *Revue de Paris)* and *La Fille d'Albano* (in *La Mode*).
April Returns to Nohant for three months. Writes *Indiana*.
July Moves to 25 Quai Saint-Michel, Paris.
December Publishes *Rose Et Blanche* in collaboration with Jules Sandeau. Book is signed Jules Sand.

1832
Travel between Paris and Nohant.
April Solange is brought to Paris.
November Move to 19 Quai Malaquais with Solange.
Indiana and *Valentine* published. Maurice sent by Casimir to Henry IV Military Academy in Paris.

1833
January Break with Sandeau.
June Meets Alfred de Musset.
Publishes *Lelia*.
September Fontainebleau with de Musset.
December 12 To Italy with de Musset.

1834

January 19 The Hotel Danieli in Venice. Musset attempts a break with Aurore, becomes ill. His physician is Pietro Pagello.

March 29 de Musset returns to Paris. Aurore remains with Pagello.

Writes *André, Mattéa, Jacques, Léone Léoni* and the first *Lettres d'Un Voyageur*.

August 15 Return to Paris with Pagello.

August 24 de Musset goes to Baden.

August 29 Aurore to Nohant.

October Return to Paris. Musset return from Baden. Pagello returns to Venice.

November 25 Begins journal to de Musset.

December Return to Nohant.

1835

January Return to Paris.

March 6 Final break with Musset.

Meets Michel of Bourges, her lawyer and political mentor. Writes *Simon*.

Autumn Return to Nohant for Maurice's holiday.

October 19 Casimir threatens her physically. Begins suit for legal separation.

December 1 Judgment in her favor won by default.

1836

February 16 She wins second judgment. Casimir bring suit.

May 10, 11 Another verdict in her favor from civil court of La Châtre. Casimir appeals to a higher court.

July 25, 26 Trial in royal court of Bourges. Jury divided. Out of court settlement. Her fortune is divided with Casimir.

August To Switzerland with Maurice and Solange and Liszt and d'Agoult.

Autumn Hotel de la France, 15 Rue Lafitte, Paris with Liszt and d'Agoult. Meets Chopin.

1837

January Return to Nohant. Publishes *Mauprat* in spring. Writes *Les Maitres Mosaïstes*. Liszt and d'Agoult visit Nohant. Fatal illness of Sophie in Paris. Visit to Fontaine-bleau, writes *La Dernière Aldini*. Trip to Gascony to recover Solange, who has been kidnapped by Casimir.

1838

Writes *L'Orco* and *L'Uscoque*, two Venetian novels.
May To Paris. Romance with Chopin.
November Trip to Majorca with children and Chopin. Writes *Spiridion*.

1839

February Leaves Majorca for three months in Marseilles. Then to Nohant. Publishes *Un Hiver À Majorque, Pauline* and *Gabriel-Gabrielle*.
October Occupies adjoining apartments with Chopin until spring of 1841 at 16 Rue Pigalle, Paris, in winter. Summer is spent at Nohant with Chopin as guest.

1840

Writes *Compagnon Du Tour De France* and *Horace*. Influenced by Pierre Leroux.

1841

Moves from Rue Pigalle to 5 and 9 Rue St.-Lazare, Square d'Orléans, with Chopin.

1842

Consuelo published.

1843

La Comtesse De Rudolstadt published, a sequel to *Consuelo*.

1844

Jeanne published, a foreshadowing of pastoral novels.

1845
Tévérino, Pêché de M. Antoine and *Le Meunier D'Angibault,* the latter two socialist novels.

1846
La Mare Au Diable published and *Lucrezia Floriani.* Solange married to Auguste-Jean Clésinger. Estrangement from Chopin.

1847
François Le Champi published.

1848
Writes government circulars, contributes to *Bulletins de la Republique* and publishes her own newspaper *La Cause du Peuple,* all for the Second Republic. Death of Solange's son. *La Petite Fadette* published.

1849
Her play based on *François Le Champi* performed at the Odéon. First of a series of successful plays.

1850
Chateau des Désertes published in the *Revue Des Deux Mondes.*

1851
Republic falls. She uses her influence to save her friends from political reprisals. Plays *Claudie* and *Le Mariage De Victorine* presented.

1852
Return to Nohant.

1853
Published *Les Maitres Sonneurs.* Play *Le Pressoir* presented.

1855
Four volume autobiography *Histoire De Ma Vie* published, carries her life to Revolution of 1848.
January 13 Death of Solange's daughter Jeanne.
Visit to Italy with Maurice and Alexandre Manceau.

1856
Does French adaptation of *As You Like It*.

1858
Holidays at Gargilesse on River Creuse at cottage given her by Alexander Manceau.

1859
Writes *Elle Et Lui*. Publishes *Jean De La Roche* and *L'Homme De Neige*.

1860
Writes *La Ville Noire* and *Marquis De Villemer*.
November Contracts typhoid fever.

1862
May 16 Marriage of Maurice Sand and Caroline Calametta.

1863
July 14 Marc-Antoine Sand born, son of Maurice and Caroline.
Mademoiselle La Quintinie published, anti-clerical novel.
Begins friendship with Flaubert.

1864
Play *Le Marquis De Villemer* presented. Death of Marc-Antoine Sand. Moves from 3 Rue Racine near the Odéon to 97 Rue des Feuillantines. Exchanges Gargilesse for a house at Palaiseau with Manceau.

1865
Death of Manceau.

1866
Visits Flaubert at Croisset, dedicates *Le Dernier Amour* to him. Birth of Aurore Sand.

1867
Return to Nohant to live with Maurice and Caroline. Writes two novels a year.

1868
Birth of Gabrielle Sand.

1870
The play *L'Autre* with Sarah Bernhardt, presented at the Theatre Francais.

1870-1871
Franco-German War. Removal to Boussac because of a small-pox epidemic at Nohant.

1876
June 8 Dies.

1.

Young Prince Karol de Roswald had just lost his mother when he first met Madame Floriani.

He was still plunged in utter grief and nothing could distract him from it. Princess de Roswald had been a tender and perfect mother. As a child Karol was weak and ailing and she had lavished on him the most constant care and devotion. Brought up under the eye of this good and noble woman the young man had only one real passion in his entire life: filial love. This mutual love between son and mother had made them as it were exclusive, and possibly a little too absolute in their way of seeing and feeling things. It must be said that the Princess was highly educated and possessed a superior mind; the lessons she gave him and her conversations with him seemed capable of satisfying every one of young Karol's needs. His delicate health had resisted the toil, rigour and harshness of classical studies which in themselves are not always as valuable as the lessons of an enlightened mother, but they have the indispensable merit of teaching us to work and are, so to speak, the key to knowledge of life. Acting on the advice of her son's doctors Princess de Roswald had dismissed the idea both of tutors and books and had resolved to form the mind and heart of her son by her conversation, by the stories she narrated, by a kind of *insufflation* of his moral being which the young man had absorbed with great delight. Thus he had succeeded in acquiring much knowledge without ever having studied anything.

But nothing can replace experience; and the box on the ear which, when I was a child, was given to youngsters to impress on their memories a great emotion, a historical fact, a notorious crime or any other example to follow or avoid, was not so stupid a practice as it appears to us nowadays. We no longer give this box on the ear to our children; they have to seek it elsewhere, and the heavy hand of experience applies it much more harshly than ours would.

So young Karol de Roswald became acquainted with people and life early, possibly too early, – but only in theory.

With the praiseworthy object of elevating his mind his mother only allowed the proximity of distinguished people, whose words and actions could only be salutary to him. He was fully aware that outside there existed knaves and fools, but he was only taught to avoid them, never to get to know them. Of course he had learned to succour the unfortunate; the doors of the palace where he spent his youth were always open to the needy; but while helping them he grew accustomed to despising the cause of their condition and regarding it as an affliction of humanity which was incurable. Disorderliness, idleness, ignorance or lack of judgement, – the fatal causes of aberration and destitution – struck him as being obviously beyond remedy in the individual. He had not been taught to believe that the masses must and can gradually rid themselves of these ills and that by grappling with humanity, chiding and caressing it in turn, like a beloved child, by forgiving it for many lapses so as to gain some little progress, one does more for it than by dropping the limited succour of compassion before its crippled or gangrened limbs.

But it was not so in Karol's case. He learned that the giving of alms was a duty; and one which no doubt will have to be performed as long as the social order makes alms necessary. But this is only one of the duties imposed on us by our concern for this immense human family of ours. There are many others, the principal one being not to pity but to love. He fervently embraced the maxim which told him to detest evil; but he clung to the letter of the law and merely pitied those who commit evil.

But again it must be said: pity is not enough. Above all one must love in order to be just and not to despair of the future. One must not be too delicate in one's sensibilities, nor be lulled to sleep by the flattery of a clear, self-satisfied conscience. This good young man was sufficiently warmhearted not to enjoy his wealth without a feeling of guilt when he remembered that the majority of men lack the necessities of life; but he never applied this pity to the moral destitution of his fellows. He did not possess sufficient mental enlightenment to tell himself that vice can rebound on the innocent, too, and that to wage war on the ills of mankind is the foremost duty of those who have not been afflicted by them.

On the one hand he saw innate aristocracy, distinction of intelligence, purity of morals and nobility of instincts, and he said to himself "Let me be with them." On the other hand he saw degradation, baseness, mental instability, but he did not say "Let me join them, to redeem them, if possible." No, he had been taught to say "They are doomed. Let us give them food and clothes, but let us not compromise ourselves by contact with them. They are hardened and sullied; let us abandon their souls to the mercy of God."

In the long run this habit of self-preservation becomes a kind of egoism and there was indeed a hint of coldness hidden in the princess' heart. She employed it on her son's account far more than for herself. Skilfully, she isolated him from young men of his own age when once she suspected they were irresponsible or merely frivolous. She feared associations for him with natures which were different from his; yet it is this contact which makes us men, gives us strength and results in the fact that instead of being led astray from the very outset, we can resist the example of evil and retain the power to bring about the triumph of good.

Without being narrowly and aggressively devout, the princess was somewhat rigid in her piety. A sincere and staunch Catholic, she was not blind to certain abuses, but she knew of no other remedy than to tolerate them for the sake of the great cause of the Church. "The Pope may err," she would say, "he is a man; but the Papacy cannot fail; it is a divine institution." As a result, her mind was hardly receptive to ideas on human progress and her son soon learned not to

question them and to refuse to hope that the salvation of the
human race could be accomplished on earth. Without being as
punctual as his mother in the performance of his religious
duties (for in spite of everything the youth of to-day soon
bursts such bonds) he remained an adherent of the doctrine
which saves men of good will and is unable to destroy the ill
will of the rest; which is content with a few chosen and is
reconciled to the sight of the many called falling into the
Gehenna of eternal evil: a sad and dismal belief which agrees
perfectly with the concept of nobility and the privileges of
fortune. In heaven as on earth, paradise for the few, hell for the
majority. Glory, happiness and rewards for the exceptions;
shame, abjectness and chastisement for nearly all.

When characters which are naturally kind and noble fall
into this error, they are punished for it by being eternally sad.
It is only the insensitive and the stupid who resign themselves
to the inevitable. The Princess de Roswald suffered for this
Catholic fatalism whose cruel decrees she could not shake off.
She had acquired a habit of solemn and sententious gravity
which she gradually communicated to her son, inwardly if not
outwardly. Thus it was that young Karol knew nothing of the
gaiety, the abandon, the blind beneficent confidence of
childhood. Indeed, he had had no childhood; his thoughts
turned towards melancholy, and even when he came to the age
of being romantic, his imagination was nourished only by
gloomy and mournful novels.

Yet in spite of the false track that it was pursuing the spirit
of Karol was by nature delightful. Gentle, sensitive, exquisite
in all things, at the age of fifteen he had all the graces of
adolescence combined with the gravity of maturity. He
remained physically delicate, as he was spiritually. But this
very absence of muscular development had the advantage of
preserving in him a charming beauty, an exceptional
physiognomy which, so to speak, was without age or sex. It did
not have the boldness and virility of one descended from that
race of ancient grandees who knew of nothing but drinking,
hunting and fighting; nor was it the effeminate prettiness of a
pink cherub. It was something like those ideal beings created
by the poetic imagination of the Middle Ages to adorn

Christian places of worship: an angel with the beautiful face of a sad woman, tall, perfect and slim of figure like a young Olympian god, and to add to all this, an expression both tender and severe, chaste yet ardent.

And in that lay the very root of his nature. Nothing was purer yet more impassioned than his thoughts; nothing was more tenacious, more exclusive and more scrupulously devoted than his affections. If one could have forgotten the existence of the human race and believed that it had been concentrated and personified in a single being, he was the one whom one would have adored over the ruins of the world.

But this being had insufficient contact with his fellows. He only understood what was identical with himself; his mother, whose pure, brilliant reflection he was; God, of whom he had a strange conception, appropriate to his particular kind of mind, and finally the vision of a woman whom he had created in his own image, whom he had not yet met, but would love one day.

All else only existed for him in a kind of wearisome dream from which he tried to escape by living alone in the midst of the world. Forever lost in his reveries, he had no sense of reality. As a child, he could not go near a sharp instrument without cutting himself; when he grew up he could not face a man different from himself without coming into painful collision with this living contradiction of himself.

What saved him from perpetual antagonism was the deliberate and later confirmed habit of not seeing or hearing anything which broadly displeased him. People who did not think as he did became like phantoms to him and as he was always charmingly polite, the cold disdain or even unconquerable aversion he really felt could be easily mistaken for courtesy and amiability.

It is very strange that with such a character the young prince could have any friends at all. Yet he did have some, not only his mother's who esteemed him as the worthy son of a noble man, but also young men of his own age, who loved him ardently and who thought themselves loved by him. He himself thought he loved them greatly, but it was with his imagination rather than his heart. He possessed a high conception of friendship, and at the age of youth's illusions he was apt to think that his friends and he, reared in the same manner and with the same principles, would never change their opinions and would never reach a situation in which they would find themselves in positive disagreement.

This did happen, however, and at twenty-four, which was his age when his mother died, he had already grown weary of nearly all of them. One only had remained very faithful to him, and that was a young Italian, somewhat older than himself, noble of features and generous of heart; ardent, enthusiastic. Very different in all other aspects from Karol, he had at least two things in common with him, namely, a passionate love for beauty in art and a devotion to the knightly ideal of loyalty. This friend it was who dragged him away from his mother's grave and carried him off to the bracing skies of Italy. Here, introduced by this friend, the prince saw Madame Floriani for the first time.

2.

You may indeed ask "Who is this Madame Floriani twice mentioned in the previous chapter, yet without moving a single step in her direction?"

I beg my reader to be patient. Just as I am about to knock at my heroine's door I realise that I have not yet made you sufficiently acquainted with my hero and that there are still certain tedious facts which I must ask you to accept.

There is nobody with a greater sense of urgency and impatience than the reader of novels; but that is a matter of indifference to me. I have a complete man to reveal to you, that is, a world, an ocean boundless in its contradictions, diversities, heights and depths, logic and inconsistency, and you expect a single small chapter to be sufficient for that! By no means. I cannot do justice to it without entering into some detail and I shall take my time. If this wearies you, omit, and if, later, you make nothing of his behaviour, the fault will be yours, not mine.

The man whom I introduce to you is himself, and no other. I cannot make you understand him by telling you that he was young, handsome, well proportioned and well bred. All heroes in novels are so, and mine is a being whom I know thoroughly in my thoughts since, whether he is real or fictitious, I am attempting to portray him. He has a very specific character and one cannot apply to the instincts of a man the standard words used by naturalists to describe the perfume of a plant or a mineral by saying that this being exhales an aroma *sui generis*.

This *sui generis* explains nothing and I maintain that Prince de Roswald possessed a character *sui generis* which it *is* possible to explain.

In consequence of his good education and his natural grace, he was so affectionate externally, that he had the gift of pleasing even those who did not know him well. His charming face predisposed one in his favour; his physical frailty made him interesting in the eyes of women; the richness and ease of his intellectual gifts, the suave and attractive originality of his conversation, won him the attention of educated men. As for those of lesser metal, they liked his exquisite politeness and they were all the more appreciative of it as they could not imagine, in their simple goodheartedness, that he was merely performing a duty and that sympathy did not enter into it at all.

Had people been able to penetrate his character they would have said that he was more lovable than loving and as far as they were concerned this would have been the truth. But how could they have guessed it when his rare attachments were so intense, so deep and so unshakable?

And so he was always loved if not with the certainty, at least with the hope of some return of affection. His young companions when they saw him feeble and lethargic in the performance of physical exercises, did not dream of despising this rather frail person, because Karol did not set great store by his own performance in this respect. When he sat down quietly on the grass, in the midst of their games, he would say to them with a sad smile, "Enjoy yourselves, dear friends, I can neither wrestle nor run. You will come and rest by my side," and as the strong are the natural protectors of the weak, it sometimes happened that the sturdiest generously abandoned their energetic sport to come and keep him company.

Among all those who were fascinated and as it were spellbound by the poetic colouring of his thoughts and the grace of his mind Salvator Albani was the most steadfast. This excellent young man was frankness itself, yet Karol exercised such influence over him that he dared not contradict him openly, even when he observed exaggeration in his principles and eccentricity in his behaviour. He was afraid of displeasing him and seeing him grow cool towards him, as had happened to so many others. He tended him like a child when Karol, not so much ill as highly strung and over-sensitive, withdrew to his room to conceal his indisposition from his mother's eyes, because it distressed her too much. Thus Salvator Albani had become necessary to the young prince. And Salvator sensed this, so that when youth and its passions urged him to amuse himself elsewhere he sacrificed his pleasures or hid them from his friend, saying to himself that if Karol happened to cease loving him, he would no longer tolerate his attentions and would decline into a solitude, deliberate and fatal.

So Salvator loved Karol on account of the need the latter had of him and, out of a strange kind of pity, he became the flatterer of his theories, however wrong-headed and extravagant. He admired stoicism with him, though fundamentally he was what is known as an epicurean. Tired by some escapade of the previous night he would read an ascetic volume kept by his bedside. He became innocently enthusiastic when his young friend depicted the sole, exclusive, undying, limitless love which was to fill his life. He regarded that as truly magnificent, and yet he himself could not live without love affairs and had to hide the number of his adventures from Karol.

This innocent pretence could only continue for a limited time, and Karol gradually discovered with sorrow that his friend was no saint. But by the time he learned the painful truth, Salvator had become so necessary to him and he had been obliged to recognise in him so many outstanding qualities of mind and heart, that he would do nothing but continue to love him, to be sure much less than before, but still sufficiently not to be able to dispense with him. However, he could never reconcile himself to the youthful escapades of his friend and his affection for him, instead of alleviating his habitual sadness became as painful as an open wound.

Salvator, who feared the sternness of Princess de Roswald even more than that of Karol, concealed from her as long as possible what Karol had discovered with so much horror. The long painful illness to which she finally succumbed also contributed towards making her less clear-sighted during the

last years of her life; and when Karol saw her cold on her
deathbed, he fell into such overwhelming despair that Salvator
resumed all his influence over him and was the only being
capable of making him abandon the intention of allowing
himself to die.

This was the second time that Karol saw death strike down
someone close to him. He had loved a girl whom he had
intended to marry. That was the only romance of his life, and
we shall speak of it in due course. There was nothing left for
him to love save Salvator. He did love him; but always with
reservations, with pain, and a kind of bitterness, when he
thought that his friend was incapable of being as unhappy as
he was.

Six months after the second catastrophe, undoubtedly the
more cruel and real of the two, Prince de Roswald was
traversing Italy in a post-chaise, carried along by his
enterprising friend in a whirlwind of hot dust. Salvator had a
need for pleasure and gaiety, yet he sacrificed everything for
the sake of the one whom others referred to as "his spoilt
child". "Say my *dearest* child," he would reply. "For however
cherished Roswald has been by his mother and me, neither his
heart nor his character have been spoiled. He has become
neither exacting, nor despotic, nor ungrateful, nor capricious.
He is appreciative of the slightest attentions, and is more
grateful than he need be for my devotion."

This was a generous admission, but it was true. Karol had
no small defects. He had only one – large, unintentional and
fatal: mental intolerance. He was incapable of opening the
floodgates of compassion fully, in general charity, when
judging things human. He was one of those who believe that
virtue consists in abstaining from evil and who do not
understand the most sublime message of the Gospel (which
they incidentally profess to the letter) and that is the love of
the repentant sinner which creates more joy in Heaven than
the perseverance of a hundred just men, and the faith in the
return of the lost sheep; in short, the very spirit of Jesus which
is evident in all His teaching and pervades all He says: namely,
that he who loves is greater, even if he strays, than the one who
walks undeviating along a cold, lonely path.

In daily life Karol behaved with the greatest charm; all forms of kindness assumed unusual grace with him and when he expressed his gratitude it was with a deep emotion which repaid friendship with interest. Even in his grief, which seemed eternal and of which he refused to foresee the end, he bore a semblance of resignation, as if he had yielded to Salvator's wish to keep him alive.

The fact is that his delicate health was not deeply affected and his life was not threatened by any serious decline; but the habit of languishing and never testing his strength had given him the belief that he would not long survive his mother. He was ready to imagine that he felt himself dying every day and, with this thought in mind, he accepted Salvator's attentions and concealed from him, how little, according to his judgement, remained of the time during which he could take advantage of his solicitude. He had much fortitude and if he did not accept the idea of an early death with the heroic unconcern of youth, he at least cherished the expectation of it with something of a mixture of bitterness and pleasure.

In this conviction he detached himself more and more each day from humanity, of which he believed he no longer formed part. All the wickedness that existed on this earth became remote to him. Apparently, so he thought, God had not given him the mission of being perturbed by it and combating it, since He had measured out to him so few days on this earth. He regarded this as a favour granted to the virtues of his mother, and when he saw the suffering which was part of the punishment for men's sins, he thanked Heaven for granting him that suffering which would purify and absolve him from all the blemishes of original sin. At such times he leapt forward in imagination towards the other world and was lost in mysterious dreams. Basically all this was a synthesis of Catholic dogma; but in the details it was his poet's fancy which was giving itself free rein. For it must be said that if his instincts and principles of behaviour were absolute, his religious beliefs were very vague, and this was the effect of an education entirely consisting of emotion and inspiration, where the arid work of examination, the rights of reason and logic – that guiding thread through the labyrinth – counted for nothing at all.

As he had not pursued and developed any course of study on his own, there were great gaps in his mind which his mother had filled, as best she could, by invoking the impenetrable wisdom of God and the insufficiency granted to men. That, too, was Catholic teaching. Younger and more of an artist than his mother, Karol had idealised his own ignorance; he had, so to speak, furnished the frightful void with romantic ideas; angels, stars, a sublime flight through space, an unknown place where his soul would repose side by side with that of his mother and his betrothed. So much for Paradise. As for Hell, he could not believe in it; but unwilling to deny its existence, he did not think about it. He felt pure and full of trust as far as concerned himself. If he had been driven to say where he relegated guilty souls, he would have sited their torments amid the turbulent waves of the sea, in the storm on high places, in the sinister noises of autumn nights, in eternal unrest. The misty, insinuating poetry of Ossian had been his companion together with the Rite of Rome.

The firm, open hand of Salvator dared not test all the strings of this subtle and complicated instrument. Therefore he could not fully realise the extent to which this exceptional being was both strong and weak, immense and incomplete, terrible and exquisite, tenacious and unstable. If in order to love him he would have had to know him completely, he would have abandoned the task very quickly, for one requires a whole lifetime to understand such natures; and even then one only succeeds, through endless study and patience, in ascertaining the mechanism of their intimate lives. The cause of their contradictions always escapes us.

One day, as they were going from Milan to Venice, they found themselves not far from a lake which sparkled in the setting sun like a diamond in the green landscape.

"Let us go no further to-day," said Salvator, who had observed signs of fatigue on the face of his young friend. "Our daily journeys are too long, and we exhausted ourselves, both body and mind, yesterday, admiring Lake Como."

"Ah, I don't regret it," replied Karol. "It is the most beautiful spectacle I have seen in my whole life. But let us spend the night where you wish. It is of little importance."

"That depends on your state. Shall we proceed to the next stage or would you prefer to make a little detour and go as far as Iseo, on the edge of the little lake? How do you feel?"

"Indeed, I don't know."

"You never know. It is enough to drive one to desperation. Tell me, are you in pain?"

"I don't believe so."

"But are you tired?"

"Yes, but no more than ordinarily."

"Well, let us go to Iseo; the air there will be milder than up here."

So they made their way towards the little harbour of Iseo. There had been a festival in the neighbourhood. Carts, harnessed with lean sturdy ponies, were returning home with girls in their Sunday best, their coiled hair pierced with long silver pins and crowned with real flowers. The men were riding on horses or donkeys, or simply walking. The entire road was covered with the merry crowd, happy women and men a little over-excited by wine and love who were shouting and exchanging laughter and broad remarks, too broad for the chaste ears of Prince Karol.

In all countries the peasant who speaks as he feels and does not change his simple manner of expressing himself, has both wit and originality. Salvator, who did not miss a single pun of the dialect they spoke, could not refrain from smiling at the swift sallies which were flung from one side of the road to the other, as the post-chaise passed between them, slowly descending a steep slope in the direction of the lake. Those beautiful women in their beribboned carts, those dark eyes, those floating kerchiefs, that fragrance of flowers, the red sunset in the background and the bold words uttered in fresh ringing voices, put him in excellent Italian humour. Had he been alone he would not have needed much time to seize the bridle of one of the little horses and slip into the cart adorned by the prettiest women. But the presence of his friend compelled him to be grave and, to distract himself from his temptations, he began to hum between his teeth. This expedient was of no avail, for he soon realised that in spite of himself he was repeating a dance tune which he had picked up out of the air from a bevy of village girls who were humming it as a souvenir of the festivity.

3.

Salvator managed to maintain an air of cool composure until a tall brunette, riding astride her horse not far from their carriage, displayed with rather excessive self-satisfaction her firm, rounded leg topped by a pretty garter. It was impossible for him not to utter an exclamation and lean his head out of the window in order to pursue the sight of this strong, shapely leg.

"Has she fallen, then?" said the prince, noticing his concern.

"She? Don't you mean what?" answered the young fool. And he went on: "Aren't you referring to the garter?"

"Garter? I am talking about the woman who rode past. What are you looking at?"

"Nothing, nothing," replied Salvator who had been unable to resist raising his travelling cap in salute to the leg. "In this land of polite manners one should always keep one's head uncovered." And as he flung himself back into the rear of the coach he added: "A vivid pink garter edged with bright blue is very fetching."

Karol's vocabulary was by no means prudish; he made no comment, but looked at the sparkling lake which shone with colours certainly far more splendid than those of a country girl's garter.

Salvator understood his silence and, as if to excuse himself, asked his friend if he were not struck by the beauty of the human race in this region.

"Yes," replied Karol, with the intention of being agreeable.

"I have noticed that the human form around here is of a sculptural type. But you know that I am no connoisseur."

"I deny it; you have an admirable understanding of what is beautiful, and I have seen you in ecstasy over ancient statuary."

"One moment! There is ancient and ancient; I love the fine, pure, elegant ideal of the Parthenon. But I do not like or at least I don't understand the heavy-muscled Roman art and the bold lines of the decadence. This country is inclined towards materialism, the race smacks of it. I am not interested in it."

"What? In all honesty, doesn't the sight of a beautiful woman delight your eyes, even for a moment, when she passes?"

"As far as I am concerned, I have accepted your easy, trite admiration for all women who pass you, however slight their pretensions to beauty. You are eager to fall in love, yet the one who is to gain possession of your being has not appeared hitherto. Doubtless, the woman God has created for you exists; she is waiting for you and you are seeking her. That is how I explain your senseless loves, your brusque bouts of disgust, and all those tortures of the soul which you call your pleasures. But, as for me, you know that I did meet my life's companion, you are aware that I learnt to know her well, you know that I shall always love her dead, as I have loved her alive. As nothing can resemble her, as nobody can remind me of her, I do not look nor do I search. I have no need to admire what exists outside the image which I carry in my thoughts, eternally perfect, eternally living."

Salvator was inclined to contradict his friend, but he was afraid of seeing him grow heated over such a subject and summoning a feverish strength for the ensuing discussion which he dreaded more for him than the languor of fatigue. He contented himself with asking him if he was absolutely certain never to love another woman.

"As God Himself could not possibly create another being as perfect as the one He, in His infinite mercy, had intended for me, He will not permit me to stray so far as to attempt to love a second time."

"Life is long, however," said Salvator in a tone of

involuntary doubt, "and that kind of oath cannot be made at the age of twenty-four."

"One isn't always young at the age of twenty-four," replied Karol, then he sighed and sank into a thoughtful silence. Salvator saw that he had aroused the idea of premature death which nourished his friend like a kind of poison. He pretended not to read his mind on that point, and tried to distract him by pointing out the pretty valley which surrounded the lake.

There is nothing imposing about the aspect of the small lake of Iseo, and its approaches are as gentle and cool as an eclogue of Virgil. Between the mountains which form its horizon and the slow, lazy ripples which the breeze traces on its banks there is a zone of lush fields literally spangled with the most beautiful meadow-flowers which Lombardy produces. Carpets of saffron of the purest pink strew its shores and even on stormy days, no waves roar in anger. Light rustic boats glide over its calm waters where the peach and almond shed their petals.

At the moment when the two young travellers alighted from their carriage, several boats were untying their mooring ropes; and the inhabitants of the lakeside parishes whom their mounts and carts had brought home from the festival dashed forward, laughing and singing, on to the small boats which were to make a tour of the lake and drop each group at its own home. Carts laden with children and noisy girls were pushed on to the bigger boats; young couples leaped into the smaller ones and challenged each other to a race. In accordance with local custom, to prevent the sweating, steaming horses from catching a chill during the crossing, they were plunged beforehand into the icy water near the shore, and these brave animals seemed to derive great pleasure from their immersion.

Karol sat down on a tree-stump by the water's edge to contemplate not the lively picturesque scene, but the vague pale blue horizon of the Alps. Salvator had entered the *locanda* to choose their rooms.

But he soon returned with a vexed look on his face. The hostelry was abominable, hot, filthy, over-crowded with animals and quarrelling drunkards. There was no possibility of resting there after the fatigues of a day's travel.

Although a bad night distressed him more than it would do anyone else, the prince usually accepted that kind of annoyance with stoic unconcern. This time, however, he said to his friend with an air of unusual anxiety: "I had a presentiment that we would do better not to come and spend the night here."

"A presentiment in connection with an inferior inn?" cried Salvator, slightly irritated with himself and therefore with his companion, because of the failure of his idea. "Upon my word, when it is a matter of avoiding the vermin of a filthy *locanda* and the stench of an unsightly kitchen, I confess that I have none of these subtle perceptions and mysterious forebodings."

"Don't mock me, Salvator," the prince resumed in a gentle tone. "It is not a question of that kind of triviality and you know full well that I bow to the inevitable more readily than you."

"Ah! Perhaps it is because of you that I do not accept the inevitable."

"I know, my good Salvator; don't distress yourself; let us leave."

"What? Leave? We are hungry and at least there are some magnificent trout leaping in the frying pan. I don't allow myself to be discouraged so quickly; let us sup first, let them serve us out there, in the open air under the carob trees. And then I shall scour the entire village and I am sure I shall find a house a little cleaner than the inn, at least a room for you, even if it is at the local doctor's or lawyer's. Surely there is a priest living here."

"My friend, you refuse to understand me; you concern yourself with childish things. . . . You know that I do not indulge in idle fancies, don't you? Well, just this once forgive me if I have a strange whim. I feel ill at ease here; the air makes me apprehensive, the lake is too dazzling. Perhaps some poisonous plant grows here which is fatal to me. . . . Let us go and spend the night elsewhere. I have a grave foreboding that I ought not to have come here. When the horses forsook the road to Venice and turned left it seemed to me as if they were resisting; didn't you notice it? And so, do not think that I have been struck by madness and do not look at me in that frightened manner. I am calm, I am resigned, if you wish, to fresh misfortunes ... but to what purpose should we brave them when there is still time to flee them?"

Salvator Albani was indeed frightened at the serious tone of conviction with which Karol had uttered these strange words. As he thought him weaker than he actually was, he imagined that he was about to fall seriously ill and that a secret uneasiness was warning him of it. But he did not think that the place entered into it at all, when nature, the human race, the sky, vegetation – everything around him was so luxuriant. However, he did not wish to come into conflict with his caprice, but he did wonder whether an additional journey, taken when he had had no food and moreover after a long day's travel, would not precipitate the illness.

The prince saw his hesitation and remembered what the kind-hearted Salvator had already forgotten, namely, that he was starving. Whereupon sacrificing his extreme repugnance and silencing his imagination, he asserted that he was hungry himself, and that before leaving Iseo, they must at least have supper.

This compromise reassured Salvator somewhat. "If he is hungry," he thought, "he cannot be under the threat of imminent illness and possibly the feeling of distress which seized him is the result of an excessive hunger of which he was unaware, a kind of moral and physical faintness. Let us eat, then we shall see."

The supper was better than the inn had seemed to promise and it was served in the innkeeper's garden, in a cool arbour which somewhat obscured the brilliance of the lake and where Karol really felt more calm. Thanks to the mobility of his temperament and mood, he enjoyed his meal and forgot the inexplicable dread which had overcome him only a few moments earlier.

While their host was serving them with coffee, Salvator questioned him about the inhabitants of the town, and was chagrined to find that he did not know a single one of them, and that there was hardly any method of going to ask for hospitality in a house which was cleaner and quieter than the *locanda*. "Ah," said he, sighing, "I once had a very good friend

who came from these regions and who had spoken to me about
them so much that perhaps it influenced me unwittingly when
the whim occurred to me to pass the night here. But I see quite
clearly that my poor Floriani had retained a memory of it
utterly devoid of reality. It is always so with our childhood
memories."

"Doubtless," said the landlord who had been listening to
Salvator's words, "Your Excellency is speaking of the famous
Floriani, the one who, born as a poor peasant girl, became rich
and famous throughout Italy."

"Indeed I am," cried Salvator. "Is it possible that you knew
her in the old days here? – for to my knowledge she never
returned to her native village since she left it at an early age."

"Excuse me, Your Lordship, she came back about a year ago
and she is here at the present moment. Her family have
forgiven everything and they live on the best of terms together
now. Look, over there, on the far side of the lake! You can see
the cottage where she was reared from here, and the pretty
villa which she bought alongside it. With the park and the
meadows they both make a single property. Oh, it's a fine
estate and she paid cash down for it! To old Ranieri, you
know . . . the miser, the father of the man who took her away,
the father of her first lover."

"You know or pretend to know more than I do about the
adventures of her youth," replied Salvator. "I only know one
thing about her, and that is that she is the kindest, worthiest
and most intelligent woman I have met. Thank Heaven! Is she
here then? What wonderful news! We are saved, Karol. We
shall go and ask her for shelter and if you wish to be kind to
me, you will make the acquaintance of my dear Floriani with a
good grace. But nobody in Milan knows that she is living
hereabouts. They told me that I would find her in Venice or its
vicinity."

"Oh, she lives almost hidden from the eyes of the world,"
said the host. "Such is her whim at the moment. However, she
is well known here, for she does much good. She is very good,
the Signora."

"Quick, then, a boat, quick," cried Salvator jumping for joy.
"Ah, what a pleasant surprise! And there was I without the

slightest sense of happy presentiment that I should find her here."

This word startled Karol. "Presentiments," said he, "act on us without our knowledge and drive us where they will."

But the irrepressible Albani would not listen. He went back and forth, he shouted, he had a boat brought up, he flung a valise into it, he entrusted the coach and bags to the care of his servant who was to remain at the inn at Iseo and he dragged the young prince on to the unsteady planks of the small boat.

He was in such a hurry to arrive and the vivacity of his character momentarily so overpowered the constraint he usually imposed on himself so as not to offend his friend's permanent sadness, that he seized an oar and himself rowed with the boatman, singing like a bird and, with the release of his impetuous gaiety, threatening to capsize the boat.

4.

They had gone half way across the lake when he noticed an increase in pallor on Karol's face. He left the rudder and sitting down near him said, "Dear prince, I am afraid you are displeased with me. Probably you did not wish to make this new acquaintance. I am sorry. When one is travelling one must depart a little from one's habits. I had promised not to vex you with such things. I had forgotten . . . because I was so pleased."

"I forgive you everything. I accept everything," replied the prince, calmly. "Friendship lives on sacrifices. You have made so many sacrifices for me that I certainly owe you some. Yet I had hoped that you would never take me to the home of a loose woman."

"Stop, stop," cried Salvator, gripping his hand hard. "Don't use such offending, wounding words. Had anyone else but you spoken of her in that way . . . "

"Forgive me," Karol said. "I had not realised that she was . . . that is, must have been your mistress."

"My mistress," retorted Salvator quickly. "Ah, if it only could have been so! But she loved another at that time, and besides, who knows if she would have liked me even if I had known her when her heart was free? No, Karol, I have not been her lover; and as I was the friend of the man she loved when we knew one another (his name was Foscari, an excellent young man) and I knew her to be loyal and faithful, I never dreamed of desiring her. Oh, if she were only living alone to-day as they

told me in Milan ... And if she wished to love me ... But no!
Come, don't frown: I do not think that I shall develop a
burning passion for her ... I haven't seen her for a long, long
time. Perhaps she is no longer beautiful. And besides, my heart
and my senses had assumed the habit of remaining calm in her
presence. My imagination would require a great effort to pass
from esteem and respect to ... Yet I'm no hypocrite and I
would not like to swear it. When there is great friendship
between a man and a woman ... But probably if she lives
alone she loves someone absent. It is impossible for that warm-
hearted creature to live without love; so I shall have no bad
thoughts towards her. I would not wish to lose her friendship
for anything in the world."

"To judge from all these twistings and turnings," said the
prince with a melancholy smile, "I see that I stand to risk
losing you, and my presentiment of misfortune could well be
no dream."

"Your presentiment! Ah, you keep on harking back to it. I
had forgotten it. Well, if it tells you that my travels will come
to an end with this enchantress and that I shall let you depart
alone, it is an impudent liar. No, no, Karol, your health, your
wish, our journey before everything else! If your presentiment
had a face I would slap it."

The two friends continued to talk a little more about
Madame Floriani. The prince, who was in Italy for the first
time, had never seen her, and all he knew of her was the fame
of her talent and the notoriety of her love affairs. Salvator
spoke of her with enthusiasm; but as one must not always
place reliance on friends, we shall tell the reader ourselves
what he must know for the moment concerning our heroine.

Lucrezia Floriani was an actress possessing a pure, superior
gift, not in the grand manner, but always moving and
sympathetic when she was playing a good part; exquisite,
admirable in all the details of mime, which help the actor to set
off to advantage the work of the true poet and to find charm in
that of the inferior one.

She had achieved great success, not only as an actress, but
also as an author; for she had carried her passion for her art as
far as to venture to write plays, first in collaboration with a few

literary friends and finally alone by her own inspiration. Her plays had been successful, not that they were masterpieces, but they were uncomplicated, their sentiment was genuine, the dialogue was good, and she acted in them herself. She had never had herself called out after performances, but her secret, for the time being, was part of the act and the public itself called out her name amid the wreaths of flowers and applause which they lavished on her.

In that country, at that time, newspaper criticism was not greatly developed. Madame Floriani had many friends and they were indulgent to her. Whole families, occupying the pit in various Italian towns showered her with ovations. They loved her; and if it is not impossible that her fame as an author was due to the benevolence of the public, it is at least certain that her character merited such indulgence and affection.

There was never a person more disinterested, more sincere, more modest and more liberal. It was either at Verona or Pavia that she managed a theatre and established a company of actors. She won the esteem of all those with whom she had dealings, was adored by those who needed her assistance and the public rewarded her for all she did. She was moderately successful financially and as soon as she felt that she had an assured competency, she left the theatre, although at the very height of her talent and charms. For a few years she lived in Milan amid the society of artists and literary people. Her home was pleasant and her conduct so honourable and dignified (which does not mean that it was conventional) that ladies of society sought her company with sympathy and even a certain feeling of deference.

But suddenly she abandoned that world and the town itself, and withdrew to the lakeside at Iseo, which is where we meet her now.

Behind the motives which drove her in these opposite directions, towards this blooming of her dramatic and literary art and towards this sudden disgust of life and noise; towards this activity of theatre administration and towards the idleness of a rustic life – behind these contradictions there lay, without the slightest doubt, an uninterrupted succession of love affairs. I shall not tell you of them now; it would be too long and without direct interest. Nor shall I waste any time in making you grasp the nuances of a character as clear and easy to understand as Prince Karol's was elusive and indefinable. As you hear it, you will appreciate this uncomplicated nature, as limpid in its faults as in its qualities. It is certain that I shall hide nothing from you in connection with Madame Floriani through prudishness or fear of displeasing you. What she had been in the past, what she was now, of this she would speak to anyone who asked her in a spirit of sympathy. But if people questioned her out of sheer curiosity and with hidden irony, to avenge herself for this patronising impertinence, she took great pleasure in shocking them by her outspokenness.

We cannot define this better than she herself did one day, when, speaking in good French, she said to an old marquis:

"You are in somewhat of a dilemma," she said to him, "to know what word, accepted in your language, would describe a woman like me. Would you say that I am a courtesan? I don't think so, since I have always given to my lovers and have never received anything, even from my friends. I owe my comfortable means solely to my work, and vanity has no more dazzled me than greed has led me astray. I have only had lovers who were not only poor, but even obscure.

"Would you say that I am a wanton? My heart, not my senses have ruled me, and I cannot even begin to understand pleasure without rapturous affection.

"Finally, am I a low, immoral woman? We must know what you mean by that. I have never sought scandal. Maybe I have caused it without wishing to, and without knowing. I have never loved two men at the same time. I have never in fact and in intention belonged to more than one man during a given time, depending on the duration of my love. When I no longer loved him I did not deceive him. I broke with him absolutely. True, at the height of passion I had sworn to love him for ever; when I did swear it, it was in perfect good faith. Each time I have loved, it was with so much of my heart that I thought it was for the first and last time in my life.

"Yet you will not say that I am a decent woman; whereas I am certain that I am. I even assert before God that I am a virtuous woman, but I know that according to your ideas and

119/143

public opinion what I have just said is blasphemy. I don't care. I offer my life to the judgement of the world without rebellion against such judgement, without acknowledging that it is right as far as I am concerned.

"Do you find that I am indulgent to myself and that I suffer from an excess of pride? I agree. I do possess great pride, but I have no vanity and one can say all possible ill of me without offending or distressing me in the slightest. I have never fought against my passions. If I have acted well or badly I have been punished and rewarded by those passions themselves. I was to lose my reputation as a result; I expected it; I sacrificed reputation to love, and that concerns me alone. What right have those people who condemn me to say that my example is dangerous? As soon as the culprit is condemned he is executed, therefore he can do no further harm; and those who might be tempted to imitate him, are sufficiently warned by the punishment."

Karol de Roswald and Salvator Albani left their boat at the entrance of the park, close to the cottage which the innkeeper at Iseo had pointed out to them. It was here that Madame Floriani had been born and here her father, an old, white-haired fisherman still occupied it. Nothing had been able to persuade him to leave this poor abode where he had spent his life and where long habit kept him; but he had consented to having it repaired, improved in sanitation and protected from the waters of the lake by a pretty, rustic terrace adorned with flowers and shrubs. He was sitting at his door amid his irises and gladioli, and was using the last few minutes of daylight in mending his nets, for, although his existence was henceforth assured, and his daughter piously watched not only over all his needs but also the anticipation of the rare extravagant whims he might have, he retained the parsimonious habits and tastes of the peasant, and he never discarded a single one of the tools of his work, as long as he could still make the slightest use of it.

5.

Karol noticed the handsome but somewhat hard face of the old man, and not dreaming that this could be the signora's father, greeted him and was prepared to pass on. But Salvator had stopped to contemplate the picturesque thatched cottage and the old fisherman who with his white beard, slightly yellowed by the sun, resembled a muddy lakeside divinity. The memories which Madame Floriani, almost weeping, had repeated to him so often, and the eloquence of her repentance, passed confusedly through his mind; moreover the austere features of the old man seemed to preserve some similarity to those of the beautiful young woman. He saluted him twice and went on to try and open the park gate, which stood ten yards away; at the same time he looked back several times in the direction of the fisherman who was watching him with an attentive and suspicious eye.

When the latter saw that the two young men were really attempting to enter the abode of Madame Floriani he rose and shouted, in a far from welcoming tone, that one was not allowed to enter there and it was not a public walk.

"I know this quite well, my good man," replied Salvator, "but I am an intimate friend of the signora and I have come to see her."

The old man approached and looked at him attentively. Then he continued, "I don't know you. You don't come from these parts, do you?"

"I am from Milan and I tell you that I am a great friend of

the signora. Tell me, which is the correct entrance?"

"You won't get in that way! Are you expected? Do you know if you will be received? What is your name?"

"Count Albani. And you, my good fellow, will you tell me your name? Aren't you, by any chance, a certain worthy man called Renzo, or Beppo, or Checco Menapace?"

"Renzo Menapace. Yes, that's me," said the old man doffing his hat in keeping with the custom in Italy where the lower classes defer to a title. "How do you know me, signor? I have never seen you."

"Nor I you; but your daughter resembles you and I know her real name."

"A better name than the one she goes by now! However, they all call her by her stage name now; it's become a habit. So you want to see her? Have you come just for that?"

"Of course, – if you have no objection. I hope she will be good enough to commend us to you and that you will not regret opening the gate to us. I presume that you have the key?"

"Yes, I have the key and yet, your Lordships, I can't open it. Is this young gentleman with you?"

"Yes, he is the Prince de Roswald," said Salvator who was fully aware of the influence of titles.

Old Menapace bowed more deeply than before although his face remained cold and stern. "My lords," said he, "have the goodness to enter my home and wait there until I have sent my servant to inform my daughter, because I cannot promise that she will be prepared to see you."

"Come," said Salvator to the prince, "We must be resigned to waiting. It appears that Madame Floriani has now developed a mania for living the life of a recluse. But as I have no doubt that we shall be well received, let us go and have a look at the cottage where she was born. It will be rather curious."

"What is indeed curious is the fact that she now lives in a palace herself and leaves her father in a cottage," replied Karol.

"I beg your pardon, your Highness," said the old man who turned around with a displeased expression, much to the surprise of the two young men, for they were in the habit of talking German when they were alone, and Karol had expressed himself in that language.

"Forgive me," continued Menapace, "if I overheard you. I have always had excellent hearing and that is why I was the best fisherman of the lake, without mentioning my sight, which was equally excellent and is still not too bad."

"So you understand German?" said the prince.

"I was a soldier for a long time; and I spent years in your country. I can't speak your language very well although I still understand it a little, so allow me to answer you in my own. If I don't live in my daughter's palace, it is because I like my cottage, and if she doesn't live in my cottage, it is because the accommodation is too small and we would interfere with each other. Besides, I am accustomed to living alone and it is only under protest that I tolerate the man servant she gave me with the pretext that at my age a man may need someone to help him. Fortunately he is a good lad. I chose him myself and I am teaching him how to become a fisherman. Come, Biffi, leave your supper for a while, my boy, and go and tell the signora that two foreign gentlemen are asking to see her. Your names, again, please, your Lordships?"

"Mine will suffice," replied Albani who, together with Karol, had followed old Menapace as far as the entrance of his cottage. From his pocket book he drew a visiting card which he handed to the youth who acted as the fisherman's servant. Biffi left in all haste, after his master had given him a key which he kept hidden in his belt.

"You see, your Lordships," said Menapace to his guests as he offered them rustic chairs which he had woven and stuffed himself with various kinds of aquatic grass, "you must not think that I am not well treated by my daughter. As far as money, friendship and attention goes, I have nothing but praise for her. Only I can't change my ways at my age. You see that, don't you? And as for all the money she used to send me when she was on the stage, I put it to better use than to lodge, dress and feed myself well. I have no taste for that sort of thing. I bought land, because that's good. It lasts and it will go back to her when I am not there any more. She is my only child. So she will have no cause to regret all she has done for me. It was her duty to give me a share of her riches and she has always fulfilled it. It is my duty to make that money prosper, to invest it well and restore it to her when I die. I have always been a slave to duty."

This narrow, selfish manner of regarding his relations with his daughter made Salvator smile.

"I am quite sure," said he, "that your daughter does not make that kind of calculation with you and she has not the slightest idea of your system of saving."

"It is only too true that the poor thing has no head for it at all," replied Menapace with a sigh, "and if I listened to her I would eat up everything, I would lead the life of a prince, like her, with her, and all those to whom she flings money in handfuls! But what is to be done? We can't agree about it. She is kind, she loves me, she comes to see me ten times a day, she brings me everything she can think of to give me pleasure. If I cough or have a headache she spends whole nights with me. But all that does not prevent her from having one great fault, and that is that she is not a good mother, as I would wish."

"What? She is not a good mother?" cried Salvator who had difficulty in remaining serious in the face of the peasant's parsimonious morality. "I have seen her in the midst of her family and I believe you are mistaken, Signor Menapace."

"Oh, if you think that a good mother should caress, tend, spoil and amuse her children and nothing more, very well. But I am not pleased to see them never being refused anything, the little girls dressed like princesses, the boy already allowed to have dogs, horses, a boat and a gun like a man! They are good children, I admit, and very pretty, but that's no reason for giving them all they want, as if it all cost nothing. I can see clearly that they run through at least thirty thousand francs a year in that house, what with pleasures and teachers for the children, books, music, excursions, presents . . . follies of all kinds. And there are charities! It is scandalous! All the cripples, all the vagabonds around here have learned the way to the house, a thing which they never knew in the days of old Ranieri, when he was the owner. *There* was a man who knew his interests well and made a profit out of his land! Whereas my daughter will be ruined if she doesn't listen to me."

The old man's avarice utterly disgusted the prince; but Salvator was more amused by it than indignant. He was well acquainted with the nature of peasants, that ruthlessness to retain things, that harshness to oneself, that thirst to acquire capital without ever enjoying one's income, that fear of the future which to these poor toiling old men stretches beyond the grave. However he felt somewhat displeased on hearing Menapace invoke the memory of old Ranieri who had played so ugly a part in the story of Madame Floriani.

"If I remember rightly what Lucrezia told me," said he, "this Ranieri was a vile skinflint. He cursed his son and wanted to disinherit him because the latter wished to marry your daughter."

"He caused us some trouble, it's true," resumed the old man, unmoved, "but whose fault was it? That young fool who wanted to marry a poor peasant girl . . . In those days Lucrezia had nothing. From her godmother, Signora Ranieri, she had learned many useless things, music, languages, elocution . . . "

"Things which have served her well since," Salvator interrupted.

"Things which ruined her," continued the inflexible old man. "It would have been better if the old Ranieri woman who could not give her anything towards setting her up in life hadn't taken such a great liking to her and had left her to remain a peasant girl, a mender of nets, the daughter of a fisherman as she was and the wife of a fisherman as she could have become. Because I knew a good one, a man who had a good house, two big fishing boats, a pretty meadow and some cows. Oh yes, an excellent match. Pietro Mangiafoco, who would have married her if she had wanted to listen to reason. But instead of that, by educating her and making her so beautiful and learned, her godmother was the cause of all the misfortune which followed. Memmo Ranieri, her son, became crazy over Lucrezia and because he couldn't marry her, carried her off. That is how my daughter was separated from me and that is why for twelve years I did not want to hear of her."

"Save to receive the money which she sent him," said

Salvator to Karol, forgetting that the fisherman understood German.

But this reflection in no way offended the old man. "Of course I received it, invested it and turned it to good account," he went on. "I knew that she was living on a grand scale and that one day she might be very pleased to find enough to live on after squandering all she had earned. And what hasn't she given away and wasted? Ah! It is a curse to have such a character."

"Yes, yes, she is a monster," cried Salvator, laughing. "But meanwhile it seems to me that old Ranieri was ill advised not to wish to marry her to his son. He would have done so had he been able to foresee that this same young peasant girl would earn millions one day with her talent!"

"Yes, he would have done," said Menapace, with the utmost calm, "but he couldn't foresee it; and in refusing his consent to a marriage so unsuitable, he was within his rights. He did well. Everybody else would have done the same and so would I, in his place."

"So you don't blame him, and very probably you remained on excellent terms with him while his son was abducting your daughter, because he was unable to extract the old skinflint's consent?"

"The old skinflint, the *avarone*, as they called him, was hard, I agree; but after all he was just, and he wasn't a bad neighbour. He never did me any good or ill. When he saw that I would not forgive my daughter he forgave me for being her father. And as for his son, he forgave him, too, when he abandoned Lucrezia to make a good marriage."

"And have you forgiven this son, so worthy of his father?"

"It was not for me to forgive him, although, after all, he was within his rights. He had promised my daughter nothing in writing; it was she who was wrong to trust his love, and when he left her they had debts; her theatre venture had gone badly at the beginning. However, he is dead and God is his judge! But, excuse me, your Excellencies, I have left my nets by the water's edge and if a storm blew up during the night they might get lost. I must bring them in. They are still in good condition and capable of catching plenty of fish. I supply my daughter's table with them, but she pays for them, of course. Oh yes, I don't give anything for nothing! And I say to her 'Eat, eat, and make your children eat. Fortunately for them, the more fish they eat, the more money I will leave them when I die.' "

6.

"What a vile nature," said Karol, when Menapace had gone.

"It is human nature in all its nakedness," replied Salvator. "He is the true type of the son of toil. Foresight without enlightenment, uprightness without delicacy, common sense devoid of ideals, honest greed, ugly and sad."

"It is more than that," said the prince. "For me it is an example of an odious lack of morals, and I cannot understand how Signora Floriani can live with such a spectacle before her eyes."

"I presume that when she came back to him she did not expect to find something so vilely prosaic. In her poetic memories of her old father and the thatched cottage, the noble creature was probably aspiring to the rustic life, the return to patriarchal innocence, to a touching reconciliation with this old man who had cursed her and whose name she could only utter with tears. But possibly there is even more virtue in staying on here than in ever having come at all and probably she understands, tolerates and even loves him in spite of everything."

"To understand and tolerate is not a sign of a delicate soul; in her place I would certainly shower the old man with benefits, but I could not live near him without unendurable suffering; the mere idea of such a disaster shocks me and cuts me to the heart."

"Where do you see all this perversity? This man does not understand the meaning of luxury nor the liberality which goes with easy circumstances among generous people. He is too old to feel that having and giving go together. He amasses what he receives from his daughter so as to preserve it for his grandchildren."

"So she has children?""

"She had two; perhaps she has more now."

"And her husband?" said Karol, hesitating, "Where is he?"

"She has never been married as far as I know," said Salvator, calmly.

The prince was silent and Salvator, guessing his thought, could think of nothing to distract him. He certainly could not invent any good excuses for *that* fact.

After a moment Karol continued: "When a person's behaviour is left to the hazards of life it is because of the lack of high standards in early youth. Could she receive any from a father who has not the slightest feeling on the subject of honour and who, amid all the irregularities of his daughter's life, saw nothing but the money she was earning and spending."

"Such is man seen at close quarters, such is life stripped of its glamour," replied Salvator, philosophically. "When my dear Floriani used to speak to me of her first error she accused only herself and did not remember her father's faults which were probably intolerable and which could have served her as an excuse. When she mentioned him, she would deplore, yet speak highly of his obstinate anger. She attributed it to an ancient virtue, to respectable prejudice. She would say, and I recollect it quite clearly, that once she had freed herself of all the ties of the world and all the fetters of love, she would go and throw herself at his feet and purify herself in his nearness. Well, the poor sinner will have found a saviour very unworthy of so noble a repentance and this disappointment must not have been one of the smallest in her life. Great hearts always see things as beautiful. They are condemned to be constantly deceived."

"Can great hearts resist many unhappy experiences?"

"The more or less harm they suffer proves their more or less greatness."

"Human nature is weak. I therefore believe that souls which

are truly attached to principles should not go out of their way to seek peril . . . Are you utterly determined to spend a few days here, Salvator?"

"I didn't say that. We shall only stay an hour, if you wish."

By always giving way, Salvator controlled Karol, at least in external matters, for the prince was open-hearted and ready to sacrifice his aversions for the sake of good breeding and those ideals of behaviour which he upheld in all his actions.

"I do not wish to thwart you in anything," he replied, "and to impose a deprivation on you or cause you regret would be unendurable to me; but at least promise me that you will try not to fall in love with that woman."

"I give you my promise," said Albani, laughing. "But it will be all to no purpose if my fate is to become her lover after being her friend."

"You invoke destiny," exclaimed Karol, "when it lies in your own hands! Here, it is your conscience and your will which should be sufficient to save you."

"You speak like a blind man talking about colours, Karol. Love breaks all obstacles which confront it, as the sea breaks its dykes. I can swear to you that I shall not remain here longer than one night, but I am not certain that I shall not leave my heart and my thoughts behind."

"So that is why I feel so weak and dejected to-night," said the prince. "Yes, my friend, I keep on returning to the superstitious fear which seized me when first I cast my eyes on the lake, even from a distance! When we entered the boat which conveyed us here, it seemed to me that we were about to drown. Yet you know that it is not one of my weaknesses to fear physical danger, that I do not dislike water, that I sailed with you calmly all yesterday, and even during a real storm on Lake Como. Well, I ventured on to the calm surface of this lake with the timidity of a nervous woman. I am only rarely subject to these kinds of superstition. I do not give way to them, and the proof that I can resist them is that I said nothing to you about it. But the same vague anxiety about an unknown danger, or imminent misfortune for you or me, has pursued me until this hour. I thought I saw familiar ghosts move over those waves, who beckoned to me to go back. In the wake of the boat the golden reflections of the dying sun assumed the shape of my mother, then the features of Lucie . . . The spirits of my lost loves stood obstinately between us and the shore. I do not feel ill, I mistrust my imagination . . . and yet I am not at ease; it is not natural."

Salvator was about to prove that this anxiety was an entirely nervous phenomenon resulting from the agitations of the journey, when a strong vibrant voice coming from behind the cottage, said "Where is he, where is he, Biffi?"

Salvator uttered a cry of joy, sprang forward on to the terrace and Karol saw him welcome in his arms a woman who effusively returned his embrace in a most sisterly manner.

They spoke to each other and questioned and answered one another with animation in a Lombard dialect which Karol could not grasp as quickly as pure Italian. The result of this exchange of rapid, contracted words was that Madame Floriani turned to the prince, held out her hand to him and without realising that he was not exactly accepting it with a good grace, pressed his cordially, telling him that he was welcome and it would give her great pleasure to receive him.

"I beg your pardon, my good Salvator," said she, laughing, "for leaving you to cool your heels in the manor of my ancestors; but I am exposed here to the curiosity of idlers and as I always have some great plan of work in mind, I am obliged to shut myself up like a nun."

"But the fact is that people do say that you almost took the veil as well as your vows some time ago," said Salvator, repeatedly kissing the hand which she allowed him to retain. "It was only with fear and trembling that I dared to disturb you in your hermitage."

"Very well, very well," she continued. "You are pleased to mock me and my beautiful plans. It is because I do not wish to receive bad counsel that I have fled from all my friends and am living in hiding. But because fortune brings you to me I have not sufficient strength yet to send you away. Come, and bring your friend with you. I shall at least have the pleasure of offering you lodgings more comfortable than the *locanda* at Iseo. But I see that you have not yet kissed my son. Don't you recognise him?"

"Indeed no. I dared not recognise him," said Salvator, turning towards a handsome boy of twelve who was frisking about and playing with a hunting dog. "How tall he has grown and how handsome he is!" And he embraced the child who did not remember his name. "And what of the other?" added Salvator, "the little girl?"

"You will see her presently, as well as her little sister and my youngest boy."

"Four children!" cried Salvator.

"Yes, four beautiful children and all with me, in spite of anything people say. You met my father, while I was being sent for, didn't you? You see, he watches over me here. Nobody enters without his permission. Good evening, for the second time, father. Are you coming to lunch with us to-morrow?"

"I can't say, I can't say," said the old man. "You will have plenty of people without me."

Madame Floriani insisted, but her father would promise nothing, and he drew her aside to ask her if she needed any fish. As she knew it was his obsession to sell her all the fish he caught and even to charge her high prices, she gave him a handsome order and left him delighted. Salvator was watching them secretly. He saw that Madame Floriani resigned herself to the old man's oddities very philosophically and even gaily.

Night had fallen and neither Karol nor his friend (who was however quite familiar with Madame Floriani's features) could see her face clearly. To the prince she appeared neither as majestic in figure nor elegant in her manners as could have been expected from a woman who had acted the part of great ladies and queens so well. She was rather small and inclined to be plump. Her voice was rather resonant, but it was too vibrant for the prince's ears. If a woman had spoken in this way in a drawing room all eyes would have turned in her direction with distaste at this breach of good manners.

They crossed the park and the garden with Biffi who carried the portmanteau and they entered a large room, simple and noble in style, supported by Doric columns, and walls of white stucco. There were many lights and flowers in the four corners of the room from which sprang brilliant, slender jets of water brought from the neighbouring lake at little expense.

"Perhaps you are surprised to see so much useless light?" said Madame Floriani, observing the pleasant surprise on Salvator's face at the sight of this beautiful drawing room. "But it is the only whim which I have retained from my days on the stage. When in solitude I like space and brilliant lights. I also like the brightness of the stars. But dark rooms sadden me."

Madame Floriani, to whom this house brought back both sweet and cruel memories, had made many changes and improvements in it. All she had left untouched was the bedroom once occupied by her godmother, Signora Ranieri, and a special patch of garden where this excellent woman cultivated flowers and taught her god-daughter to love them. Signora Ranieri had loved Lucrezia tenderly; she had done her utmost to induce the old miserly lawyer, of whom she had had the misfortune to be both wife and slave, to unite her son in marriage to this peasant girl whom she had brought up and educated. But she had failed; and now the whole Ranieri family was gone. Madame Floriani cherished the memory of some of them, forgave the others and, after much emotion, she had become accustomed to living here without thinking too much of the past. It was because she had made several necessary and tasteful improvements to this house, which was basically very simple, that old Menapace who could not understand these needs of hers for elegance, harmony and style, accused her of ruining herself.

The appearance of this drawing room pleased Karol, too. This kind of Italian luxury which concentrates on satisfaction to the eye, beauty of line and monumental elegance rather than profusion, comfort and richness of furniture, was exactly in keeping with his own tastes and corresponded to the ideas he held of an existence both noble and simple. In accordance with his habit of not wishing to probe too far into the soul of another person and looking at the frame rather than studying the picture he sought something in her outer behaviour which might comfort him for what he thought must be scandalous and culpable in her intimate life.

But while Karol was occupied with admiring the brightly coloured walls, the limpid fountains and the exotic flowers,

Salvator was preoccupied with something entirely different. He was looking at Madame Floriani both anxiously and eagerly. He was afraid he would not find her beautiful and perhaps at the same time bearing in mind the solemn promise he had made to leave the following day, he partly wished that it would be so.

As soon as he saw her in a light sufficiently bright he did indeed observe a definite change in her freshness and beauty. She had put on a little weight; her delicate complexion had given way to a uniform pallor; her eyes had lost some of their brilliance, the expression of her features was no longer the same. In short, she was less vivid and less animated, although she appeared more active and better in health than ever. She was no longer in love; she was a different woman, and it required a few moments for him to adjust himself to this change.

At this time Madame Floriani was thirty, and Salvator had not seen her for five years. He had left her in the midst of emotions resulting from work, love and fame. Now he found her a mother, a country woman, a retired genius, a star grown dim.

She was quickly aware of the impression made upon him by this change, because they had taken one another by the hand and were looking at each other closely, both smiling, she calm and radiant, he anxious and melancholy.

"Well," she said to him in a frank, resolute tone, "we have both changed, haven't we? And we both have something to correct in our recollections. The change is entirely in your favour, dear Count. You have gained much. You used to be an amiable and interesting young man. And now you are still a young man, but at the height of your physical powers, darker, stronger, with a handsome black beard, magnificent eyes, a lion's mane and an air of triumph and success. You are at the most beautiful moment of life's blossoming and you are enjoying it to the full. That is obvious from your look which is more assured and brilliant than it was in the old days. Possibly you are surprised that you are more good-looking to-day than I am. You will remember the time when it was the opposite. There are two reasons for it: you are less impetuous and I am less young. I am in the process of descending the slope which you are still climbing. You used to raise your head to look at me and now you bend to seek me below you, on the far side of life. Do not pity me, however! I believe I am happier in my cloud than you are in your bright sunshine."

7.

Madame Floriani's voice had a certain individual charm. In truth, it was too strong a voice for a lady of society, but it had retained its pristine freshness, and its timbre had not suffered from her life on the stage. Above all, the tone of her voice possessed a frankness which never left the slightest shadow of doubt of the sincerity of feeling she was expressing; and in her diction which had always been as natural on the stage as in private, nothing reminded one of the ranting and bombast of the boards. However, everything she said bore the stamp of tremendous vitality. From the accuracy of the modulation of her voice, Karol judged that she must have been a perfect actress of irresistible appeal. It was on this head that he expressed his approval, determined as he was never to see anything interesting in her save as an artist.

Salvator knew that she was too sincere by nature to pretend detachment from herself. But he believed that she was deluding herself, and he thought of something to say which would soften the somewhat cruel effect of his first look at her. But in such cases we cannot find anything delicate enough to console a woman for her decline and all he could do was to kiss her and tell her that she would still have lovers when she was a hundred, if she so wished.

"No," said she, laughing. "I don't wish to be another Ninon de Lenclos. So as not to grow old one has to be cold and idle. Love and work do not allow one to preserve oneself in that way . . . I hope I shall be able to retain my friends, that is all.

And that will be indeed enough."

At that moment two charming little girls came hurrying into the drawing room, saying that supper was served. The two travellers, having had theirs at Iseo, insisted that Madame Floriani should sit down to eat with her children. Salvator picked up the little girl he knew and the one he did not know and carried them both into the dining room; Karol who was afraid of being in the way, remained in the drawing room. But the two rooms were adjoining; the door remained open and the stucco walls were resonant. Although he wished to remain plunged in his own private world and take no part in the events around him while he was in this house, he could see and hear everything, and he even listened, somewhat to his own annoyance.

"Now then," Salvator was saying as he sat down at the table beside the children (and Karol noticed that when he was not in his immediate presence Salvator found it natural to use the familiar form of address with Madame Floriani) "allow me to wait on your children and yourself. I already adore them as I always did, and even this charming little blond fairy who was not born then. You are the only one, Lucrezia, who can do everything better than anyone else, and that includes producing children."

"You should say *especially* children. God has blessed me in this respect. They are as good, sweet and easy to rear as they are fresh and healthy. Ah, look, here is another coming to say good night to me. Another one for you to meet, Salvator."

Karol, who after trying to glance through a news-sheet had begun to walk about in the drawing room, cast an involuntary glance in the direction of the dining room, and saw a beautiful village girl enter, carrying a sleeping child in her arms.

"What a magnificent nurse," cried Salvator, innocently.

"You slander her," said Madame Floriani. "Say rather a Correggio Virgin with *il divino bambino*. In fact, my children had no other nurse but myself, and the two youngest were often fed in the wings, between two acts. Once I remember the public calling for me with such insistence after the first act, that I was obliged to come and take my bow with my child under my wrap. The two youngest were brought up in less disturbed conditions. This baby was weaned a long time ago. He is a child of two."

"Upon my word, the one I see last always seems the most beautiful," said Salvator, as he took the *bambino* from the maid's hands. "He is a real cherub! I would very much like to kiss him, but I am afraid I will awaken him."

"Don't be afraid. Children who are healthy and play all day in the open air sleep very soundly. One should never deprive them of a caress; even if it gives them no pleasure, it brings them luck."

"Oh yes, that's *your* superstition," said Salvator. "I remember! It's a sweet idea, and I love it. You extend it even to people who have died. I remember that poor stage hand who was killed during one of your performances, when some scenery fell."

"Ah yes, the poor man! You were there . . . It was during the time when I had my own company."

"And you, so brave and admirable, had him carried to your dressing room, where he uttered his last sigh. What a scene!"

"Yes, indeed, it was more terrible than the one I had just played to the public. My costume was covered with the blood of the unfortunate man."

"What a life was yours! You hadn't the time to change, the play went on, you reappeared on the stage and the audience thought that this blood was part of the drama."

"He was a poor fellow, married, with a family. His wife was there and from the stage I could hear her screaming and moaning in my dressing room. One has to be made of iron to endure the life of an actress."

"Outwardly you are of iron, but I know that inwardly there is no one more humane and compassionate than you. I well remember that after the performance, when they removed the dead man, you approached him and kissed him on the forehead, saying that it would help his soul to enter his eternal rest. Moved by your example, the other actors did likewise, and I myself, to please you, had the courage to do the same, although men possess this virtue to a lesser degree than women in such cases. At the time it looked odd and seemed somewhat exaggerated; but things done from the heart go straight to the heart. His wife, to whom you promised a pension, was even more moved by the kiss from the beautiful queen of the play, given to the bleeding corpse of a hideous workman (for he was hideous) than by all your other kindnesses. She embraced your knees, she felt that you had made her husband illustrious and that with your kiss on his brow his soul would never descend to hell."

During the story the eyes of Madame Floriani's elder son had been flashing like jewels.

"Yes, yes," cried the handsome boy who had his mother's pure features and intelligent expression. "I too was there and I have forgotten nothing. It happened just as you say, signor; and I too kissed poor Giananton."

"My good Celio," said Madame Floriani, kissing him, "You must not remember such emotions too much; they were too strong for your age; but on the other hand you must not forget them. God forbids us to shun the misfortune and suffering of others; one must always be ready to run towards them and never believe that there is nothing one can do, even if it is only to bless the dead and give a little support to those who weep. That is your way of seeing things, isn't it, Celio?"

"Yes," said the child with the tone of candour and firmness which he had from his mother, and he embraced her so hard and so wholeheartedly that for a moment her round, strong neck bore the mark of his sturdy little hands.

Madame Floriani ignored the roughness of the embrace and did not reproach him for it. She went on eating with an excellent appetite, but even in the midst of her lively conversation with Salvator she was still the mother concerned with her children and carefully watched that he measured out the food and wine to each of them correctly, according to his age and temperament.

Hers was a nature which was active amid calm, indifferent to herself, attentive and vigilant for others; ardent in her affections, but without excessive anxiety, always concerned to make her children think without impairing their gaiety, always ready to play with them (and on this point very much a child herself), gay by instinct and habit, yet surprising one by a seriousness of judgement and a firmness of opinion which did not preclude a maternal tolerance extending well beyond the family circle. She had a clear, profound and lively mind. She said amusing things with a calm manner and made others laugh without laughing herself. It was her system to maintain good humour and to see the amusing side of annoyances, the acceptable side of suffering and the salutary side of misfortune. Her state, her whole life, her very being were an incessant education to her children, friends, servants and the poor. She existed, thought and breathed as it were for the moral and physical well-being of others, and in the midst of this work, so simple apparently, she did not seem to remember the possible existence of regrets or desires for herself.

And yet, as Salvator well knew, no woman had suffered so much.

Towards the end of supper, the little girls prepared to go to their mother's bedroom and join their younger brother who was already asleep. The handsome Celio who, by reason of his twelve years enjoyed the privilege of remaining downstairs until ten o'clock, took his dog for a run on the terrace which overlooked the lake.

It was a beautiful sight to watch Madame Floriani at dessert receiving the last caresses of her children, while at the same time these charming youngsters were themselves saying good night and kissing each other in a sprightly ritual of embraces half loving, half teasing. With her profile like that of an antique cameo, her hair artlessly and unaffectedly coiled around her shapely head, her gown loose and unadorned, behind which one had difficulty in surmising the statuesque figure of a Roman empress, her calm pallor flushed by the violent kisses of her children, her eyes tired but serene, her beautiful arms whose round firm muscles were gracefully outlined when she encircled the whole of her brood, she suddenly became more beautiful and alive than Salvator had ever yet seen her. Hardly had the children gone when, forgetting the ghost of Karol which was moving fitfully against the background of the far wall, he poured out his heart to her.

"Lucrezia," he cried, covering with kisses those arms tired after so many games and maternal embraces, "I do not understand where my mind, heart and eyes were when I imagined that you had aged and lost your looks. Never have you been younger, fresher, sweeter, more capable of driving a man frantic. If you wish to drive me into that state you only have to say one word, and maybe you would have to say more than one to prevent it. I have always loved you with friendship, esteem, admiration, and now . . . "

"And now, my friend, you are mocking me or raving," said Madame Floriani, with the calm modesty which results from the habit of holding sway over others. "Let us not speak lightly of serious matters, please."

"But nothing is more serious than what I am saying . . . Come," he said, lowering his voice a little out of instinct rather than real caution, for the prince was not missing a single word, "Tell me, are you free at the present moment?"

"Not in the slightest – indeed, even less than ever. Henceforth I belong entirely to my family and my children. Those are chains that are more sacred than all others, and I shall not break them."

"Of course! Who would wish to break them? But what about love? Tell me, is it true that for the past year you have renounced it?"

"It is very true."

"What? No lover? And what of the father of Celio and Stella?"

"He is dead. He was Memmo Ranieri."

"Yes, that's true . . . But the little girl's father?"

"Beatrice's? He left me before she was born."

"So he was not the father of your youngest boy?"

"Salvator's? No."

"Is your last child called Salvator?"

"In memory of you, and in gratitude, because you never made love to me."

"Divine and cruel woman! But tell me, where is the father of my namesake?"

"I left him last year."

"Left him? *You* left *him?*"

"Yes, indeed! I was weary of love. I had found nothing but torment and injustice in it. I had either to die of sorrow under the yoke or live for my children by sacrificing to them a man who could not love them all equally. I chose the latter; I suffered, but I do not repent of my decision."

"But I was told that you had had a liaison with a friend of mine, a Frenchman, a man of some talent, a painter."

"Saint-Gély? We loved one another for a week."

"Your adventure caused a stir."

"Perhaps. He was impertinent to me. I asked him never to come back to my house."

"Is he the father of Salvator?"

"No. Salvator's father is Vandoni, a penniless actor, possibly the best and most honest of all men. But he was consumed by childish, wretched jealousy. Would you believe it, his jealousy was retrospective. Unable to suspect me in the present, he overwhelmed me with my past. It was not difficult; my life is vulnerable to the attacks of moralists, and he was incapable of generosity. I could not endure his quarrels, reproaches and tantrums, which soon threatened to explode in my children's presence. I fled. I remained hidden here for some time and when I learned that he had accepted the inevitable I bought this house and settled here. However, I am still slightly apprehensive, for he loved me greatly, and if his present mistress hasn't the skill to hold him, I may find myself burdened with him once more."

"In that case," said Salvator, laughing and holding out his arms to her, "keep me here as your knight. I shall cleave him in twain if he appears."

"No, thank you. I shall protect myself quite well without you."

"So you don't want me to stay?" said Salvator, whose natural gaiety had been somewhat heightened by a few glasses of maraschino, and who had completely forgotten his friend and his own solemn promises.

"Oh yes, stay as long as you wish," replied Madame Floriani, giving him a little pat on the cheek, "but on the old footing."

"Let it be on a war footing, so that I can rebel."

"Take care," said she, freeing herself from his arms, "if you are no longer my friend as you were in the old days, I shall send you away. Let us go and find your travelling companion who must be bored there, all alone, in the drawing room."

Karol who had been leaning against a column had heard all this dialogue. It seemed to him now that he was coming out of a dream and he moved away so as not to be accused of eavesdropping, whereas in reality he had been standing there lost to his surroundings. He passed his hand over his brow as if to efface the memory of a nightmare. The involuntary effort he had made to enter into the mind of a being so stormy and anarchic, a mixture of things so magnificent and so deplorable, had shattered his soul. He could not understand how Salvator's passion could grow stronger as this woman disclosed her successive errors more and more boldly, and how the very things that would have repelled him, attracted this irresponsible young man like a moth attracted by light.

He felt incapable of facing them. He was afraid of being unable to hide his displeasure from Salvator and his pity from Madame Floriani. He left hastily through another door and, meeting Celio, asked him to show him the room which they had been good enough to place at his disposal. The boy took him to the upper floor, then to a handsome apartment where two beds, beautifully fresh and downy, had already been prepared for him and Salvator. The prince asked the boy to tell his mother that, feeling exhausted, he had retired, and begged her to accept his respects and his apologies.

Remaining alone, he tried to collect his thoughts and recover his composure, but he found it impossible to regain his habitual calmness of mind. It seemed as if a brutal influence had deeply disturbed his inner peace. He determined to lie down and go to sleep, but he sighed and tossed in vain in his luxurious bed. Sleep would not come and he heard midnight strike and he still had not slept a wink. Nor did Salvator appear.

8.

And yet Salvator Albani was a great sleeper. Like all fit, robust, active and easy-going men he ate voraciously, tired ,himself out the livelong day, and did not need much persuasion to go to sleep as quickly as the prince who, because of his regular habits and indifferent health, was obliged not to keep late nights.

If however since first they began travelling together, the occasion arose when Salvator's evening engagement was unusually long, he never failed to go two or three times and reassure himself that his *child* (as he called him) was sleeping quietly. He had a paternal instinct and though he was no more than four or five years older than Karol, he cared for him just as he would have done for his own son, so great was his need of serving and helping people who were weaker than himself. In this there was some resemblance between Madame Floriani and him, and that is why he could appreciate better than anyone else the deep love she bore her children.

In spite of everything, Salvator for once forgot his usual concern, and Madame Floriani, unaware of the attentions and considerations to which the prince was accustomed from his friend, did nothing to remind him to return to Karol.

"Your friend has already left us," she said to him after receiving Celio's message. "He appears to be unwell. What did you say his name was? How long have you been travelling together? One has the impression that he is grieving over something . . . "

When Salvator had answered these questions she continued: "Poor boy! He interests me. It is beautiful to love a mother so much and mourn for her so long. His face and manners went straight to my heart. Ah, if my dear Celio lost me, how sad for him! Who would love him as I do?"

"One should adore one's children and live for them, as you do," said Salvator, "but one must not accustom them overmuch to living for themselves or for the tender mother who dedicates herself to them. There are grave dangers and drawbacks in not giving their minds all the development of which they are capable, and my friend is an example of this. He is an adorable being, but unhappy."

"How is that? Why? Explain it to me. When it is a matter of children, character or education, I am always ready to listen and consider."

"Oh, my friend has a strange character and I could not possibly define it, but, in a word, I can tell you that he takes everything to excess, affection as well as aversion, happiness as well as sorrow."

"Well, that means an artistic nature."

"That's exactly it, but he has not been sufficiently developed in that direction. His emotions are intense and keen, but they are too generalised for art. He is exclusive in his tastes, but he is not dominated by a special passion which would occupy him and compel him to abstract himself from real life."

"Well, that is a feminine nature."

"Yes, but not like yours, my dear. Although he is capable of as much passion, devotion, delicacy and rapture as the tenderest woman . . . "

"In that case he is indeed to be pitied, for he will go through life searching in vain for a heart which will match his."

"Ah, Lucrezia, did you yourself search far enough? If you only wished, your quest need go no further."

"Tell me more about your friend."

"No, I am not talking about him, but about myself."

"I understand and I shall answer you presently, but I don't like to change the subject every minute. Tell me this first: while asserting that there are similarities between us, why do you say that your friend is so different from me?"

"Because there are a thousand nuances in your mind, and he has none. Work, children, friendship, the countryside, flowers, music – everything that is good and beautiful – you feel it all so deeply that you can always find something to distract and console you."

"That's true. And what about him?"

"He loves all these things in relation to the being he loves, but none of them for themselves. If the object of his love is dead or absent, nothing exists for him any longer. Despair and boredom overwhelm him and his soul hasn't sufficient strength to start life once more for the sake of a new love."

"That is indeed beautiful," said Madame Floriani, overcome with genuine admiration. "If I had come across such a soul when I fell in love for the first time, I should have had but one love in my life."

"You frighten me, Lucrezia. Are you going to fall in love with my little prince?"

"I don't like princes," she answered simply. "I could only fall in love with paupers. In any case, your little prince could well be my son."

"You are mad! You are thirty and he is twenty-four."

"Ah! I would have thought he was only sixteen or eighteen. He looks like an adolescent. And as for myself, I feel so old and staid that I think I am fifty."

"It makes no difference. I am not easy in my mind. I must take the prince away to-morrow."

"You may put your mind entirely at rest, Salvator. I shall never love again. See," she said, taking his hand and putting it on her heart, "Henceforth a stone lies here. But I am wrong," she went on and placed Salvator's hand on her forehead. "Love of one's children and charity still dwell in one's heart; but the main abode of love is here, in the head, and my head is turned to stone. I know that love is said to be seated in the senses, but this is not true of intelligent women. With them it follows a progressive course: first it takes possession of the brain and knocks at the doors of the imagination. Without this golden key it could not enter. Having triumphed thus far, it descends into the emotions, it steals into all our faculties and we then love the man who dominates us like a God, a child, a brother, a husband – like everything that a woman can love. It stimulates and subjugates all our vital forces, and the senses duly play their own important part. But the woman who can know pleasure without rapture is an animal, and I tell you now that rapture, – ecstasy – is dead inside me. I have had too many disappointments, I have too much experience, and above all, I am too tired. You know how I suddenly became sick of the theatre, through lassitude, although I was physically perfectly well. My imagination was satiated, exhausted. I could no longer find a single rôle in the world's repertoire which seemed genuine and when I tried to make one myself to my own liking I realised after one single performance that I had failed to convey my feelings in my words. I did not play this rôle well, because it wasn't good, and I was not deluded when the public tried to deceive me by applauding. Well, I have reached the same point in the matter of love. The music of illusion has died for me too soon.

"Love is a prism," she went on. "It is a sun which we wear on our brows and through which our interior being is illumined. When once it is extinguished, everything sinks back into night. Now I see life and men just as they are. Now I can only love through charity, which is what I did for my last lover, Vandoni. I had no more ecstasy, I was grateful for his affection; touched by his suffering, I devoted myself to him. I was not happy, I did not even experience excitement. It was a perpetual sacrifice, senseless and unnatural. Suddenly the whole situation horrified me, I felt myself degraded. I could not endure to be reproached by my past, because among all the loves into which I had flung myself innocently and blindly none appeared so culpable as the one I was trying to maintain in spite of myself. Oh, my friend, what things I could tell! But you are still too young and you would not understand."

"Speak! Speak!" cried Salvator who had grown deeply thoughtful. Still clasping her hand he said, "Let me learn to know you well, so that I can continue to love you as if you were my sister – or inspire me with the courage to love you otherwise. See, I am calm, because I am listening to you."

"Love me like a sister and not otherwise," she said to him,

"for I can only look upon you as a brother. That is how I loved Vandoni, for years. I had known him at the theatre where he did not shine on account of his talent, but where he made himself useful with his activity, his devotion and his kindness. One night – in the country near Milan, it was a beautiful summer night like this one – he made me tell him the story of my break with the singer Tealdo Soavi, the father of my darling little Beatrice. I had loved that man passionately, but his was a cowardly and depraved soul. He kept telling me that he wished to marry me, and he was already married! I did not value marriage as such, but I was horrified when I realised that he could lie to me so long and so cunningly. I was bitter and furious in my reproaches. He left me at the moment when I was about to become a mother. I would not have had the courage to send him away, but I had sufficient not to ask him to return.

"Beatrice was only a year old when poor Vandoni who had become my servant, my squire, my instrument, and who had loved me for a long time without daring to tell me so, heard my sad story and when I had finished he threw himself at my feet and said 'Love me and I shall console you for everything. I shall heal and obliterate all the wrong that has been done to you. I know full well that you have no passion for me; but yield to mine and maybe the love which is consuming me will spread to your heart. Moreover having your friendship and your trust I shall be the happiest and most grateful of men.'

"I resisted for a long time. I liked him so much that it was impossible for me to love him. I wished to send him away, but he spoke seriously about suicide. I tried to live chastely with him. He became like one demented. I yielded; and I thought I was committing incest when instead of feeling the intoxication of passion, I lay in his arms, ashamed, sorrowful and weeping.

"However, his rapture moved me to pity, and for some time life with him was fairly pleasant. But he had expected that his heightened emotion would be requited ultimately. When he saw that he was mistaken and that I still remained nothing but a gentle companion to him, he did not have the modesty to tell himself that I knew him too well to be ecstatic over him, and that the more I knew him the less likely it was for the ecstasy to come. He was young and handsome and a man of feeling; he lacked neither intelligence nor education – but he could not imagine that he would never influence me by the charm of his personality. (And you would not, either, Salvator . . .) I shall tell you why he could not influence me.

"We must not measure the power of the love we experience by the merit of the beloved one. For some time love feeds on its own flame and is even kindled in us without consulting our experience and reason. What I have said is commonplace, and every day one sees noble natures meeting nothing but ingratitude and treachery, whilst depraved, wretched souls inspire violent and lasting passions.

"We see it, we note it and are constantly astonished by it, because we do not inquire into its cause, love being a sentiment of a mysterious nature which everybody experiences without understanding it. This subject is so profound that it is terrifying to think of, and yet, couldn't one make a serious effort to examine something which hitherto has only been vaguely glimpsed? Couldn't one study, analyse, understand and get to know something of this delightful, yet terrible emotion, the greatest which the human species feels, the one that no one can escape and which, however, assumes as many forms and varied aspects as there are individualities on this earth? Couldn't one at least grasp its metaphysical essence, discover the law of its ideal, and then find out, by questioning oneself, if it is a noble and sincere love one is harbouring in oneself or a baleful, destructive emotion?"

"These are weighty matters, Lucrezia," said Salvator. "From the fact that you have given this subject so much thought I see quite clearly that you are no longer under the sway of passion."

"That would hardly follow," she retorted. "One can experience great emotions, yet consider them critically. Perhaps that is a misfortune, but I possess that faculty and I have always possessed it. In the midst of the greatest storms of my youth, my thoughts used to consume themselves in the attempt to make sense of the storm which was causing this confusion. I fail to understand how, when it is a matter of love, the mind can have any other application than this. I am fully aware that it achieves nothing, that the more one tries to see clearly into oneself, the more one's vision becomes blurred, but that is because, as I have already said, the law of love is not known, and the catechism of our affections is still to be made."

"So," said Salvator, "you have striven, yet have not solved the riddle?"

"No, but I have a presentiment that it lies in the Gospel."

"My poor friend, the love we are speaking of is not in the Gospel. Jesus forbade it; He knew nothing of it. The love He teaches us extends to humanity as a whole and does not concentrate on one individual being."

"I know nothing about that. But it seems to me that not everything that Jesus said and thought is sufficiently understood. And I could swear that He was not as ignorant about love as we are led to believe. That He lived chaste I accept, which was all the more reason why He understood the metaphysical side of love. That He is God, that, too, I accept; therefore I see in the Incarnation a marriage with matter, an alliance with woman, and that leaves me no doubts about the divine thought. So do not mock me when I tell you that Jesus understood love better than anyone else. Note His behaviour with the woman taken in adultery, with the Samaritan woman, with Mary and Martha, with Mary Magdalene, the parable of the labourers at the twelfth hour, so sublime and so profound! All that Jesus does and says and thinks is intended to show us that love is greater in its cause than in its object and that it overlooks human imperfections. The more culpable, feeble and unworthy men are of this generous love, the more it strives to envelop them in its ardent embrace."

"You are describing Christian charity."

"Well, isn't love, great, real love, Christian charity applied and as it were concentrated in a single being?"

"That's Utopia. Love is the most selfish of feelings and the most incompatible with Christian charity."

"That is your love, such as you have made it, miserable men!" cried Lucrezia passionately. "But the love which God gave us, the kind which, fresh and pure, should have passed from Him to us, the kind which I understand, which I have dreamed of and sought, the love which I thought I had grasped and possessed once or twice in my life, – alas, it lasted the space of a dream and a startled awakening – the kind which I shall believe in as a religion, although I may be its only adept, and I have died in the pain of its pursuit . . . that is the kind which is patterned on the love which Jesus Christ felt and manifested to mankind. It is a gleam of the divine charity, it obeys the same laws; it is calm, mild, and just, with those who are just. It is restless, ardent, impetuous, in a word, passionate, only for sinners. When you see a man and wife loving one another tenderly and faithfully, you can say that that is friendship. But when you, a decent man, will feel yourself madly enamoured of a wretched courtesan, you may be sure that that, too, is love, and do not blush for it! That is how Christ loved those who were unworthy of Him.

"And that is how I loved Tealdo Soavi. I knew quite well that he was selfish, vain, ambitious and ungrateful, but I was madly in love with him. When I learned that he was vile I cursed him, but I still loved him. I wept over him with a bitterness so great that since that time I have lost the faculty of loving any other man. It seemed as if I found consolation very quickly, and now I certainly am consoled; but the blow was so violent, the wound so deep that I shall never love again."

Madame Floriani wiped away a tear which fell slowly down her pale cheek. Her face expressed no pain, but there was something terrifying about her stillness.

9.

"So it was because of a scoundrel that you were unable to love a decent man?" said Salvator, deeply moved. "You are a strange woman, Lucrezia."

"Well, why did this man need my love?" she retorted. "Wasn't he sufficiently happy in himself, knowing that he was sensible, well balanced, at peace with his conscience and the world? He asked for my friendship and offered me in return a loyal and long devotion. He had my friendship and was not satisfied with it. He demanded passion; he was asking for turmoil and torment. It was not in my power to make myself unhappy on his account. And he could not forgive me for wishing to make him happy."

"Those are paradoxes indeed ! They terrify me. What you say is very beautiful, but difficult to summarise. You say that love is generous, sublime and divine. Christ Himself taught it to us indirectly by teaching us charity. It is compassion driven to transcendence, devotion driven to ecstasy. Consequently it only happens to noble hearts. And thus such hearts are condemned to hell for the whole of this life, since they only burn with this sacred fire for the wicked and the ungrateful."

"Yes, that is just how it is," sighed Madame Floriani. "The riddle of life has no other solution. It is sacrifice, suffering and weariness; sacrifice in youth, suffering in the prime of life, weariness in old age."

"Consequently good persons will not know the happiness of being loved?"

"No, as long as this world will not change, and with it the human heart. If Jesus returns one day, as He promised, I hope He will give gentler laws to a new race of men, which will be better than ours."

"So, no requited love, no pure intoxication for the generations of the present?"

"No, no, and again, no."

"You frighten me, you soul in despair!"

"The fact is that you wish to see happiness in love. It is not there. Happiness means tranquillity and friendship; love is storm and conflict."

"Well, let me define another kind of love: friendship, that is tranquillity combined with sensual pleasure – that is to say, enjoyment and happiness."

"Yes, that is the ideal of marriage. I have not known it, although I have dreamed of it and pursued it."

"And because you do not know it, do you deny its existence?'"

"Salvator, have you ever known two lovers or two married people who loved one another absolutely in the same manner? – with the same strength or the same calmness?"

"I don't know . . . I don't think so."

"I am sure not. As soon as passion seizes one of the two (and that is inevitable) the other grows cool, suffering comes and happiness is disturbed, if not completely lost. In youth one tries to find love; in maturity love is accompanied by torture; in old age one tries to love, but love has gone."

"Well, when you have reached a mature age, you will get married, I can see that. You will make a gentle and understanding marriage based on reason and you will be happy in conjugal love. That is your dream, isn't it?"

"No, Salvator. I *have* reached mature years. My heart is fifty years old, my brain is twice that age, and I do not think that the future will give me back my youth. I ought to have loved only one man, traversed all life's vicissitudes with him, suffered with him and for him and reserved for him the angelic devotion that Christ has taught us. This virtue would then have been able to count on its own reward. Old age would have come to heal everything and I would have gone peacefully to my rest alongside the companion of my life, sure that I had done my duty to the end and given him a worthwhile devotion."

"Why did you not do so? You forgave your first lover so much! When I knew you, you seemed resolved to go on forgiving the second one, too, endlessly."

"I lacked patience and faith forsook me, but I yielded to the weakness of human nature, to dejection, and later to the wild hope of finding happiness with another. I was wrong. Men find it impossible to be grateful to us for worshipping those who preceded them. On the contrary, they look upon it as a crime and a reproach and the more devoted we were before we knew them the more they judge us to be incapable of devotion to them."

"Isn't that true?"

"It does become true after a number of errors and involvements. The soul is exhausted, the imagination freezes, courage departs, strength forsakes us. That is the stage at which I am. If I told a man now that I am capable of love, I would be lying shamelessly."

"Ah, you have never been a coquette, my dear friend, and I see that you could never become a cold sensualist."

"Do you pity me then on that account?"

"I pity myself, for in spite of and possibly because of all you say I feel I am desperately in love with you."

"In that case, my dear Salvator, good night – and you will be leaving to-morrow."

"Do you wish it? Ah, if you could really wish it."

"What does that mean?"

"It means that then I would stay in spite of you and that I would hope."

"Do you imagine that I am afraid of you? You used not to be conceited, but now you have become so."

"No, I haven't grown conceited, but I do not know why you wish to make me believe that you have become invulnerable. Have you never had any sudden impulses?"

"Never."

"Ah, I can't believe it."

"Listen, I have had violent, blind, culpable relationships, I won't deny it. But they were never an impulse. That is another word for a pleasurable affair which lasts a week. . . But there can be genuine passions which only last a week."

"There are even passions which last only an hour," cried Salvator, with emotion.

"Yes," she replied, "Illusions so sudden and so powerful that they are followed by aversion and terror as they vanish. The shortest lived passions can be the deepest felt; one mourns them and blushes for them all one's life."

"Why blush for them if they are sincere? One can be quite sure that these at least were requited."

"One can't be more sure of these than of the rest."

"What is spontaneous and irresistible is legitimate and divinely right."

"The right of the stronger is not divinely right," said Madame Floriani, freeing herself from Salvator's arms. "My friend, why have you come to insult me, and under my own roof? I can feel no love for you."

"Lucrezia! Lucrezia! You would not kill yourself to-morrow morning, would you?"

"The Lucrezia you speak of was wrong to kill herself. Sextus had not possessed her. A man who takes a woman by surprise is not her lover."

"Ah! You are right, my dear friend," said Salvator, kneeling at her feet. "Will you forgive me?"

"Yes, of course," she answered, with a smile. "We are alone and it is midnight. I have no protector and perhaps I have been too kind to you. What is happening to you is not your fault, but mine. So I will have to abandon the idea of seeing my friends for another ten years. It is sad."

"Oh, my dearest, you are weeping. I have offended you."

"No, not offended. My life has not been chaste enough for me to have a right to be offended by a desire expressed plainly."

"Do not speak in that way. I respect and adore you."

"That is impossible. You are a man and you are young. That is all."

"Trample me underfoot, but do not say that I only feel sensuality towards you. My heart is deeply moved, my mind uplifted, and your refusal, far from vexing me, increases my respect and affection even more... Forget that I have distressed you. Heavens, how pale and sad you look! Wretched fool that I am, I have awakened the memory of all your sorrows. Ah, you are weeping, weeping bitterly. You make me wish to kill myself, I despise myself so much."

"Forgive yourself as I forgive you," said Madame Floriani gently, as she rose and offered him her hand. "I am wrong to be affected by a chance meeting which I should have foreseen. I would have laughed at it once... If I weep about it now it is because I thought I had already entered for ever on a life of calm and dignity. But it is not sufficiently long since I broke with weakness and folly for others to think me sober and strong. These conversations about love, these outpourings, these confidences between a man and a woman at night are dangerous, and if you have had bad thoughts, all the fault lies in my imprudence. But let us not take it too seriously," said she, wiping her eyes and smiling at her friend with wonderful gentleness. "I must accept this mortification as an expiation of my past sins, although I myself do not regard them as such. Perhaps I would have done better to be wanton rather than passionate. It would have harmed no-one but myself, whereas my passion has broken other hearts than mine. But what can you expect, Salvator? I was not born to have philosophical morals, as they used to be called once... Nor you, my friend... You deserve better than that! Ah, out of respect for yourself do not ask women for pleasure without love. Otherwise you will cease to be young before you are old and that is the worst of all moral states."

"Lucrezia, you are an angel," said Salvator. "I have insulted you and you speak to me as a mother would to her son. Let me kiss your feet, I am no longer worthy of kissing your brow. I do not think I shall ever dare to do so again."

"Come and kiss more innocent brows," she said, slipping her arm through his. "Come into my bedroom."

"Your bedroom?" said he, trembling.

"Yes, my bedroom," said she, with a frank laugh which no longer held any hint of bitterness. Leading him through her boudoir she brought him into a room draped with white, in which four little pink beds stood around a kind of quilted hammock suspended by silk cords. Madame Floriani's four children were sleeping in this sanctuary and formed a kind of rampart around her aerial couch.

"I used to be very greedy for my sleep once," she said to him, "and I had difficulty in awakening during the night to attend to my children after the fatigues of the theatre and society. Since I have been enjoying the happiness of living for them and with them at all hours of the day and night, I have grown accustomed to more vigilant habits. I perch like a bird on a branch close to its nest and my children cannot make a single movement without my hearing and being on the alert for them. You see, because I left them for two hours to-night I have been punished and have been troubled. Had I gone to bed with them as usual, at ten o'clock, I would not have remembered the past . . . Ah, the past, that is my enemy."

"Your past, your present and your future are admirable, Lucrezia, and I would have given my whole life to have been you for a single day. I would be proud of it, and that day would be the most memorable in my life . . Farewell! My friend and I will leave to-morrow at daybreak. Allow me to kiss all your children, and give me your blessing. It will sanctify me, and when we see one another again, I shall be worthy of you."

When Salvator Albani entered his bedroom it was nearly one o'clock in the morning. He went in cautiously and approached the bed on tiptoe, for fear of waking his friend whose silence and stillness made him think he was asleep.

However, before extinguishing the light, the young count, as was his habit, went and gently drew apart the curtains of the prince's bed to make sure that he was sleeping peacefully. He was surprised to see that his eyes were open and staring at him as if questioning all his movements.

"Aren't you asleep, my good Karol?" he said. "I have wakened you . . . "

"I haven't been sleeping," answered the prince in a voice which held a tinge of sadness and reproach. "I was worried about you."

"Worried?" said Salvator, pretending not to understand. "Are we in a robbers' lair? You are forgetting, we have made a stop at a pleasant villa among friendly people."

"A stop," said Karol, with a strange sigh. "That is just what I feared."

"Oh! Oh! So your presentiment has not gone? Well, you will soon be rid of it. Our stop will not last much longer. I shall throw myself on my bed for a couple of hours and we shall be away even before sunrise."

"To meet again, and part thus," said the prince, tossing on his bed in distress. "How strange . . . How horrible . . . "

"What? What did you say? Do you want us to stay?"

"No, certainly not for my sake, but for yours. I am frightened at so easy a separation after so easy a reunion."

"Come, my dear Karol, you are wandering," said Salvator, forcing a laugh. "I understand your suspicions and accusations which are somewhat rash . . . and harsh! You imagine that I have just come from an intoxicating tête-à-tête and that content with a pleasant and easy adventure I am preparing to leave without formal leavetaking, without regrets, in short, without love . . . Thank you for such generous thoughts . . . "

"Salvator, I said nothing like that; you are making me speak so as to pick a quarrel with me."

"No, no. Let us not quarrel. This is not the time. Let's sleep. Good night." And as he reached his bed and flung himself on it, slightly ill tempered, Salvator muttered: "You do jump to conclusions, don't you? How charitable you virtuous people are! Ah! It is really very amusing."

But his laughter was not exactly hearty. He felt that he was guilty and that if Madame Floriani had wished to be as foolish as he, Karol's accusation would have hit the mark only too well.

10.

Karol was extraordinarily sensitive. Temperaments which are delicate and intense possess a kind of divination which often deceives them because it goes beyond the truth, but never falls short of it and which consequently seems magical when it hits the target.

"My friend," he said to Salvator, trying to settle down quietly on his pillow, which was not easy because he was trembling like a man stricken with fever, "you are cruel. Yet God knows that I have suffered greatly on your account for the last three hours and that one suffers in proportion to the affection one has for people. I cannot endure the idea that you have committed a fault. It is more cruel to me, it causes me more shame and regret than if I had committed it myself."

"I don't believe anything of the sort," retorted Salvator coldly. "If you had a slightly improper thought you would blow out your brains. Consequently you are implacable when others think that way."

"So I am not mistaken," said Karol. "You have made that unhappy creature commit another indiscretion."

"I am a blackguard, a villain, anything you say," cried Salvator, sitting up in his bed and opening his curtains to see Karol as he spoke to him, "but that woman is an angel, I tell you, and so much the worse for you if you haven't sufficient heart and mind to understand her."

This was the first time that Salvator had uttered a harsh, insulting word to his friend. He was over-excited by the emotions of the evening and he could not endure this undeserved blame.

He had no sooner given vent to his resentment then he regretted it bitterly; for he saw Karol's expressive face grow pale, change terribly and betray great pain.

"Listen, Karol," said he, kicking the wall hard so as to make his bed move nearer to his friend's, "don't be angry, don't be distressed. It is bad enough for me to have done so earlier this evening to a being whom I love almost as much as you, if that is possible. Pity me, scold me, I don't mind, I deserve it; but don't accuse this excellent and admirable woman. I shall tell you everything."

And Salvator, unable to resist the silent domination of his friend, related to him most truthfully, in every slightest detail, all that had taken place between their hostess and him.

Karol listened to him with great inner emotion, a fact of which Salvator, carried away by his own confession, did not take sufficient notice. This description of the noble instincts and the reckless life of Madame Floriani was the final blow, and his imagination was deeply impressed by it. He could picture her in the arms of the wretched Tealdo Soavi, then as the companion of a common actor, accommodating through kindness, degraded through nobility of soul. And now he could see her insulted by the blind desires of this same good Salvator who, according to his own admission, would have been ready to make love to the maidservant at the inn at Iseo, if he had spent the night on the other side of the lake. Finally he pictured her in her bedroom, in the midst of her sleeping children. He saw her throughout as great by nature and degraded by life. He felt himself growing deathly cold and burning hot, leaping towards her and swooning at her approach. When Salvator had finished speaking, a cold sweat bathed Karol's brow.

Why should the shrewd reader be surprised? Surely he has guessed already that Prince de Roswald had fallen madly in love, at first sight and for life, with Lucrezia Floriani!

I promised or rather threatened not to give the reader the pleasure of the smallest surprise throughout the whole of this book. It would have been fairly simple to conceal our hero's sufferings before the explosion of an emotion increasingly unlikely and difficult to foresee. But the reader is not as simple as is believed and knowing the human heart just as well as those who write about it, knowing full well from his own experience that those loves which are reputed to be impossible are the very ones which burst forth with the greatest violence, he would not have been deceived by the would-be cunning of the novelist. What would be the purpose then of trying the reader's patience by skilful manoeuvres and false circumventions? He reads so many novels that he knows all the tricks of the trade and as far as I am concerned, I have resolved not to trifle with him, even if he should regard me as a simpleton and take it ill.

Why should this woman who was no longer very young nor very beautiful, whose character was the exact opposite of Karol's, whose indiscreet behaviour, unrestrained passions, tenderness of heart and boldness of mind seemed a violent protest against all the principles of society and established religion, why, in short, had the actress Floriani without wishing or even thinking of it succeeded in casting such a spell over Prince de Roswald? How did this man, so handsome, chaste, poetic, so fervent and refined in all his thoughts, affections and behaviour, fall suddenly and almost without a struggle under the sway of a woman worn out by so much emotional stress, disillusioned by so many things, sceptical and rebellious with regard to everything which he most respected, faithful to the point of fanaticism to ideas which he had always denied and would always deny in the future? This, I need scarcely say, is one of the most inexplicable problems in logic, but it is that part of my novel which is truest to life, since the lives of all poor human hearts offer each one of us a page, if not a whole volume, of this fatal experience.

Isn't it possible that in the midst of her paradoxes Madame Floriani had laid her finger on the very heart of the truth when, as she spoke to Salvator Albani about love, she had said that generous or tender souls are condemned to love only those whom they pity and fear?

People have long said that love attracts the most opposite elements, and when Salvator reported to his young friend the slightly confused, wild but enthusiastic and possibly sublime theories of Lucrezia, it is certain that Karol felt that he had fallen beneath the law of this appalling fatality. The dread and horror which he felt were so violent and, at the same time, the fascination of which his presentiment had vaguely warned him waged such battles in his poor soul that he had not the strength to make the slightest remark to his friend.

"So we shall leave in an hour," he said, at last. "You can rest for an hour, Salvator. I do not feel sleepy. I shall wake you when it is daylight."

Salvator, yielding to the urges of youth, fell soundly asleep, relieved no doubt to have opened his heart and given utterance to his emotions. He was not ashamed that he had made what a *roué* would have called a blunder with regard to Lucrezia. He was sincerely sorry for it, but knowing she was good and true, he counted on her forgiveness and did not make the rash vow never to attempt a similar move with other women.

Karol did not fall asleep. He became feverish and because he felt ill he tried to tell himself that the moral perturbance which he had just undergone was merely a symptom of physical illness. "These are mere hallucinations," he kept on saying. "The latest new face I have come across on this journey has fixed itself in my brain and is now haunting my fevered thoughts like a phantasm. It could just as well have been any other person whose image tortured my insomnia in the same way."

The early morning whitened the horizon and Karol arose so as to dress slowly before waking his friend; for he felt extremely weak and more than once he was obliged to sit down. When Salvator, observing the heightened colour of his cheeks and the occasional convulsive shiver that shook him asked if he was ill, he denied it, determined as he was that nothing should keep him here. The house was already astir, they had to cross the ground floor to reach the garden and the lakeside where they hoped to find a fishing boat. Just as they were setting foot outside, they found themselves face to face with Madame Floriani.

"Where are you going so quickly?" she asked, taking each of them by the hand. "They are putting the horses to my carriage and Celio, who drives delightfully, is looking forward greatly to being your coachman as far as Iseo. I don't wish you to cross the lake at this time of the day. There is still a cool little mist which is very unhealthy, not so much for you, Salvator, as for your friend, who is not very well. No, you are certainly not well, Monsieur de Roswald," she went on, taking Karol's hand again and holding it between both hers with the simplicity of maternal instinct. "I was struck a moment ago by the heat of your hand and I am afraid you are slightly feverish. The nights and mornings are cold here. Come in, come in, I insist. While you are taking your chocolate, the coach will be ready, you will settle in it comfortably, and at Iseo you will meet the first rays of the sun, which will dispel the evil influence of the lake."

"It is true, then, dear siren, that your mirror has a somewhat baleful influence?" said Salvator, allowing himself to be persuaded to return to the house. "My friend was saying only yesterday that he was conscious of it, but I did not believe it."

"If by mirror you mean the lake, dear Ulysses," replied Lucrezia, laughing, "may I tell you that it is like every other lake and when one is not born on its shores, one must mistrust it a little. But I do not like the dryness of this hand," said she, examining Karol's pulse. "This little hand, for it is a woman's hand . . . *Che manina!*" she exclaimed, turning to Salvator artlessly. "But take care; your friend is not well. I know what I am talking about; my children have had no other doctor but me."

Salvator too wished to examine the prince's pulse; but the latter pretended to be a little annoyed by this anxiety. Abruptly he pulled away from the count the hand which he had tremblingly abandoned to Madame Floriani. "Please, my good Salvator," said he, "do not try to persuade me that I am ill and do not remind me too much that I am never in good health. I slept rather badly, I am a little agitated, that's all. The movement of the carriage will restore me. The signora is too kind," he added, somewhat reluctantly and dryly, as if to say "I should be much obliged to you if you allowed me to leave as quickly as possible."

Madame Floriani was struck by his tone; she looked at him in surprise and thought that the brevity of his speech was another indication of his fever. He was indeed suffering from a high degree of feverishness now, but Lucrezia in her simplicity was far from imagining that the seat of his disease was in his soul and that she was its cause.

A collation was served. While Salvator was eating with his usual hearty appetite, Karol was reluctantly having some coffee. Nothing could be more disagreeable to him at that moment, for he never took it. But he felt so close to fainting that he insisted on giving himself some artificial strength so as to be able to depart without betraying his deep discomfort.

Indeed he thought he felt better after taking this stimulant, and the sight of Salvator losing all sense of time while overwhelming Madame Floriani with endless compliments made him keenly impatient. In fact he was hard put to it not to interrupt him with spiteful words. At last the coach rolled to a halt on the gravel outside the house and the handsome Celio, leaping up with pleasure, seized the reins of two pretty little Corsican horses which were drawing a light carriage. An attentive faithful servant was sitting on the seat by his side.

Just as he was leaving Lucrezia, Count Albani, who truly loved her, felt a regret and an upsurge of affection which were translated into expansive and exaggerated caresses, as was his habit. After begging her forgiveness a thousand times in a low voice, he wrenched himself away from an emotion which, against his will, reminded him of the wrongs he had done her, for he took remarkable pleasure in kissing the cheeks, the soft hands and the velvety neck of his beautiful friend. She, without prudishness, yet without coquetry, tolerated these voluptuous and tender farewells, possibly with too much kindness and amusement for the liking of Karol, who at that moment felt that he hated her. So as not to see their final embrace which was almost passionate as far as his friend was concerned, he flung himself back into the furthest part of the carriage and averted his eyes. But just as they were setting off he encountered the face of Lucrezia close to the window. She was saying goodbye in a few friendly words and was offering him a box of chocolates. He took it mechanically and gave her a low, frigid bow, then flung the box peevishly on to the nearby seat.

Salvator did not notice the action. Half out of the carriage he was still throwing kisses to Madame Floriani and her little daughters who, having left their beds and still partly dressed, were waving gracefully to him with their pretty bare arms.

When there was nothing more to see than the trees and the walls of the villa, Salvator felt his warm Italian heart, so fickle, yet so sincere, swell and burst. He covered his face with a handkerchief and shed a few tears. Then, ashamed of this sign of weakness and afraid of appearing ridiculous to his friend, he wiped his eyes, turned to him, slightly shamefaced, to say: "Come, don't you agree that Madame Floriani is not exactly what you thought her?"

But the words died on his lips when he saw the drawn features and the livid pallor of his friend. Karol's lips were as white as his cheeks, his eyes were glazed and lack-lustre, his teeth were clenched. Salvator called out to him and shook him, but to no avail; he neither felt nor heard anything; he had fainted. For a few moments Salvator hoped to restore him to consciousness by rubbing his hands. But seeing that he was icy cold and apparently dead, he was seized with sudden panic. He shouted to Celio, had the carriage stopped and opened all the doors to give him air. Everything was useless. Karol gave no other sign of life save deep sighs and convulsive shudders.

Young Celio who had his mother's courage and presence of mind went back on to his seat, whipped up the horses and brought Prince Karol back to the house where fate had decreed that he should learn to know a new life.

11.

Towards the end of the last chapter the reader will have anticipated that Prince de Roswald would develop an illness which would compel him to remain at the Villa Floriani. I hope you do not consider the incident extraordinary and that is why I do *not* pass over it in silence.

If I had made a mystery of it, how would the development of this story remain true to life? It is evident that if there is something fatal about great passions, the fulfilment of this fatality is always explained and supported by very natural circumstances. If by symptoms preceding the illness, and if by the overwhelming nature and disorder of the illness itself, Karol had not been predisposed and constrained to come under the influence of passion, it is probable that he would have resisted the attacks of this strange and wild emotion.

He did not resist because he was indeed very ill and because for several weeks Madame Floriani almost never left his bedside. This excellent woman, as much from friendship for Salvator Albani as in obedience to a feeling of religious hospitality, made it her duty to nurse the prince, just as she would have done for his best friend or one of her own children.

In this time of trial Providence had indeed sent to Karol the person most capable of helping and saving him. Lucrezia Floriani had an almost miraculous instinct for judging the condition of a patient and the treatment he required. Perhaps this instinct was merely a matter of memory. At the age of ten, in this same house of which she was now mistress, she had been a servant, just a servant of her godmother, the Signora Ranieri, a sickly, nervous woman whom she had nursed with a love, devotion and tenderness beyond her age. This was the primary reason for the signora's affection for her which went as far as securing for her an education above her station and later wishing to marry her to her son.

So Lucrezia had learned very early to be a nurse and almost a doctor when the necessity arose. Later she had had sick friends, sick children and sick servants, as everyone is likely to have, and she had tended them herself, as everyone does not do. By making passionate efforts to discover what could relieve them and by noting attentively and scrupulously the good or bad effects of any particular medical treatment, she had acquired some very sound ideas on what suits different physical constitutions, and an excellent memory for infinite detail. She remembered the harm which had been done to her beloved mistress by the rule-of-thumb methods of the Italian doctors; she was convinced that after she herself had left the village, they had killed her. So she did not wish to summon them for the prince and she took it upon herself to treat him.

Salvator was very frightened at the responsibility which she wanted to assume and which weighed heavily on him too. But Madame Floriani's confident and courageous character won the day. Salvator wearied her with his anxieties and indecision; so she sent him away from the sick-room, saying: "Go and look after the children, amuse them, take them for walks and forget that your friend is ill; for I assure you that you are utterly useless with your childish, anxious solicitude. *I* shall look after him. He is my responsibility, I shan't leave him for a single minute."

Salvator had great difficulty in keeping calm. Karol's prostration terrified him and seemed to call for prompt and active help.

Madame Floriani had seen such nervous phenomena before and when she looked at the prince's delicate hands, his white transparent skin and his fine, silky hair, the whole picture both collectively and in detail was so significant that she easily recognised certain similarities between his and Signora Ranieri's illness which did not deceive her woman's heart.

Her main object was to calm Karol without weakening him, and being convinced that for such highly sensitive constitutions there are magnetic influences of a superior order which elude common observation, she often summoned her children to the prince's bedside, when once she had made sure that his condition was not contagious. She believed that the presence of those strong, young, healthy beings would have a mysterious beneficent power, both morally and physically, which would kindle the flickering flame of life in the young patient.

And who can say with certainty that she was deluding herself in this matter? Whether or no the imagination plays a considerable part in nervous illness, the fact remains that Karol breathed more easily when the children were there and their pure breath, mingled with that of their mother, made the air seem easier and milder to his fevered breast. We are prepared to accept that patients experience repugnance when they are approached by people who fill them with disgust and anxiety; consequently we should also recognise the physical well-being which they feel when they are cared for or merely surrounded by beings who are sympathetic and pleasant-featured. If, when our last hour comes, instead of the sinister trappings of death we could bring down celestial figures to surround our bed and lull us with the music of the seraphim, we should endure the bitter moment of death without effort or agony.

Karol, tossed by painful dreams, awoke at times in terror and despair. When this happened he instinctively sought some place of refuge from the phantoms that beset him, and it was the maternal arms of Madame Floriani which were to surround him as if they were a rampart, and her bosom on which to rest his aching head. Then, when he opened his eyes and gazed wild and distraught around him, he would see the beautiful, loving faces of Celio and Stella smiling at him. He returned their smile mechanically, as if he were making an effort to please them, but meanwhile his nightmare had faded and his panic was forgotten. His brain, which was still weak, also developed strange fancies. They would bring little Salvator's rosy face close to his and when he looked at the child it seemed to him that he had wings like a cherub and fluttered round his head so as to cool him. Beatrice's voice was unusually sweet and when she chattered quietly with her brothers, he thought he could hear her singing. In the fresh, soothing tone of her voice he could hear musical notes discernible to him alone, and one day when the little one was quietly arguing about a toy with her sister, Madame Floriani was surprised to hear the prince tell her that the child sang Mozart better than anyone else alive. "She has a beautiful nature," he added, making a great effort to convey his thought. "She has probably heard a lot of music, but she can only remember Mozart, never anything from the other masters."

"And doesn't Stella sing too?" asked Lucrezia, who was trying to penetrate to the meaning behind his words.

"She sometimes sings Beethoven, but it is less consistent, less sustained, less uniform."

"And what about Celio? He never sings."

"I can only hear Celio when he walks. There is so much grace and harmony in his person and his movements that the ground echoes beneath his footsteps and the room is filled with long, vibrating sounds."

"And the little one?" asked Lucrezia, offering him the cheek of her *bambino*. "He is the noisiest one, he sometimes shouts. Doesn't he hurt you?"

"He never hurts me. I can't hear him. I think I have become deaf to noise. But melody and rhythm still affect me. When that cherub," he added, pointing to little Salvator, "is before me, I see a kind of shower of bright colours dancing around my bed, which are shapeless, but dispel the evil visions. Ah! Do not remove the children. I shall be free of pain, as long as the children are there."

Hitherto Karol had lived with the thought of death. He had grown up so accustomed to it that, before he had been stricken with this illness, he had reached the stage when he believed that he belonged to death and that every day of respite which he had been granted was by mere chance. He even went so far as to joke about it; but when we form that kind of idea when we are well, we can accept it with philosophical calm, whereas it is rare not to be driven to panic when it invades a mind weakened by illness. In my opinion the only sad thing about death is that it comes to us when we are so prostrated and demoralised that we can no longer see it for what it is and that it even terrifies souls which are in themselves calm and resolute. Thus, what happens to most sick people happened to the prince. When he had to pit himself at close quarters against the idea of dying in the spring time of life, the sweet melancholy on which he had fed hitherto degenerated into black despair.

If his mother had been his nurse in the present situation, she would have raised his spirits in a way entirely different from that used by Madame Floriani. She would have spoken to him of the life hereafter, she would have surrounded him with the austere external succour of religion. The priest would have come to his aid and Karol, prepared by ritual pomp, would have accepted and endured his fate. But Lucrezia proceeded otherwise. She thrust aside from him the idea of death and when he gave her the impression that he thought it imminent and inevitable, she teased him tenderly and pretended to a calmness of mind she did not always have.

She applied so much prudence and apparent serenity to the matter that she succeeded in winning his confidence. She soothed him, not by telling him what it is too late to tell the sick, namely to despise life (that is a form of courage which is not to be relied upon, because this courage can very often kill,) but she cheered him by making him believe in life, and she quickly realised that he still loved, and fiercely loved, this physical life which he had scorned so much at the time when it was not menaced.

Salvator was afraid, because he thought that his friend would not have the moral strength to resist the disease. "How do you hope to save him?" he would say to Madame Floriani, "when he has been weary of life so long and especially since his mother's death, and when he is slowly and gently yielding to consumption? From the almost pleasure which this idea gave him I had the feeling that he was already stricken and that when he fell he would never rise again."

"You were wrong then and are wrong now," answered Lucrezia. "No one has a taste for dying unless he is a monomaniac and your friend is certainly not that. He is well balanced and this nervous perturbation which was making him so gloomy will vanish when the present crisis passes. I assure you, he wishes to live and he *will* live."

Karol did indeed wish to live, he wished to live for Lucrezia Floriani. To be sure he did not realise it and for the fortnight during which he was suffering the worst of the illness he forgot the shock which had precipitated it. But this love continued and grew without his awareness, like that of a child in the cradle for the woman who feeds it. An instinctive attachment, indissoluble and imperious, took possession of his poor distressed soul and tore him away from the cold fingers of death. He fell under the ascendancy of this woman to whom he was no more than a patient to be nursed and to whom he transferred all the love he had felt for his mother and the love he thought he had had for his sweetheart.

In the early stages of his delirium he was obsessed by the idea that his mother, by a miracle of maternal love, had left her grave to come and help him to die and he kept on mistaking Lucrezia for her. It was this delusion which explained why she found him submissive to all her treatment, attentive to all she said and forgetful of all the mistrust with which her character had originally inspired him. When he was oppressed to the extent of being unable to breathe he sought her shoulder on which to rest his head and sometimes he would doze for an hour in that position without suspecting his mistake.

Then, one day, his delirium was gone and as his sleep had been more unbroken and wholesome he opened his eyes and fixed them, astonished, on the pale face of this woman, wearied with all the attentions and sleepless nights she had devoted to him. It seemed to him that he had come out of a long dream and he asked her if he had been ill long and was it she whom he had always seen by his side. "Good heavens," he said when she had replied, "you certainly do look like my mother. Salvator," he went on, recognising his friend who was approaching his bed, "doesn't she look like my mother? I was completely thunderstruck by it when I saw her the first time."

Salvator did not consider it opportune to contradict him, although he could not see the slightest similarity between the beautiful, shapely Lucrezia and the tall, gaunt, austere Princess de Roswald.

On another occasion, Karol still leaning on Madame Floriani's arm, tried to support himself unaided. "I feel better," he said. "I have more strength. I have tired you too much. I don't understand how I could take advantage of your kindness to such an extent."

"No, no, lean on me, my child," she answered gaily, using the familiar form of address which was a habit she easily adopted with people who interested her, and in Karol's case she had come to regard him almost as a son.

"Are you my mother, then? Are you really my mother?" asked Karol whose mind was beginning to become confused again.

"Yes, yes, I am your mother," she replied, without thinking that for Karol such a statement might be sacrilege. "Rest assured that at this moment it is absolutely the same thing."

Karol said nothing, then his eyes filled with tears and he began to weep like a child and pressed her hand against his lips.

"My dear son," she said, kissing him on the brow several times, "you must not weep, it may overtire you. If you think of your mother, think that she sees you from Heaven and blesses you, knowing that you will soon be better."

"You are wrong," Karol replied. "High in Heaven, my mother has been calling a long time and urging me to go and join her. I can hear her clearly, but I, in my ingratitude, haven't the courage to give up life."

"How can you argue so mistakenly, child that you are?" said Lucrezia, with the tender seriousness and calm she would have used in chiding Celio. "When it is God's will that we should live, our parents cannot summon us to them in the other world. They neither wish it nor should wish it. So you must have dreamed it all; when one is ill one has many dreams. If your mother could make herself heard by you she would tell you that you have not lived long enough to deserve to go and join her."

Karol turned round with an effort, possibly surprised to hear Madame Floriani preaching to him. He looked at her again, then as if he had not heard or understood what she had just said, he cried: "No, I haven't the strength to die. You are holding me back and I cannot leave you. May my mother forgive me, I want to stay with you."

And exhausted by his emotion he fell back in Lucrezia's arms and sank into sleep once more.

12.

One evening, when the prince who was convalescing by now, had apparently fallen gently asleep, and Madame Floriani had put the children to bed, she was sitting with Salvator on the terrace, enjoying the cool air.

"My dear Lucrezia," he said to her, "the time has come at last for us to speak of real life, for we have been traversing a twenty day nightmare which is now fading, thank God, – I should say thank *you*, for you have saved my friend, and you have added to my affection for you a gratitude which it is impossible to express. But now tell me, what are we going to do when once our dear patient is fit to travel?"

"We haven't reached that stage yet," she replied. "He will not be able to leave even after a fortnight. He can barely walk round the garden at present and, as you know, strength returns much more slowly than it goes."

"Let us suppose that this convalescence lasts another month. There is an end to everything. We can't remain a burden on you eternally, and we shall have to part one day."

"Certainly, but I want it to be delayed as long as possible. You are no burden to me; I am well rewarded for the attentions I have given to your friend by the happiness I feel in knowing that I have saved him. Moreover, his gratitude is so great, so genuine and tender, that I have begun to love him, almost as much as you love him yourself. It is natural to nurse and comfort those whom one loves. So I do not see that there is any occasion for thanking me so much."

"You seem unwilling to understand me, my dear Lucrezia. It is the future which disturbs me."

"What? The prince's life? It has not been imperilled at all by this illness. I have studied him. He has an excellent constitution. It is even possible that he will outlive both of us."

"I too am almost sure of it. The occasion has shown me what resources these nervous temperaments possess. But have you thought about his moral future, Lucrezia?"

"It seems to me that that is not my responsibility. Why do you ask me that?"

"I ought not to be surprised that a nature as loyal and generous as yours should carry simplicity as far as blindness, yet it is strange that you don't understand me."

"Well, then, I don't understand you. Come, speak clearly."

"To speak clearly on so delicate a matter to someone who gives no help at all is brutal. And yet I must. Well – Karol loves you."

"I should hope so! And I love him too; but if you are trying to tell me that he is in love with me, I cannot take your fears seriously."

"Oh, my dear Lucrezia, please don't make light of it. Everything is serious with a character which is as deep and intense as my poor friend's. Believe me, it is frightfully serious."

"No, no, Salvator, you are talking nonsense. That your friend should have a serious feeling of affection for me, keen, ardent gratitude if you wish – that is possible for a being as gentle and noble as he is. But that this boy should be in love with your old friend is impossible! You see him over-excited when he speaks to us and that is the effect of his weakness and the aftermath of his previous nervous condition. You hear him thank me in terms which are not proportionate to the services I have rendered him, and that is the effect of the beautiful language which comes from a beautiful soul, from a noble habit of thinking and saying things well, and from the distinguished education and exquisite manners he has acquired. But love me? What madness! He does not know me and if he did know me, if he knew my past life, the poor boy would be afraid of me. Fire and water, heaven and earth are not more dissimilar."

"Heaven and earth, fire and water may be opposing elements, but they are always united or ready to unite in nature. Clouds and rocks, volcanoes and seas embrace each other when they meet. They shatter and merge together in the same eternal disasters. Your comparison affirms my assertion and must explain my fears."

"You are being poetic to no purpose. I tell you that he would despise and maybe hate me if he realised that the sister of mercy who had waited on him was a sinner. I know all about his principles and ideas from what you tell me every day – for I must admit that he himself has never preached morality to me. But after all, how can you, who know his character and opinions so well, suppose that there could be any possible relationship between us in the future? Come, I know quite well what he will think of me when he recovers his health and clarity of judgement. I hve no illusions. Six months hence, in Venice, Naples or Florence someone will relate in his presence the sad adventures which have befallen me and those even sadder which they attribute to me – for there is nothing which they don't ascribe to the rich . . . Well, remember at that time what I am telling you now. You will see your friend defend me a little, sigh a great deal and then say to you, 'How unfortunate that so good a woman, for whom I feel so much friendship and gratitude, should be vilified so!' That is all that La Floriani will mean to this proud young man. It will be a sweet but sad memory and I do not expect anything more, for what do I need save the truth? You are fully aware, Salvator, that I have the strength to accept all the consequences of my past, that they neither perturb nor offend me, and that they in no way affect the serenity of my conscience."

"All you say saddens me, my dear Lucrezia," replied Salvator, taking her hand tenderly, "because it is all true, save one point. My friend will leave you, certainly. He will flee you as soon as he has the strength to do so and has seen clearly into himself. Yes, he will hear fools tell the story of your life without understanding it and cowards slandering it. And he will suffer and sigh bitterly. But that that will be all, that his grief will fade with a few words and that your memory will be effaced by an effort of reason and will-power, that I deny! At this very moment Karol is more unhappy than he has ever been, and he will be unhappy for ever, although he does not yet realise it, lost as he is in the intoxication of first love."

"I must interrupt you at the words 'first love'," said Lucrezia, who had been listening attentively. "It is because you yourself have told me that I would not be his first love that I cannot be too afraid of this one, assuming, as you do, that it exists. But did you not tell me that he had been betrothed to a beautiful girl of his own station, that he had been inconsolable when she died and that he would probably never love another woman? That is what you told me earlier on and if that is true, he does not love me, or if he is capable of loving me, it is not impossible that another woman will obliterate me from his thoughts."

"But that would mean another five or six years of suffering for him – for he was eighteen when Lucie died and until he met you he had not even looked at another woman."

"There is no possible comparison between two such different loves. For six years he may have mourned an angelic creature similar to himself, whom duty and attachment required him to prefer above all others. But in the case of a poor old theatrical like me, the widow of... several lovers, (I have never counted how many) he would not require six weeks to regain his senses, that is, if he ever lost them. Come, Salvator, let us drop the subject. That idea of yours distresses and offends me somewhat. Why must your poor Lucrezia to whom you have shown proof of trust and rare brotherly love for the past three weeks – why must she necessarily be the object of everybody's gross desires, and even of the most chaste and ailing of your friends? When I have expiated all my faults by so much suffering and made some slight amends for them with good deeds, why can I not be treated like a motherly friend by young men of good character? Must I play the part of Satan in connection with them, when in fact there is as little evil in me as there is in Stella or Beatrice? Am I a coquette? Am I still beautiful? *Corpo di Dio*, as my father would say, I so much wish to be left in peace that I do my utmost to give people cause for neither fear nor envy of me. Rest, oblivion, that is what I ask for, what I sigh for, what I sometimes moan for like the hart panting for the water brooks ... When, then, will I cease to hear the word 'love' jarring on my ear like a false note?"

"My poor beloved sister," said Salvator, "you are struggling in vain. For many a day to come you will have to resist, if not yourself, then at least the men who see you. It is useless for *me* to try to be absolutely calm when I am with you. Even I can't do it and yet ... "

"Come," cried Lucrezia in frank and almost comical desperation, "are you starting again? Et tu, Brute ... Kill me without delay. I would prefer that. At least in that way I would be rid of that eternal refrain!"

"I'll say no more," exclaimed Salvator, who dreaded the sight of her grief coming so soon after that small flash of playfulness. "I shall never speak again, I shall never mention myself even if it should kill me. I have given you my promise and I swear to keep it. But it will not be so with all men. It will be useless for you to say that you are old: they will look at you and see the vivid flame of life coursing through your generous veins. You will screw your hair up as negligently as you do now and hide yourself in that eternal dressing gown which looks more like a penitent's sackcloth than a woman's garment, but it will all be to no purpose: you will still be beautiful in spite of yourself, still more beautiful than any other woman in the world! What other woman besides yourself could show herself in broad daylight dressed so casually, expose her neck and arms to the blazing sunshine, tire her complexion and her eyes watching a patient throughout endless nights, after feeding half a dozen children, working, weeping, suffering ... Oh, what haven't you endured? What other woman could, after all this, still inflame the imagination of men, whether they be as chaste as my friend Karol or as experienced as your friend Salvator?"

'I tell you," cried Madame Floriani, losing her patience, "if you continue talking in that way and succeed in convincing me that I shall fall in love again one day, I can see myself this very night putting acid or some other corrosive on my face so as to be hideous to-morrow."

"What?" cried Salvator, taken aback, "Would you really be so savage to yourself?"

"No, I didn't mean it," she answered, candidly. "I have suffered enough not to have the slightest wish to look for more suffering."

"But supposing you could disfigure yourself without making yourself blind or doing yourself any real harm . . . You wouldn't do it, would you?"

"I would not do it lightly, for I am an artist. I love beauty and I do my utmost to shield my children's eyes from the sight of ugliness. I would terrify my own self if I became an object of horror and disgust, and yet I assure you that if I had to choose between the tortures of a new love and the unpleasant consequences of disfiguring myself I would not hesitate in my choice."

"You sound so sincere as you speak that you terrify me. A person like you is capable of anything. Lucrezia, don't take it into your head to commit that kind of madness, – like Frederick the Great's sister who, they say, disfigured herself, so as not to be sought in marriage, and so preserve herself for her lover."

"That is indeed sublime," said Lucrezia, "for it is the greatest sacrifice a woman can make."

"Yes, but the story adds that with the destruction of her beauty the princess also destroyed her health and that she became unbalanced and ill-natured. So remain beautiful. Otherwise you may be running the risk of losing your goodness of heart, which is no mean treasure."

"Friend," said Madame Floriani, "time will settle everything. Little by little I shall grow ugly without thinking about it, possibly without realising it, and then I believe I shall be happy at last. Through fatal experience I have learned that there is no happiness in love and so I still maintain the dream of a certain state of calm and innocence which I believe I feel at this moment and which seems to me full of delight. Don't tell me then that your friend is about to disturb it with his own suffering. I shall do something to prevent him from loving me."

"And how will you set about it?"

"By telling him the truth about myself. Help me. Don't spare him . . . But all this is nonsense. I am mad to believe what you have said. He cannot be in love with me. Doesn't he still wear the portrait of his beloved on his heart?"

"Do you really think he loved her?" said Salvator, after a short silence.

"You told me so," replied Lucrezia.

"Yes, I thought so too, because he believed it himself, and spoke of it so eloquently. But, between ourselves, wouldn't you say that the love which a man has for a woman is not complete unless he has possessed her? True love cannot feed eternally on desires and regrets. And when I come to think now of the relations between Prince Karol and Princess Lucie, I am convinced their love existed only in their imagination. They had seen one another five or six times, perhaps, and even then, always in the presence of their parents."

"Is that all?"

"Yes, Karol told me so himself. They barely knew one another when they were betrothed and she died so soon afterwards that they had no time to become better acquainted."

"Did you yourself ever see Princess Lucie?"

"I saw her once. She was a pretty creature, slight, pale – and consumptive. I could tell that immediately, although no one else thought so. She was very elegant and graceful. She dressed exquisitely and had a grand air, which I considered somewhat too affected, blue eyes, a cloud of hair, a delicate complexion, the reputation of an angel and a poetic aura. I did not like her. She was too romantic and too disdainful. She was one of those beings to whom I am always tempted to say: 'Do open your mouth when you speak, do put your feet down on the ground when you walk, do eat with your teeth, do cry with your eyes, do play the piano with your fingers, do laugh with your throat, and not with your eyebrows, do bow with your body and not with your chin. If you are a butterfly or a flower, fly away into the wind and don't come to flutter round our eyes or ears. If you are dead, say so immediately.' In short: she made me impatient. She was like something which resembles a woman, but is nothing more than her shadow. She had a mania for covering herself with flowers and perfume which gave me the migraine on the day when I had the honour of dining with her. She had the fragrance of an embalmed corpse, and I would have preferred a sachet in my wardrobe rather than a woman like that by my side – at least I would not have been obliged to inhale its perfume all the time."

"I cannot help laughing at the portrait," said Lucrezia, "and yet I feel that it is exaggerated and that there is a hint of spite in it. The princess did not like you, that's obvious. You probably paid her a compliment which was not too refined. Let us leave the dead in peace and respect this memory in the pure soul of Prince Karol. Indeed, it is my intention to make him speak of her and rekindle that love in him; it will be salutary for him at this moment. Good night, my friend. Don't worry, Karol will never love anyone but a sylph."

Lucrezia was genuinely convinced that Salvator was mistaken. She was well aware that his own love for her was generous and, so to speak, good-natured, a love very sincere but very matter-of-fact, one which would have imposed no chains but would equally have accepted none; in a word a good, warm friendship with a few pleasures now and again, and as many infidelities as could or would be permitted by either partner.

Madame Floriani wanted no more chains and thought herself proof against all passion, but she had formed too high a conception of love, she had felt it too deeply and indeed was too uncomplicated and ardent by nature for such an arrangement not to appear revolting to her. She did not know the meaning of doing things by halves and if, without her knowledge, she was still harbouring certain feelings, she preferred to conquer and silence them rather than satisfy them without rapture and without the conviction, possibly illusory, but nevertheless sincere, of a life shared with another in eternal fidelity. That is how she had always loved and whether her passion had lasted a week or perhaps even a day, as Salvator had said, it had been in the firm belief that it was for life. Great facility in self-delusion, blind benevolence in judgement, inexhaustible tenderness of heart, resulting in over-haste, errors and weakness, heroic devotion to unworthy objects, unparalleled energy applied to a wretched goal in actual fact yet sublime in intention – such was the generous, extravagant and deplorable story of her entire existence.

As ready to respond to desire as to renounce it, she had thought for the whole of the past year that she was finally free of love and that nothing could bring her back to it. Her mind was so quick to accept a resolution and accustom itself to a certain manner of looking at things, that she was convinced that her victory was won for ever, and if she could have based the length of time on the intensity of her conviction, she would have sworn on oath that she had not known love for more than twenty years.

And yet the last wound was barely healed and like a good soldier who rejoins his comrades when his legs can hardly support him to the ambulance, Lucrezia bravely faced daily contact with these two men in love with her, each in his own way. She comforted herself by saying that she had never felt any love for the one, nor could she ever feel love for the other, and that as Providence had meant her to be necessary to them, there was no reason for her to torture herself by dwelling on the possible dangers of the situation.

Still thinking of all that Salvator Albani had just said, she sat down in her boudoir before entering her bedroom and began to loosen her hair and arrange it for the night in a charmingly casual manner. "Perhaps," she said to herself, "it may be a harmless ruse on Salvator's part to discover what I think of his friend and whether I am to be approached by way of impertinence or sentiment. He had invented this story of Karol's love to renew those outbursts of passion which I have forbidden him."

And yet there were words which the prince had let slip, exclamations, certain looks which should surely have enlightened a woman of Lucrezia's age and experience. But she had preserved a child-like modesty and innocence despite everything, and this trait of her character was not one of the least of its charms. Perhaps that was why she always appeared young, and why people suddenly found that they liked her.

As she was arranging her hair before a mirror by the light of a single candle, she looked at herself carefully for a moment, as she had not done for the past year; but she possessed the instinct for living for herself to such a slight degree, that she saw nothing more in her face than the memory of the men who had loved her. "Nonsense," she said to herself, "they would not love me if they saw me now. How could I really please others when the ones who had so many greater reasons for loving me than my youth and beauty are now indifferent to me?" She had not been happy in her loves and yet she had kindled passions so violent that it was no compliment to her to inspire a passing fancy, and after being an idol to become a diversion.

She therefore felt very resolute when, lowering the gauze curtains over the mirror on her dressing table, she promised herself that no one would ever have any rights over her again; but as she was taking up her candle to return to her children, she started at the sight of a ghost in front of her.

"My dear prince," she said after a moment of uncontrollable panic, "there you are out of your bed when we thought you sound asleep! What is the matter? Are you in pain? And to think you were alone! Salvator has just left me. Didn't he go back to you? Speak please, I am very uneasy about you."

The prince was so pale and agitated and was trembling so much that there was indeed cause for anxiety. He had difficulty in replying. At last he seemed to come to a decision.

"Don't be afraid of me, and don't be afraid for me," he said. "I am well, very well. But I could not sleep. So I went and stood near the window. I heard voices. I was sorely tempted to go down and join in your conversation. But I did not dare . . . I hesitated a long time. At last, when your voices died and I saw Salvator wandering alone far in the garden, I made a great resolution . . . I came to look for you . . . Forgive me, I am so confused that I do not know what I am doing, nor where I am, nor how I had the audacity to penetrate into your own private apartments."

"Set your mind at rest," said Madame Floriani as she made him sit down on her divan. "I am not offended. It is quite clear that you are ill. You can barely stand up. Come now, my dear prince, you must have had a bad dream. I thought I had left

Antonia by your bedside. Why did the young scatter-brain leave you alone?"

"It was I that asked her to leave me. I am going now. Forgive me again. I think I must be mad to-night."

"No, no, stay here till you feel better. I shall go and find Salvator. Between us we shall distract you, you will forget your malaise as you talk to us and when you are more yourself, Salvator will take you back to your room. You will sleep calmly when he is near you."

"Don't go for Salvator," said the prince, and with an impetuous movement seized both her hands. "He can do nothing for me. You alone can do everything. Listen, listen to me and let me die afterwards if the little strength I have regained fades in the supreme effort I must make in order to speak to you.

"I heard everything that Salvator said to you this evening and all that you answered. My window was open; you were standing below it. At night voices carry in the solemn silence here. So I know everything: you do not love me and you do not even believe that I love you."

"Here it starts again," thought Lucrezia, overcome with distress and weary in anticipation of what she would have to say in self-defence without wounding his sad heart. "My dear child," she began, "listen . . . "

"No, no," he cried with an energy of which one would have thought him incapable. "I have nothing to listen to. I know everything you will say, I do not need to hear it and it is not even certain whether I have the strength to do so. It is I who must speak. I ask nothing of you. Have I ever asked you for anything? Would you even know my thoughts if Salvator had not guessed them and betrayed them? But there is one thing in all this which is intolerable to me, something which has pierced me to the heart, because it was you who said it. You believe that I cannot love a woman like you. You speak evil of yourself to prove that I must think it too. And lastly you think that I shall forget you and that when people will speak ill of you in my presence I shall sigh like a coward and express regret for being linked to you by gratitude. These thoughts are horrible, they kill me! Tell me that you deny them or I do not know what I shall do in my despair."

"Don't be so distressed by a few thoughtless words which I do not even remember," cried Lucrezia, alarmed by the growing excitement of the prince. "I never dreamed of accusing you of arrogance and I know that you are incapable of ingratitude. Didn't I say rather that your gratitude to me was greater than the very natural services I rendered you? I implore you, forget the words which offended you; I withdraw them and I am ready to beg your pardon for them. Calm yourself and prove the sincerity of your friendship for me by not torturing yourself unnecessarily."

"Yes, yes, you are good, entirely good," said Karol, clinging to her convulsively, for he could see that she was anxious to put an end to this tête-à-tête, "but for the first and probably the last time I must speak. Know then that if anyone, whether it be Salvator or anyone else, if anyone ever tells you that my feelings for you are not those of respect, adoration and worship – the same worship that I gave to the memory of my mother – then he will have lied like a coward, he will be my enemy and I shall kill him if I meet him! I who am gentle, weak and reserved will become venomous, violent and implacable, stronger to punish him than all your pugnacious swash-bucklers. I am aware that I have the appearance of a child, the features of a woman . . . but they don't know what there is inside me. They cannot know, I never speak of myself. I do not wish to be noticed, I do not know how to set about making myself loved, I am not loved . . . I will never be loved. I do not even ask that people should believe me capable of great love . . . what does it matter to me? But you, you . . . Ah, you at least must know . . . Know that this dying man belongs to you like a slave belongs to his master, like blood to the heart, like the body to the soul. What I cannot accept is that you should doubt it, that you should say that I cannot love another human being. Am I not a man? All men love God and I love you as the ideal, as perfection. I fear you as I fear God, I venerate you so much that I would die at your feet rather than express an outrageous desire before you . . .

"Nor do I see you as a phantom, like the one I carried within me for so long. I know full well that you are a woman who has loved before and may love again . . . . someone, not me. Well, so be it, I accept everything and I do not need to understand the mysteries of your heart and your life in order to adore you. Be anything you wish, abandon your children, deny God, drive me away from you, love the man who seems most worthy of it. If Salvator finds favour in your eyes, if he can give you a moment's happiness, listen to him, make him happy. I shall surely die in consequence, but no thought of blame will enter my mind, no feeling of vengeance will touch my heart. I shall die blessing you, proclaiming that you have the right to do everything which is forbidden to others and that what is a crime and a reproach in them is a virtue and a glory in you. I tell you, I am so unhappy in this world and the love which I bear you is gnawing at my heart with such agony, that at this moment I only have one wish, the desperate wish to die. But if you want me to go away to-morrow, never to see you again yet go on living, I shall live and be content to live in torment in order to obey you. Do you think that I have loved anyone more than you? It is untrue! I have never loved anyone. I realise now that what I once thought was love was just imagination, for, as Salvator has told you, it was in my brain, I had not felt it devour my heart. She was a pure woman and I respect her memory so much that I do not wish to lie to her any longer by wearing her portrait on my heart. Take it, hide it, keep it. I no longer understand it. When I look at it now I always see your features on it, not hers. I give it to you and beg you to accept it because it must not be profaned and because there are only two places where it can be sanctified: your hand and the grave of my mother . . . Do not think that I am delirious. If I were calm I would not have the courage to speak; but the courage I have now reveals the truth and proclaims what I have been thinking every hour since I have known you. And I would tell it to the whole world. I would swear it solemnly on the heads of your children. I shall tell Salvator himself. Let him hear me, let him know and never have the folly to deny it. I love you . . . you who for me have no name, you whom I could not describe in words. I love you . . . Fire is consuming me . . . I am dying!"

And Karol, exhausted by this ardent declaration, fell at

Lucrezia's feet and lay there writhing and wringing his hands with such violence that he tore them till they bled.

"Love him! Love him! Have pity on him," cried Salvator. He had sought the prince in vain in his room and throughout the house and had just entered here. Terrified he had overheard Karol's last words. "Love him, Lucrezia, or you are no longer yourself – or a horrible egoism has withered your generous heart. He is dying, save him! He has never loved. Restore him to life or I curse you."

And this man, strangely generous and impetuous despite his personal zest for the pleasures of life, this priceless friend who preferred Karol to everything, to Madame Floriani and himself, raised him from the floor where he lay convulsed in some kind of death agony and, as it were, flinging him into Lucrezia's arms, he rushed towards the door as if not to hear her reply or witness a happiness which he could not renounce without effort.

Lucrezia, distraught, held Karol and clasped him to her heart tenderly; but more terrified than conquered, she indicated with a peremptory gesture to Salvator that he must on no account go. "I shall love him," she said, pressing a long, firm kiss on the prince's pale brow, "but it will be as his mother loved him – as passionately and as steadfastly, I swear it. I can see that he has a need to be loved thus and I know that he deserves it. This motherly love, which I had developed for him instinctively and without thinking of prolonging beyond his recovery, I swear to give to him for ever and to the exclusion of all other men. For you, my son, I renew the vow of chastity and devotion which I made for Celio and my other children. I shall keep the portrait of your betrothed piously and respectfully, and when you wish to look at it we shall speak of her together. We shall weep together over your beloved mother, and finding her heart in mine you will not forget her. I accept your love on those terms, and I believe in that love, however disillusioned I may be about all others. That is the greatest proof of affection I can give you."

This promise appeared to Salvator to be a very incomplete remedy and more dangerous than useful. He was about to say something more, when the prince, regaining his strength and his speech cried: "Be blessed, adored woman! I shall never ask for anything more and my happiness is so great that I have no words to thank you."

Bursting into tears as he spoke he prostrated himself at her feet and embraced her knees passionately. Then tearing himself away from her he followed Salvator, and that night slept more calmly than he had ever done before.

"What a strange and hopeless predicament," said Salvator, trying to fall asleep too.

14.

I hope that the reader already knows what is about to happen in this chapter, and that nothing that has occurred hitherto in the monotonous course of this story has caused him the slightest surprise. I should like to be present when he approaches the outcome of each stage of some novel or other he happens to be reading, for then, according to his forecasts, I would be able to say whether the book in question is following the path of logic and truth. I greatly mistrust a dénouement impossible to foresee by anyone but the author, because there are no two courses to be taken by any given characters; there is only one, and if no one suspects it, it is because the characters are false and impossible.

Perhaps you will tell me that Prince Karol has been shown yielding to an outburst of emotion and an unleashing of passion utterly outside his nature as I have described it hitherto. But I am sure that you will not make such a naive observation, for I would refer you to yourself and I would ask you if in matters of love what seems to us the very opposite of our own tastes and faculties is not precisely what we rush to embrace with the greatest fervour and whether in such cases the impossible is not the inevitable.

Indeed life as it takes place before our eyes is certainly insane and odd enough; the human heart as God has made it is fickle and inconsistent enough; in the natural course of events there are disorders, cataclysms, storms, disasters and accidents enough for it to be unnecessary to torture one's brain so as to devise strange facts and exceptional characters. All that one needs is to narrate. Moreover, what are these exceptional characters which the novelist is constantly seeking so as to surprise and interest his public? Aren't we all exceptions in relation to others, in the infinite detail of our make-up? If certain general laws make humanity a single being, when we analyse this great synthesis, do we not find as many distinct and dissimilar beings as there are individualities? Genesis tells us that God made man from a little clay and water in order to show us that the same elementary matter was used to create us all. But in the combination of the constituent parts of this matter lies eternal and infinite diversity and this explains why it is impossible to encounter two identical leaves in the vegetable kingdom, and why it is futile to seek two identical hearts in the human race. Let us then recognise this commonplace: that each one of us is an unknown world to his fellows, and he could relate a history of himself which is similar to, yet not the same as that of anyone else.

The novel is not required to do more than to relate faithfully one of these personal histories and to make it as clear as possible. I have no objections when the writer adds a large number of external facts and there is much interplay of varied personalities, but for me such additions complicate the novelist's work considerably without much benefit to the reader's moral instruction. Besides, it makes it very tiring for the reader, who is lazy! Let my lazy reader be happy then in discovering a writer even lazier than he!

You already have the feeling that when Madame Floriani made the agreement with Prince Karol she was committing herself more than she thought and that a platonic yet passionate maternal love could not continue endlessly between a man of twenty-four and a woman of thirty, both of them beautiful, both of them warmly emotional and hungry for love. It lasted six weeks, possibly two months, during which time they were both blissfully serene, and this, it must be mentioned, was the most beautiful period of their lives. Then came the storm and it was in the young man's soul that it broke first. Then came a few hours of rapture when for both of them heaven seemed to descend and absorb the earth. But when human happiness has reached its peak it is nearing its end. The inexorable law which rules our fate has ordained it so, and it would be the greatest folly to urge man to aspire to a state of absolute happiness without telling him that this happiness cannot be anything but a flash of lightning in the course of his life, and that he must be reconciled to vegetating for the remainder of his days, tolerably content with some hope or some memory.

It is the same in real life as it is in the novel; for life to be perfect one would have to die the moment after the greatest ecstasy. In order for the novel to flatter the imagination it is usually ended on the wedding day; in other words, in the course of a number of more or less masterly volumes the writer aspires towards the sight of a shining light, whose brilliance and beauty no art can express and which the reader colours according to his own fancy, for that is the point at which the author puts down his pen and takes his leave.

Well, to make some attempt to leave the beaten track, we shall not end the book at this fatal page. We shall pause for a moment at the top of the hill which we have seen climbed and we shall descend it again at a later stage – but the reader may be excused from accompanying us on this part of the journey if he does not like sad stories and painful truths.

So the reader has been given fair warning. He knows everything which is still to happen. I repeat: stop here, if you wish. You know the synthesis of these two existences who have come together from the two opposite ends of the social horizon. *Details* are my concern, and if you are not interested in them, leave me to write in peace. Do you think that a writer is always obliged to bear you in mind and that he can never give himself the pleasure of forgetting you and writing for himself? *You* rarely feel any embarrassment when you forget him, which makes us quits . . .

When she renounced love and sought solitude, Madame Floriani had been mistaken about the stage she had reached in her life. At that moment she was absolutely convinced that the calm of old age had come miraculously to bring her its benefits prematurely. The fifteen years of passion and torture she had undergone seemed so cruel and burdensome to her that she deluded herself into thinking that they would be counted as double that time by the great Dispenser of our trials. But implacable destiny was not satisfied. Because she had been mistaken in her choices, because she had given sublime affection to beings who pleased her without deserving to please her, because she could not love those who deserved her love without pleasing her, because she had loved too well those whom Jesus Christ wished to redeem, and because she had not sought the tranquillity, security and calm triumph of the elect – the intolerable righteous ones who from their golden seats look down in scorn on the miseries and sufferings of humanity – for all these reasons this poor sinner was to expiate her past misfortunes by more and more misfortunes. Become a sister of mercy, go and gather the broken bodies scattered on the field of battle, drive the filthy flies away from the wounded left to die – and you will be killed by a bullet or treated like a camp-follower by the brutal conqueror! But live with those who are perfect, love none but the beautiful, the rich, the wise, the happy ones of this world, steep your delicate soul in an ethereal atmosphere, be like a flower in its garden, like Princess Lucie on her cloud, and you will be canonised!

So Madame Floriani was deluding herself greatly when she imagined that she would escape so lightly and that henceforth she would be able to live for her children, her old father and herself. A heart which has experienced such terrible suffering as she had undergone is not cured by a few months of rest and solitude. Solitude and inaction are perhaps the very things which are *not* advisable. The transition had taken place too abruptly and by accepting her cure as a fait accompli Lucrezia in her simplicity had not been sufficiently aware of her own character. When instead of the exacting personal love which had been the tragedy of her life, the noble romantic Prince de Roswald offered her absolute devotion and respect worthy of a saint and when he not merely accepted, but accepted with rapture her vow of chaste friendship, she thought she was saved. Was it permitted for a woman burdened with so many lapses to be deluded to such an extent and really imagine that Providence was about to reward her for her errors instead of punishing her for them? No, it was not permitted, yet Lucrezia accepted everything with her usual naïvety.

At the beginning she found utter happiness and unadulterated joy in the arrangement. Karol was so unassertive, so submissive, he had pledged himself so completely, he was so greatly under her spell that a single word, a glance, an innocent caress was sufficient to send him to the heights of indescribable ecstasy. At the surface of his being there was angelic purity, and the acrid passions which were fermenting unknown and latent in the depths of his soul did not awaken immediately. He had never burned with the flame of love, he had never felt the heart of a woman beat against his, and the first emotions of this nature were sharper and deeper for him than for an adolescent at the first awakening of the senses.

These desires had been growing in him for a long time now, but he did not wish to recognise them. He had deceived them with the help of poetry and the religious feeling he had entertained for his beloved Lucie whose hand had barely ever brushed his own. Therefore his dreams came into contact with reality in all their freshness, timidity and tremulousness. He still had the terrors of a child, but also the energies of a man. This mixture of modesty and latent passion gave him an irresistible charm which Lucrezia had never yet encountered. And so, every day he stirred her with an ever increasing sympathy, admiration and finally ardour of which she was utterly unaware.

Always brave to the point of recklessness and careless of herself in relation to those whom she loved she did not see the storm approach. Why should she believe anything save what he told her and why should she worry about a future which seemed as if it must inevitably be the indefinite continuation of the present celestial love?

This sweet yet terrible young man who, utterly vanquished and consumed by passion, could still not believe in it, who had lived on illusions and relied on the power of words without appreciating the subtleties of the ideas and facts they represent – this sweet yet terrible young man was deceiving himself and the woman he loved. When he had addressed her as 'mother', when he had pressed the hem of her garment to his burning lips, when he had said as he fell asleep: "I would rather die than profane you with my thoughts", he judged himself to be stronger than human nature and scorned the storm which was muttering in his breast.

And she, the blind girl – for she was a child even more ingenuous and credulous than Karol – this woman whom one would have described in accepted language as a fallen woman, she believed in this calm which seemed so beautiful, so new and so wholesome to her. She experienced it in herself because lassitude and disgust had calmed her blood and protected her from any sudden emotional onslaught.

And yet, through this mutual trust, so absolute and sincere that the presence of Salvator did not embarrass them, and their chaste kisses hardly feared the children's glances, an abyss was being dug, widening with the passing of the days. Karol no longer existed through himself. His family, his faith, his mother, his betrothed, his instincts, his tastes, his associations – he had lost sight of them all. He only breathed through Lucrezia's breath; he did not breathe nor did he see, he did not understand nor did he think unless she stood between him and the outer world. His intoxication was so complete that he could no longer take a single step in life by himself. The future meant as little to him as the past. The idea of departing from her had no sense for him. It seemed as if this frail, diaphanous being had been consumed and absorbed in the furnace of love.

Gradually however the flames emerged from the clouds of perfume which concealed them. Lightning traversed the sky, the voice of passion rang out like a cry of distress, like a question of life and death. An unconscious neglect of all fear and all caution had gradually brought about the imminent defeat of that reason whose supremacy had been Lucrezia's great pride. As for Karol, an invincible attraction, a progression of delicate, consuming sensations, the delights of a strange, all-powerful intoxication had silenced and annihilated one by one his religious fears, and this triumph of the senses which he had thought would be degrading for both of them, gave his love an added exultation and intensity.

He had spent his life duelling in the name of the spirit against the flesh. In the sanctification of marriage and the blessed union of two chaste beings he had seen the only possible rehabilitation of an act which was only divine in his eyes because it was necessary. For a long time he had thought that to ask for this expression of love from a woman who gave her favours easily, or even from a woman who had had intimate knowledge of only one other man would be an irreparable moral fall for which he could never forgive himself. But now he was greatly surprised to feel flooded with so much joy that his conscience was dumb; and when he questioned this same conscience he found that it was intoxicated; and when it did answer him it was to the effect that it was not concerned with his sin, that it felt at ease, that it did not know why he had always wanted to prevent it from making common cause with his heart, in short, that it thirsted for fresh delights and would talk morality and wisdom to him when it would be satiated.

Lucrezia who had never made these metaphysical distinctions, who had only renounced love because hers had caused unhappiness to others, felt very calm and very proud when, infected by the illusions of her lover, she thought that he was and would remain the happiest of men. She did not even regret her beautiful dream of being stoical and becoming old at an early age. Her pride did not reproach her and she did not mourn over its fall. Always naïve and trusting she only answered Salvator's fears by asking him if Karol had any regrets or cause to complain. And as Karol at that moment was dwelling in the highest heaven of bliss and Salvator himself was stupefied with astonishment, jealousy and admiration, he could find nothing to say.

Our good friend Count Albani who would not have felt this happiness with the same force as his young friend, but who on the other hand would not have suffered from it as cruelly later, was seriously troubled by the entire affair. He was so perturbed by it that he lost his sleep and nearly all his appetite and gaiety. But his soul was so noble and his friendship so loyal that he triumphed over himself. He thanked Lucrezia effusively if not for curing the mind and heart of Karol for ever (which he did not think possible in such conditions) at least for initiating him into a happiness which no other woman would have ever shown him. Then excusing himself on the grounds of important business in Venice he departed, without making any definite plans with them for the future. "I shall return in a fortnight," he said, "and you will tell me then what you have decided."

The fact was that he could not continue to endure the sight of such happiness, although he approved of it and encouraged it with all his heart. He set off without telling them that he was going to seek philosophical distraction with a certain dancer who had given him an encouraging sign from the wings of La Scala in Milan . . . .

"I would never have thought," he said to himself as the coach left, "that my young Puritan would eat the forbidden fruit with such violence and such forgetfulness of the past. Lucrezia is certainly more of a temptress than was the serpent, for Adam wept immediately over his sin, whereas Karol glories in his . . . Well, may Heaven grant that it lasts and that on my return I do not find him full of shame and despair."

The reader will soon know what happened, if he does not know already, and if he does not wish to remain suspended between the gates of heaven and hell.

15.

In spite of the affection which the prince bore the count, in spite of the gratitude inspired in him by his devotion, his fond attentions and the approval he had just given to his happiness, happiness is so selfish that Karol saw Albani leave with something akin to joy. The presence of a friend always tends to hamper the continual effusions of an impassioned heart and although the prince had been utterly unrestrained in proclaiming the strength of his love in the presence of Salvator, it is no less true that he was somewhat displeased when he did not see him welcome with absolute certainty his own conviction that this felicity was to last for ever and would not be marred by a single cloud.

A soul less pure and less loyal than his would have been humiliated to appear so different from its usual self in front of a friend who could compare the present with the past and accuse him of inconsistency, or merely smile to see him so suddenly swept off his feet, just as he had smiled in the past at his exaggerated restraint. But if the prince's character contained certain elements of narrow-mindedness, they were never of a mean and shabby nature – indeed, they could have been described as touches of a charming childishness. He too was artless, but it was less obvious and less extensive than in Lucrezia, and his was more subtle and interesting in contrast to the basis of his character. Thus, he did not deny that he had been a rigorist in the past and that he was now blinded by passion; but it was impossible for him to admit it. He did not remember it and was almost unaware of his transformation. He persisted in the belief that he hated the transports of a mind without rules or restraint and if anyone had spoken to him of a woman exactly resembling Madame Floriani in behaviour and experience but not possessing that mysterious charm which enthralled him, he would have averted his eyes from her in horror and disgust. In short, his eyes were covered by the bandage which the poets of antiquity, those masters of the art of symbolising the passions, placed over the eyes of Cupid. His mind had not changed, but his heart and his imagination adorned his idol with all the virtues which he wished to adore.

Understandably, Madame Floriani grew easily accustomed to being the object of a worship which she had never believed to exist. To be sure, she had been loved and she herself had loved very passionately. But people of such delicate sensibilities as Karol are very rare and she had never encountered any. As she had told Salvator, she had loved only poor creatures, that is men without family, fortune or fame. A shy kind of pride had always made her repulse the attentions of men in high society. Anything remotely resembling an intimate relationship based on considerations of fortune, success or vanity had always found her mistrustful and almost haughty. Given the excessive kindness of her nature, the care she took to flee and reject great lords and great artists had appeared odd; but in fact it was a consequence of her courageous and independent character, possibly too of the maternal instinct which prevailed in all she did. The idea of being protected was unendurable to her. She preferred to be subject to the quirks of a lover with refinement than to undergo the pompous discipline of a perfumed pedagogue.

Basically it had been she who had always protected and rehabilitated, saved or attempted to save the men she cherished. Chiding their vices with tenderness, rectifying their faults with devotion, she had almost made gods of these mere mortals. But she had sacrificed herself too completely to succeed. Since Christ, crucified for having loved too much, until the present day, such is the story of all devotion. The one who imposes it on himself is its inevitable victim, and as

Lucrezia was, after all, only a woman, she had practised patience to the point of self-destruction. Moreover, she had harboured too many loves in her heart simultaneously, that is to say, she had wished to be the mother of her children, and these two affections, always battling with one another, had inevitably to resolve their conflict by the extinction of the less persistent of the two. It was the children who always triumphed and, to speak metaphorically, the lovers who had been taken from the orphanages of life, were destined to return there sooner or later.

The result was that she was often hated and cursed by the men who owed her everything and who after being spoilt by her, could not understand that, being weary and dispirited, she was trying to recover herself. They accused her of being capricious, pitiless and mad in her haste both to surrender and withdraw herself; (the latter complaint was not entirely ill-founded). Madame Floriani cannot therefore seem to the reader to be exactly perfect, and my intention was never to make you see her as the divine being of Karol's dreams. It is a human being that I am analysing here, with its noble intentions and its feeble achievements, its vast enterprises and its limited means.

There were many charming men who thought her rude, absent-minded, odd and undiscerning because she did not welcome their insipid compliments. Had she the right to gain the respect of these people, she who chose the objects of her preference so badly and soon broke with them only to choose others who were even worse?

So she had enemies, but because she had even more friends, she was hardly aware of them and she completely ignored what people said of her because her heart was engrossed by so many warm affections. But all this did not prevent her from continuing to regard noblemen and privileged personages as her natural enemies. She had remained a woman of the people to the backbone even at the height of her stage career; and in the very course of acquiring social graces she retained an element of savage pride against society. If the circumstances required it she could display true distinction of manners and when she acted on the stage or wrote for the theatre one would have said that the had been born on a throne. But she could not tolerate the thought that it should be assumed tht she owed this noble air and superior style of speech to association with titled people. She was convinced that she derived her nobility from her own sense of the high rules of her art, from her instinct of what constituted true elegance and from the innate pride of her mind. She laughed heartily when a marquis with common features and ridiculous appearance came to her dressing room to tell her what people admired most in her was her ability to *guess* good breeding. One day when a great lady (who unfortunately had a raucous voice, purple hands and a bearded chin) complimented her on the way in which she played a duchess, she answered in a voice full of conviction: "When one has models like Your Ladyship before one's eyes, one cannot go wrong in knowing what befits a noble role." But when the great lady had gone Lucrezia and all the other actors burst out laughing. Poor duchess! And she had thought she was bestowing so much honour and pleasure with her praise!

All these digressions are meant to tell you that it would have required nothing less than a miracle to make this proud plebeian develop an infatuation or affection for a prince. We have seen how this miracle happened by degrees and how it was accomplished as if by surprise. And now Madame Floriani, no longer concerned in defending herself but in admiring, discovered in the object of her love charms which she had always refused to appreciate in other members of his caste. Faithful to her prejudices, she was reluctant to ascribe so many graces and such delicate courtesy to the education he had received and the habits he had acquired. From that point of view, she would have preferred to criticise them. But on the assumption that he owed them entirely to the perfection of his innate character, the sweetness of his soul and the tenderness of his feelings for her, she was intoxicated by them. It seemed to her that all her past loves had been orgies in comparison with the feast of ambrosia and honey which was served to her by the chaste lips, sweet words and divine ecstasies of her young lover.

"I do not deserve such adoration," she would say to him, "but I love you because you are capable of feeling and expressing it thus. I used not to love myself and I have never loved myself hitherto. But it seems to me that I am beginning to love myself in you and that I must respect the being whom you venerate in this way."

At other times she would cry out in the sincerity of her heart: "No, no, I have never been loved and you are my first love! Parched with thirst, I used to search for what I have at last found now. I tell you, my soul which I thought was exhausted, was as virgin as yours. I am sure of it now and I can swear it before God."

Love is full of such blasphemies uttered in good faith. The most recent always seems the first to deeply emotional natures, and it is certain that if affection can be measured by exultation. Lucrezia had never loved to such an extent. The ecstasy which she had felt for other men had been of brief duration. They had been unable to maintain or renew it. Affection had survived disillusion for a certain time, then had come generosity, solicitude, compassion, devotion, – in short, maternal feeling. It was indeed a miracle that passions born in such frenzy could have endured so long, although the world, judging merely by appearances, would have been astonished and scandalised to see her end them so swiftly and with such finality. In all these passions she had been happy and blinded for barely a week, and when one or two years of absolute devotion survive a love which almost at once is recognised as absurd and misplaced, is it not a great expense of heroism, more costly than would be the sacrifice of an entire life for a being whom one always felt worthy of it?

In that case, is it very difficult and meritorious to submit and immolate oneself? Coriolanus was greater in pardoning his ungrateful fatherland than Regulus in suffering martyrdom for his grateful country.

And so this time Lucrezia was dazed by her happiness. This time, too, she had begun with devotion, since she had tended, nursed and saved this sick child, at the cost of great mental anxiety and physical fatigue. But what was that in comparison with the suffering she had endured in saving depraved souls and distracted minds?

Indeed, nothing, less than nothing. Hadn't she lavished care and attention on paupers and strangers? "And for the little that he owes me," she said to herself, "see how he loves me – as if I had opened the heavens to him! From now on I shall never say to myself that I am loved because I am needed or because a little glamour surrounds me. He loves me for myself, for myself alone. He is rich, he is a prince, he is virtuous, he has no debts, he does not feel weak in spirit or carried away by evil passions. He is neither a libertine, nor a gambler, nor a spendthrift, nor an egotist. He has only one ambition: to be loved. And he expects no service and no support from me, but only the happiness which love can give. He never saw me in my days of glory. It was not the artificial beauty created by costumes, the display of my talents, my triumphs, the infatuation of the crowd and the rivalry among my admirers which drew him to me. He has only seen me in retirement, stripped of all glamour. It is me, yes, it is my own self that he loves."

She did not tell herself what was indeed even more difficult to conceive and to explain, and that is that this young man, consumed by the need of an exclusive affection and recently deprived of that of his mother, had reached a point in his life where he must attach himself to someone or die; that chance or fatality having sent him to find care, tenderness and kindness at the hands of a woman still beautiful and very gentle, his inner life, too long repressed, had exploded; in short, that he loved passionately because he could not love otherwise.

Salvator's absence which was only supposed to last a fortnight lasted more than a month. Who was keeping him so long from his friends? Possibly it was someone not worth mentioning; so I shall not mention him. Evidently Salvator was of the same opinion, for he never spoke about it to Karol or Lucrezia. He returned to them when he had reached the conclusion that he would have done better never to have left them at all.

For our two lovers, during this month in which they were together, paradise had remained radiant and serene, drenched in sunshine and profuse in riches. The absolute and continual possession of the being he loved was the only existence that Karol could endure. The more he was loved, the more he wished to be loved; the more his happiness possessed him, the more determined he was to possess his happiness.

But he could only possess it on one condition: that nothing should come to stand between him and the object of his passion, and this miracle was produced for him for more than a month, thanks to a combination of utterly exceptional circumstances. Lucrezia's children were in perfect health, and not a single one suffered the slightest indisposition for five weeks. If Celio had had a touch of sunstroke or little Salvator had cut a big tooth, Lucrezia would have been absorbed by the attentions they would have required and for a few days her interest would have to be diverted from her dear prince. But as the two boys and the two girls were enjoying wonderful health there were no fits of temper, tears or quarrels among them – at least, if there were any, Karol was not aware of them, for he was not yet conscious of the small details or rare interruptions in his happiness; and Lucrezia only needed to devote very brief moments to discipline or maternal intervention. She exercised her assiduous shrewd supervision of them with her customary calm, but they made her task so easy, that the prince only saw the admirable side of these motherly duties.

Old Menapace caught many fish and sold them at a good profit both to his daughter and to the innkeeper at Iseo. This put him in a good mood and prevented him from coming to administer tiresome rebukes to Lucrezia. She went to see him several times a day, as usual. Karol never dreamed of acompanying her, so that he forgot the aversion and disgust the mean old man had inspired in him when first he saw him. In short, no one came to the Villa Floriani and nothing disturbed their divine intimacy.

16.

It must also be said that the prince assisted fate by the happy
disposition of his mind and that he did nothing to appreciate
the strangeness of his situation. Skilled in self-torture,
accustomed to dark and taciturn reveries, he allowed
Lucrezia's tranquil nature and sweet serenity to drive away his
sad thoughts and maintain his spiritual well-being.

They almost never conversed together – an admirable and
indeed the only method of always agreeing in everything! As
their love was at its highest point it expressed itself in nothing
but ecstatic and incoherent utterances, mutual caresses, silent
contemplation of each other, impassioned exclamations,
burning looks and gentle reveries.

Yet if one had been able to see into these two souls plunged
in their dreams of the ideal, one would have noted a great
absence of similarity and unity between them. Whereas
Madame Floriani, in love with nature, associated with her
intoxication the earth and the sky, the moon and the lake, the
flowers and the breeze, above all her children and often, too,
the memory of her past griefs, Karol, insensitive to the external
beauty of the world and the realities of his own life, drowned
his more exquisite and untrammelled imagination in an
exalted monologue with God Himself. He was no longer on
earth, but in an empyrean of golden, fragrant clouds, at the feet
of the Lord, between his cherished mother and his adored
mistress. If a ray of sunshine set the landscape aglow, or the
scent of a plant was wafted through the air and Lucrezia

commented on it, he saw the splendour and the delight through his dreams; but in reality he had seen nothing and smelled nothing. Sometimes, when she said to him: "See how beautiful the earth is!" he would reply: "I do not see the earth, I only see the sky." And she would admire the passionate depth of this reply without exactly understanding it. As she looked at the crimson clouds at sunset she never thought that the soul of Karol could see beyond those clouds an imagined Eden where he thought he was talking with her, but where he was really alone. In a word, one can say that Lucrezia saw reality with the poetic feeling of the author of *Waverley,* whereas her lover, idealising poetry itself, peopled the infinite with his own creations, after the manner of *Mannfred.*

In spite of these differences, their love had soared to the highest heaven, and things of this earth found no place in their effusions. This was utterly contrary to the active, succouring and so to speak militant instincts of Lucrezia. She moved about in these regions like one blind from birth who has suddenly recovered his sight and tries in vain to understand all these strange new things. The prince could only convey to her a vague impression of his own vision. He would have thought he was wronging her by thinking that her insight was not greater than his and that she was unable to explain the miracle to herself a thousand times better than he could have done. As for Lucrezia, lost in this immensity, yet enraptured by this adventurous journey through a new world, she scarcely thought to question him on what he was experiencing. For the first time she felt the inadequacy of human speech, she who had studied it so much and used it to such purpose! But with the humility of one who idolises a person other than oneself, she thought that anything she could have said or understood was as nothing in comparison with what her lover thought or felt.

She had not yet experienced the lassitude inseparable from the tensions of a soul which dwells in a region above its natural abode, when Salvator came to put an end to their tête-á-tête; yet she greeted his arrival with instinctive satisfaction and received him with open arms. His coming was utterly unexpected. He had not written for a week and they were rather anxious about him, Lucrezia more so than Karol however, for although she did not love him as much as the prince was supposed to love him, she felt a concern for Salvator which was natural to her but which found little room in the superhuman ecstasy of the young prince.

Karol came forward, ready to be pleased at the return of his faithful friend; but when he heard the sound of the bells of the post-horses stop at the entrance to the villa, even before he knew who it was, his heart sank. The old presentiment, obliterated and forgotten, suddenly awoke. "Oh God," he cried, pressing Lucrezia's arm convulsively, "we are no longer alone. I am lost! Ah, if I could only die now."

"Oh no," she replied, "if it is a stranger I shall not receive him. But it can only be Salvator, my heart tells me so, and that makes our happiness complete."

But Karol's heart told him nothing and in spite of himself he wished the visitor was a stranger so that he could be sent away. However, he received his friend with deep emotion, but an involuntary sadness had already taken possession of him. This new presence was a change in an existence which could ensure his happiness only as long as it was perfect; *any* modification would ruin it.

Salvator seemed to him to be more noisy, more crudely alive than ever. He had not felt happy away from them, but he had found distraction and amusement despite the disappointments and irritations one encounters in a life of pleasure. He related as much as he could of his stay in Venice. He described a ball at an old palace, excursions on the lagoons, music in churches and processions around St. Mark's Square; then spoke of accidental but pleasant meetings, a Parisian friend, a beautiful English acquaintance, distinguished German and Slav personages, relatives of Karol – in short, over the dazzling prism in which Karol had forgotten himself, he projected the small magic lantern of society.

In everything he said there was nothing in any way unpleasant or perturbing. Yet Karol felt a horrible unease as if in the midst of a sublime concert a screeching old woman had suddenly added shrill sounds and a vulgar musical theme to the divine thoughts of the great masters. There was no one who interested him, nor anything which did not seem inferior to his situation and which did not seem unworthy of mention. He tried not to listen but, in spite of himself, he heard Salvator say to Lucrezia: "Now then, let me give you some news which will interest *you*. I met many of your friends, or rather, everybody, for everybody adores you, and not a single one of those who saw you even for one night, on the stage, can forget you. I saw Lamberti, your former fellow-producer, who still bewails your retirement and says that the theatre in Italy is now dead. I saw Count Montanari, of Bergamo, who until his last breath will speak of the day when you deigned to visit his villa; and young Santorelli who is still in love with you . . . And Countess Corsini who knew you in Rome and at whose home you consented one evening to read a drama written by her friend, the Abbé Varini, – a poor play, apparently, but you spoke it so well that everyone thought it good and all eyes were bathed in tears."

"Do not remind me of my past sins," said Lucrezia. "It may even be a mortal one to declaim a platitude carefully and conscientiously; it means deceiving the author and the audience. Thank heaven, I am no longer exposed to committing similar mistakes. And tell me, whom else did you meet?"

The prince sighed. He could not imagine that all this could interest his mistress. Salvator mentioned half a dozen other people and although Madame Floriani did not feel any positive interest in them, she listened with the kindliness which one owes to one's friends. But there was one name which she took up, however, with a certain amount of concern. It was that of Boccaferri, an unfortunate artist whom she had rescued several times from destitution, although she had never had the slightest love for him nor even the remotest hint of infatuation.

"What! In debt again and to such an extent?" she said, after Salvator had given her some details about Boccaferri. "Is it impossible then to save the wretched man from his disorderly and improvident way of living?"

"I am afraid so."

"No matter, we must try again."

"I anticipated your wish; I gave him a little help."

"Oh, thank you for that. You are kind. I shall return it to you, Salvator."

"Nonsense. Are you trying to prevent me from giving a little charity?"

"No, but in this case it is possibly misguided, and you did it out of consideration for me, because you only knew Boccaferri slightly and I am sure that he used my name to win your interest in his sad story."

"What does it matter? He could not call upon a protectress whose name would be more effective. I like the rascal, he amuses me; he is so witty."

"And so talented," added Madame Floriani. "If he could only make use of his gift and wished to do so . . . Poor Boccaferri . . . "

Karol heard no more. He had walked a little behind the others, as they chatted and strolled along a path in the park. Then he stopped to see if when she reached a bend in the path, Lucrezia would turn round to look at him. But she did not turn round: she was engaged with Salvator in seeking some means of employing Boccaferri's skill to paint scenery in some theatre other than Milan, Naples, Florence, Rome, Venice, etc. – all of them towns from which he had been driven through loose living and a capricious temperament.

"You say that an extra three hundred francs might induce him to undertake a journey to Sinigaglia where he could find employment, at least during the festival time? Well, I shall send it to him, because I can appreciate his disgust, pressed for money and compelled to put himself at the mercy of those who employ him. It is thus that extreme poverty breeds and increases itself tenfold."

As she spoke Lucrezia's only thought was that she was fulfilling a duty of pity and charity. By one of those instincts of modesty which go with true benevolence she had even lowered her voice and walked a little faster so as not to be heard by Karol, and possibly also because she sensed that the subject was too ordinary to interest him.

But for the first time she was mistaken in her idea of what suited Karol's state of mind. He was only too interested in what she was saying. He would have wished not to miss a single word of it and yet he would have blushed to try and hear anything against her wishes. He stopped and hesitated for a moment and when she had vanished from sight, he was seized by vertigo and it seemed to him that an abyss had just opened between them.

What had happened and what was it that could cause him so much suffering? Nothing! But one who aspires to the glory of the gods requires nothing and less than nothing to make him fall from the heights of the empyrean to the lowest depths of hell. The old classical writers whom we so foolishly scorn created the image whereby a fly had sufficed to plunge into the abysses of space the bold mortal who wished to steer the chariot of Phoebus along its celestial course. Let us, if we can, try and find a more apt and ingenious metaphor to express the little that we are, and the little that is required to trouble our happiness. *I* cannot do so. All I can say, in humble prose, is that Prince Karol had soared too high to descend by slow degrees. His fall had to be sudden and without apparent cause. The giant steeds of the sun were certainly very fiery and powerful, and the gadfly which made them bolt was a very poor and very small insect!

Karol left the garden, ran and shut himself in his room and paced about in it, pursued by the Furies. This soul, only a few moments ago so magnanimous and strong, was now nothing but the plaything of the meanest delusions. Who was this Boccaferri who interested Lucrezia so much? Some former lover perhaps! He remembered something which he had completely forgotten since the first day they met, namely that she had had many lovers. And why should she return with so much concern to a memory unworthy of her, when he, the betrothed of Lucie, had sacrificed the very portrait of this pure virgin, in order not to have even the likeness of any other woman than Lucrezia in his possession?

The more he strove to explain naturally so simple a fact, the more mysterious and hopeless were the complications he encountered. She had lowered her voice and she had walked faster as she spoke to Salvator. That was undeniable. She had not turned round at the end of the path to see if he was following her – she who for a whole month had not lost a single second of the time she could devote to him without neglecting the duties she owed to her family! And now she was still walking, leaning on the count's arm, probably speaking warmly of this terrible memory and the mysterious person whom she had not even mentioned to him! He was amazed at this, as if Lucrezia had never told him anything of her life, forgetting, on the contrary, that he had always implored her never to accuse herself before him and to erase altogether the emotions of the past in order to concentrate on the enjoyment of the present.

So she was not returning... She was not wondering where he might be or why he had left her! The minutes seemed to him like hours and years... And Salvator, too, that insensitive, tactless friend who had come to entertain her with such problems and drop poisoned names into the cup of their happiness! Karol suffered so much in the space of a quarter of an hour that he felt that he had aged a whole century. Suddenly he shuddered as he heard the voices of Lucrezia and Salvator beneath his window. She was laughing! The count was reminding her of Boccaferri's witticisms and eccentricities. She was laughing... and he, her lover, was enduring tortures without her even suspecting it!

Certainly poor Lucrezia was far from suspecting it. She was only a little uneasy not to see him near her and merely said to herself that as the subject of her conversation was strange to him he had preferred to plunge into his usual reveries. When she used to go to Menapace's cottage, how many times had he told her that he preferred not to go in, but he had waited under the pink acacias, by the lakeside, to continue to converse with her in imagination!

Yet the instinct of her heart drew her back towards him more quickly than Salvator would have wished. He would have liked to keep her in the park and make her speak of her love. But she had progressed too fast along the path of exclusion which Karol had opened for her, to be in such a hurry as she usually was to give way openly to confidences and friendship. This time she was afraid of expressing the immensity of her happiness badly or of not being understood even partially.

She answered briefly; and with a subtlety which she

discovered for the occasion, she led the conversation back to Boccaferri and directed their walk towards the house, for Karol was nowhere to be seen in the garden.

She was hardly in the drawing room when, making some excuse or other, she went up to the prince's apartments.

The violence of his condition was revealed in his distracted face. A secret fury was seething deep in his breast. Afraid that he would be unable to pretend and not wishing to appear in this condition and lose all control of himself, as soon as he heard footsteps in the gallery, he rushed through another door and down the staircase. As he fled towards the shore of the lake he thought he could hear Lucrezia looking for him and calling his name.

But presently he saw issuing from a clump of trees a cloud of tobacco such as Salvator always trailed around his head like a halo. He thought that his friend was about to join him and fearing his looks even more than Lucrezia's he dashed into old Menapace's cottage, in the knowledge that no one would come and look for him in a place he was never known to enter. He had just seen the old man, accompanied by Biffi, leave the shore in his fishing boat and Karol felt sure that he would be left alone for as long a time as was necessary for him to regain command of himself and at least the appearance of calm.

After a while he did indeed grow calmer and he began to reproach himself for having dreamed a monstrous dream. The sight of this cottage in which he had never set foot since the day of his arrival nor ever closely examined until that moment filled him with a strange sensation when he found himself alone there in this emotional state.

The interior of this rustic dwelling which, thanks to Biffi's efforts, was clean and tidy, had undergone no change since Madame Floriani's childhood, and if the old fisherman had agreed, but only reluctantly, to the necessary repairs involving the fabric and the sanitation of the house, he had positively refused to allow the furniture to be renewed or the coarse material of the curtains to be renovated. The only object which gave evidence of civilisation was a large engraving framed in rosewood which stood in the alcove behind the old man's bed. Karol leaned forward to look at it. It was Madame Floriani in all her beauty and all her glory, in the costume of Melpomene, bare-shouldered, wearing the antique diadem and with a sceptre in her hand. A beautiful vignette encircled the noble face and was ornamented with the attributes of several muses: the mask of Thalia, the sock and the buskin side by side, the trumpet, the pearls, the myrtles of Calliope, Erato and Polyhymnia. A couplet in classical Italian expressed the idea that as an actress of tragedy and comedy, as a heroic and historic poetess, as a *letterata* etc. etc. Lucrezia Floriani combined in herself all the talents and all the skills which are the glory of the theatre and letters.

This engraving was a tribute from the dilettanti of Rome, which Lucrezia had not wished to put in her villa; but her father had taken it because he had heard a servant say that such a beautiful print was worth at least two hundred francs.

He had set it up above a small pastel drawing which interested Karol much more and which represented a little girl of ten or twelve, in peasant costume, with a rose above her ear, a large silver pin in her hair, a delicate white chemisette and brick-red bodice. This portrait, though lacking skill in execution, possessed a charming naïvety. It had captured the frank, innocent air of a child, intelligent in thought and simple in feeling and upbringing. Below it ran the words: Antonietta Menapace, aged ten, drawn from life by her godmother Lucrezia Ranieri.

On seeing these two portraits which presented so strange a contrast here in the cottage of her birth: the humble, happy child and the famous hapless woman, the former so pretty, so untroubled, with her innocent, bright and carefree smile, her firm, boyish breast chastely covered by a thick, coarse bodice; the latter, so beautiful, so severe, with her expressive look, her noble attitude, her proud bosom hardly veiled by the classical drapery – on seeing this contrast Karol experienced a feeling of terror and pain. He could not deny that both portraits were true to life and that Lucrezia, in the calm of her present life, had preserved or regained much of the sweet and touching expression of the innocent Antonietta Menapace. But the nobility, grace and allure which she had acquired in becoming Madame Floriani had also left an impression which for the first time frightened Karol when he saw her image ornamented and indeed revealed through the admiration of the painters of the portrait. This aureole seemed to burn his eyes and he was forced to turn them away and let them rest on the wild rose which adorned the brow of the little girl. He had the feeling that the past, fighting for the muse of the picture, was stealing her away from his jealous possession, whereas the child, belonging to God, remained with him, undisputed.

Yet he had the courage to examine the muse minutely, and one may judge of his dismay when he read in small letters below the vignette that this decoration had been composed and drawn by Jacopo Boccaferri!

He had forgotten the accursed name, and there it was once more, the name which, perhaps wrongly, had obsessed and shaken his imagination for the past hour. Boccaferri was not the author of the portrait. That bore the signature of a more famous artist, but at all events Boccaferri had had a hand in the work. Perhaps he had seen the actress Floriani pose before the painter wearing that transparent tunic and in the splendour of youth, strength and beauty which Karol only possessed in their decline. In short, this Boccaferri must have known her very well and very intimately, seeing that he accepted help from her without blushing. Unless one were a scoundrel, how close would one have to be to a woman in order to take charity from her? And if here were indeed an artist degraded by loose and debauched living to the point of begging for alms, how could Lucrezia, that saint whom Karol adored, have such friends?

"When one is the mistress of a Prince Karol, how can one even remember such previous associates?"

The insane pride which is born of love and gives birth to jealousy does not express such follies in clear words in the conscience of the man who is obsessed by it. Instead, it whispers them low in his ear, so low that even as he is beside himself with fury he cannot understand what is causing this inner rage and pain.

Karol took his head in both hands and was tempted to beat it against the wall. If acts of violence had not been outside his habits and the principles of his education he would have destroyed the fatal portrait. But he gradually grew calmer as he contemplated the proud serenity of the gaze fixed on him. The eyes of a well-rendered portrait have in themselves something terrifying by virtue of their pensive stare which seems to be asking you what you think of them. Karol fell a victim to this influence. It seemed as if the tragedienne was saying to him: "By what right are you questioning me? Do I belong to you? Was it you who gave me my sceptre and my crown? Lower your inquisitive and insolent eyes, for I never lower mine, and my pride will break yours."

Karol's brain, already weakened by this violent struggle against himself, passed through a succession of hallucinations. He averted his eyes with a feeling of childish terror and brought them to rest on the charming pastel. He discovered fresh graces in it and, gradually overcome by the purity of its sweet, profound gaze, he finally burst into tears with the sensation that he was pressing to his heart the dark head of the angelic Antonietta.

Lucrezia who had been searching everywhere and had now come to ask her father or Biffi if they had seen the prince, entered at that moment. Thoroughly frightened at seeing him weep so, she rushed towards him and anxiously clasped him in her arms, lavishing the sweetest names on him and pouring out a stream of questions which betrayed the greatest concern.

He neither could nor wished to answer. How could he possibly have confessed to her and made her understand all that had just been going on inside him? He blushed for it, and, to the great credit of love, it must be added that if Karol had recently shown the excessive haste and injustice of a spoilt child, he now equally quickly displayed the love and gratitude of a child whom one has every reason to adore. Scarcely had he felt the embrace of those strong arms which had served him as a refuge against the terrors of death, scarcely was his heart, paralysed by suffering, restored to life through contact with this maternal heart than he forgot his madness and once more felt that he was the happiest, most willingly submissive and trusting of mortals.

He would have preferred to die at that very moment rather than insult his dear mistress by confessing to the slightest suspicion. He had a very touching and very simple pretext close at hand in explanation of his emotion and his tears, which was to show her the little pastel drawing, and Lucrezia, moved by this delicacy of heart, passionately pressed against her lips the beautiful hands and beautiful hair of her young lover. Never had she felt so happy and so proud of inspiring great love. The poor woman could hardly suspect that only a few minutes earlier she had been almost an object of horror to him.

"Dear angel," she said to him, "*I* would never have dared conquer the repugnance you felt on entering here. Although you had never spoken to me about it, I had more than guessed that the peculiarities of my old father could not seem attractive to you. But since fate, or some instinct of the heart, has brought you to the cottage of my birth and we are alone, I would like to show it you in detail. Come!"

She took him by the hand and led him to the back of the room in which they now stood and which, together with the one they were about to enter and a kind of store-room cluttered with old furniture, broken and unserviceable (of which Menapace did not wish to lose the pieces), made up the whole of this rustic building.

The room which Lucrezia opened to the prince was the one which she had inhabited during her childhood. It was a kind of garret, lighted by a single narrow skylight, its walls mantled on the outside with wild vine and clematis. A ramshackle bed with a reed mattress covered by a calico sheet patched again and again, crudely coloured plaster figurines of saints, some drawings stuck on the wall and so blackened by time and damp that they were totally unrecognisable, a stone floor, rough and uneven, a chair, a chest and a small deal table – such was the wretched place in which the fisherman's daughter had spent her first years and felt the gifts of energy and genius smoulder within her.

"This is where my childhood was spent," said she to the prince, "and whether it was through a spirit of preservation or a remnant of affection ill-stifled under his stern resentment, my father did not change or disturb anything in it during my long hard peregrinations through the world. That is the bed I had when I was a little girl. I remember sleeping in it with my legs bent and aching as I grew too big for it. Look, at the head of the bed, a branch of hazel catkin which is crumbling into dust and which I put there on Palm Sunday, on the day before my departure, my flight with Ranieri. That crude plaster statuette is the portrait of Joachim Murat, but a pedlar sold it me as the effigy of my patron saint, Saint Anthony, and I said my prayers before it for a long time in all faith. And over there you can still see a spool, some pins and needles which I used when making fishing-nets. The number of times I dropped or broke the mesh when my thoughts carried me far away from this monotonous work, the only kind which my father allowed me to do outside the household tasks! How I suffered from cold, heat, gnats, scorpions, from loneliness and boredom in this dear little prison! How happy I was to leave it and without even dreaming of bidding it farewell on the day when my beloved godmother said to me, 'You will become ill or deformed if you remain in that room and that bed. Come and live with me. You will not be as comfortable as I would like or as you could be, because my husband, although richer than your father, is no less careful with money than he is. But I will look after your needs secretly, I will teach you everything that you are thirsting to know, you will look after me when I am ill and you will keep me company. You will pass for my servant, for Signor Ranieri would not allow me to take you as my friend. But we shall be no less friends in this exchange of services.' What an admirable and excellent woman she was! She sensed my abilities and revealed them to myself. Alas! It was she too who made me pluck the fruit of good and evil from the tree of knowledge . . .

"And later when her son fell in love with me and old Ranieri drove me from his house, I returned once more to my wretched little room. I was fifteen then. My father wished to force me to marry a loutish friend of his, too old for me, grim, obstinate, greedy, violent and well nick-named Mangiafoco. I was afraid of him. I used to hide in the bushes near the lakeside so as to avoid him, and whem my father went fishing at night by torchlight, I barricaded myself in this poor garret, in dread of Mangiafoco whom I could see prowling around the house. My young lover wished to kill him. I lived in constant terror, because Mangiafoco was capable of killing him first.

"This existence was intolerable. When I implored my father to protect me from this ruffian, he would say: 'He doesn't mean you any harm. He is madly in love with you. Marry him, he is rich, he will make you happy.' And when I tried to rebel he reproached me for my insane love for the son of my employers and threatened to deliver me to the brutal passions of Mangiafoco who would thus be able to force me to become his wife. I knew quite well that my father would never have done so, for I had heard him tell the fellow that he would kill him if he as much as tried to frighten me. But if my father was capable of avenging his family honour in this, he had not sufficient delicacy not to attempt to do violence to my inclinations by frightening me. Moreover, I was consumed with boredom. When I was with my benefactress I had acquired the gentle art of intelligent occupation. The tedious work on the nets left too much freedom to my imagination. I was obsessed by the desire for an existence utterly different from the one which was being imposed on me. I therefore accepted the offer of Ranieri which I had so long rejected. Our love was still pure. He swore to me that it would always be so and that when his father saw him run away, he would consent to our marriage. He carried me off and it was through this little window and over a plank thrown across the stream below the cottage that I ran away in the middle of the night.

"This time, however, I was not happy to leave my cottage. Besides fear and remorse for the error that I was committing, as I parted from this room and its old furniture, the calm and silent witnesses of my games of childhood and the restlessness of puberty, I experienced an incredible regret, as if I had had a sudden revelation of all the sorrows and misfortunes which lay before me, or perhaps it was the result of the attachment which we develop for the very places where we suffer most."

Lucrezia was wrong to relate part of her life thus to Karol. It gave her pleasure to open her heart to him, and as he was obviously moved as he listened to her, she thought she was fulfilling a duty towards him and that he was grateful to her for it. But at that moment he had not sufficient strength to receive confidences of this nature, nor to hear the mere mention of the name of a former lover. He was too oppressed to interrupt her with even the slightest remark, but a cold sweat appeared on his brow, and his mind, seizing upon the pictures which she set out before him, was harrassed by them in the most agonising manner conceivable.

However, this account was a truthful vindication of Lucrezia and her first error – the fatal source of all the others. Karol felt that he had not the right to refuse to listen to it and that the place and the moment held a certain solemnity which he could not flee.

"I had no need to hear all that," he finally said with an effort, "to know that you have never obeyed evil instincts. I told you once: what would be wrong in others is right in you. A daughter who abandons her old father is guilty, but you, Lucrezia, were perhaps authorised to escape from his brutal and impious law. Heavens! How right I was when I could not bear to look at that old man without the utmost dislike!"

"Do not hasten to condemn him in order to diminish my wrongs," she retorted. "You misjudge him and do not know him. After accusing him to you, let me now show you the fine side of his character. It is a duty I must perform, isn't it?"

Karol sighed and nodded agreement. His principles commanded him to respect her filial piety, but his instinct could not accept the avarice and narrow despotism of such a father. What he did not realise was that he himself was much more tyrannical towards Lucrezia in his jealousy than Menapace had ever been with his paternal authority and his money.

18.

"Men are never logical or consistent in their best or their worst qualities," said Lucrezia, "and in order to avoid passing from one extreme to the other, from an excess of esteem to an excess of blame, in order to preserve affection and trust for those whom duty tells us to love, we must form a fair picture of them, see the good and the bad with some degree of calmness and, above all, remember that in most men a vice is sometimes a virtue carried to extremes.

"My father's vice is parsimony. I must mention this without delay for otherwise we would not recognise that his virtue is a spirit of equity and a fanatical respect for established rule. Loving money passionately – like all peasants – he is distinguished from them in that the theft of a blade of grass appears as a crime to him. His meanness lies in his eternal fear of waste which leads to destitution. His greatness is this same instinct of avarice put to the service of those whom he loves to the detriment of his own well-being, his health, and almost his life.

"Thus he has amassed – admittedly in a mean and ugly way – a miserable sum, buried no doubt in some recess in the cottage. From time to time he buys small plots of land in the belief that this will ensure the honour and future dignity of his grandchildren. To attempt to persuade him that a good education and talents are a better investment would be utterly futile. Having remained a peasant both in body and soul, he only understands what he sees. He knows how grass grows and seed germinates and without suspecting that that is a greater miracle than all human achievement, he calmly says that it is a natural fact. Speak to him of things which can be proved and explained, of a steamship, for example, or a railway, and he will smile and say nothing. He does not believe in the existence of what he has not seen and if he were told to go to the other side of the lake to convince himself of it with his own eyes he would not go for fear it was a hoax.

"My life has taught him nothing of society, the arts, the power of intellectual gifts or the exchange of ideas. He never asks questions about such matters nor does it please him to hear conversations on subjects which are utterly unfamiliar to him. He believes that if I have made a fortune in my artistic career it is due to fortuitous circumstances which he would advise me not to risk again. Then he advances the following argument which is both very plausible and very ingenuous: 'You artists earn a lot of money, but you need to spend even more. You acquire this taste from associating with one another and from gadding about. So that you work to excess to enable you to have a little pleasure. I who spend nothing and have no taste for pleasure earn less, but what I have acquired I keep. Therefore my work is more pleasant and more lucrative than yours. You are poor and I am rich; you are slaves and I am free.'

"This explains his lack of esteem and admiration for the fame I have acquired. He is not flattered by it and, if you ask my opinion, I regard this kind of scorn for my futile triumphs as one of the most interesting aspects of his character and most worthy of respect. The career which I pursued has conflicted too much with his ideas of elementary order for him to have retained much affection for me; in any case he has never felt real affection for anyone. With him everything is transferred to principles of cold, rigid equity. When my mother died on giving birth to me he made an oath never to remarry if I survived, in the conviction that a stepmother could never love the children of a previous marriage. And he kept his word, not out of love for the memory of his wife, but through a sense of his duty towards me. He brought me up with every possible care and watched over me in a way of which few men are capable when dealing with a small child; but I don't think that he ever gave me a single kiss. He never thought about it. He never felt the urge to clasp me to his heart and he thinks that I spoil my own children because I caress them. He asks what good it does them and what advantages they derive from it. When, after an absence of fifteen years, I came here and flung myself at his feet, begging his forgiveness and trying to justify my behaviour, he said: 'None of that concerns me, I know nothing about what is permitted or forbidden in the world you speak of. You refused the husband I meant for you, you disobeyed me – that is what I blame you for. You loved your master's son and you turned him away from the obedience he owed his father, which was a bad thing and could have done me harm. None of those people are left now; you have come back and you have given me a lot of presents. I know how I am to behave towards you. Let us never speak of the past, there is an end to everything and I forgive you on condition that you bring up your children with a sense of order and good behaviour.' Thereupon he shook my hand and that was all.

"Well, my dearest, in the course of my life on the stage I have seen something of the private lives of many artists and I am going to tell you what happens in nine cases out of ten. The artist and in particular the dramatic artist always comes from the poorest and humblest ranks of society. Whether his parents have intended him to be the bread-winner or chance and outside influence have revealed and utilised his talents, even if he is still only a child, he immediately finds himself burdened with maintaining, carrying, clothing, feeding and even amusing his family. It will be he who will pay his brothers' debts, it will be he who will find suitable husbands for his sisters, it will be he who will invest all the fruits of his labour in safe funds to ensure a handsome pension for his father and mother against the day when he will wish to buy his freedom from them.

"It is women above all who suffer most in the world of art. This would be reasonable if it did not take shameful advantage of their strength, their health, and what is worst, alas! their honour, in order to make quicker profits, and by means of prostitution protect them from failure before their audiences.

In this case the theatre also serves as a showcase, and more than one stupid and beautiful young woman pays for the privilege of showing herself – if only for a moment – on the boards, wearing provocative clothes, so as to make herself known and find clients.

"When this gullible young woman, this poor victim happens to have character and pride, whether she has managed to preserve her innocence or has yielded to infamous suggestions and justifiably resents it, as soon as she threatens to break with her family they collapse, tremble, flatter and crawl. I have seen these shameless fathers and odious mothers waiting in the wings, holding their daughter's shawl, almost kissing the feet which have danced at a thousand francs per evening, performing the office of lackeys at home, making a downy nest for the goose that lays the golden eggs, in short, stooping to unparalleled servility, despicable complaisance and the vilest of flattery – all to retain the glory and profit which are to be gained by belonging to the great coquette, the prima donna or merely the courtesan of the moment.

"That kind of family would have made me weep with shame, and whenever I thought of my old father, the peasant, who had not wished to leave his nets so as to come and share my luxury, who refused to answer my letters, accepted my remittances of money solely to build up a dowry for my daughters, yet insisted on rising before the dawn, living in a thatched cottage and existing on two penn'orth of rice daily, it seemed to me that I was of illustrious birth, and I felt proud of the plebeian blood that flowed in my veins.

"It is quite true that as in all things human all this has its occasional touches of pettiness and absurdity. It is true that my father refused to accept my letters if I ever forgot to stamp them; it is true that to-day he deplores what he calls my prodigality and that when he has sold his fish he shows a silver coin to Celio with a look of triumph and says: 'At your age I was already earning this amount and at my present age I am still earning it. I will give it you to help you when you go out into the world and wish to earn some money too.' It is also true that if he saw me give a hundred francs to an unfortunate penniless friend he would almost heap curses upon my head. I am often obliged to tolerate his oddities, but I am also always compelled to respect his pride and his homespun stubbornness. If he is harsh to others, he is even more so to himself. He works with the zeal of a young man, he is never indiscreet or importunate, he lives in his stoicism without ever verifying what he does not understand. Many another parent would have filled my existence with annoyances, drunk himself into a stupor at my table or made me blush for his coarseness. The situation of my father in relation to me was very delicate, and without any attempt to reason or calculate, he has kept it dignified, independent, and from his point of view, generous. Although showered with gifts from me he can still regard himself as the head and protector of the family, since he works and amasses money for the sake of my children's happiness. I smile at his manner of doing things, but not at his intentions. And now, Karol, do you understand why I love and still bless my old father? Haven't you noticed that I look like him and don't you think that I have something of his character?"

"You?" cried Karol. "Good Heavens! Nothing at all."

"Oh yes, I have," Lucrezia insisted. "I owe something to the pride of the blood which he has transmitted to me. I have found myself in difficult situations; I have been loved by rich men; I had friends from whom I could have accepted help without dishonour. But the idea of imposing privations or an excess of work on others when I felt young, strong and industrious would have been intolerable to me. I have been accused of many faults and those which I have committed have been cruelly exaggerated; but not even the people worst disposed towards me have ever harboured the slightest shadow of a doubt concerning my independence and my integrity. I have been the manager of a theatre, I have handled practical matters, I have done what is called business – even complicated, difficult, delicate business. When I dealt with so many pretentious, vain or unreasonable people, my principle, in doubtful cases, was always to pay double my debt rather than argue; without being thrifty I have always been orderly, and although I have been charitable I have not jeopardised my fortune. The fact is I have never been extravagant for reasons of self-satisfaction. The woman who gives what she has to the less fortunate is more sober and sensible than the woman who mortgages what she does not have in order to procure jewels and carriages for herself.

"I myself have never had a taste for empty luxury. The possession of a small, valueless object which reveals the intelligence and taste of its maker is much more precious to me than that of a diamond necklace. I prefer what is good and true to what is showy and the object of envy. Without disciplining myself to a life as frugal as my father's, I have trained myself to habits of moderation. Affection is the only instinct which I do not rule with temperance of the mind, and that is the only thing in which I differ from him. But if I have not been a kept woman, if the bribes of corruption did not tempt me when at sixteen I found myself at grips with the difficulties of existence, if I can still command respect from those who criticise me, you may be sure it is because I am the daughter of old Menapace. Admit then, that appearances are deceptive and that nature establishes strong ties and profound relations between beings who at a first glance seem utterly different."

"All you say is admirable," replied the prince, overwhelmed with sadness, "and you must be right in everything. But let us go and join Salvator who is looking for us, no doubt."

"No, no," said Lucrezia, "he was tired from his journey and is sleeping in the garden in the shade of the myrtles. Let us go and join the children. I haven't seen them for the past hour."

For the first time she had spoken at length to Karol about real things and she flattered herself that she had taken advantage of a good opportunity to rehabilitate in his mind the father whom she loved sincerely. But there are arguments which the mind accepts but which fail to win the heart. Karol acknowledged that Lucrezia had made a wise speech in defence of tolerance and in the wish to justify human nature. This did not minimise his revulsion for reality, nor his inability to accept human faults with any other feeling than that of politeness, that perfidious magnanimity which leaves the heart cold and aversion triumphant.

In his opinion Lucrezia ought to have had an environment more worthy of her, that is to say, an environment such as exists for no one: a lake which was more expansive without ceasing to be as peaceful, a dwelling place more picturesque without ceasing to be as comfortable and healthy, a fame less dearly achieved without ceasing to be as brilliant, and above all a father more distinguished, more poetic, without ceasing to be a fisherman. He did not possess a narrow aristocratic spirit: the rustic origin, the paternal cottage, the nets hanging on the willow trees at the lakeside pleased him, but to be entirely happy he would have asked for a peasant such as one encounters in poems or plays, one of Byron's or Schiller's mountaineers. He liked Shakespeare, but with great reservations: he regarded his characters as based on too close a study of real life and the language they spoke as too earthy. He preferred epic and lyrical syntheses which leave the sad details of humanity in the shadows. That is why he spoke little and hardly listened, only wishing to express his thoughts or gather those of others when they had attained a certain loftiness. To burrow below the surface of the earth in order to analyse the wholesome or noxious vapours it contains, for the purpose of planting appropriately and making full use of what it can produce, would have been for him a vile and revolting labour. But to pluck flowers, admire their brightness, beauty and perfume, without concerning himself with the toil and skill of the gardener, such was the gentle occupation which he reserved for himself in life.

So when Lucrezia thought that she was convincing him it was like a voice speaking in the wilderness. He had listened to her thoughtfully, and in everything she had said he had admired the composition, the ingenious aspects of her system of tolerance and the kindness of her instincts. But in order not to ignore good it was not necessary to accept evil. Her ideas about human relations were diametrically opposed to his. And yet he had a high conception of filial duty. But he was able to make a distinction between duty and feeling, actions and sympathies, which was utterly unknown to Lucrezia. Thus, in her place, he would not have attempted to defend Menapace's avarice, because in order to find an acceptable side to this vice, one would have had to begin by admitting that it existed in him. Karol would have denied it or would never have uttered a single word about it – which, one must admit, is much simpler. . . .

Then again, when speaking of herself, Lucrezia had hurt him deeply. She had used words which had burned him like a red-hot iron. She had said that she had never been a kept woman, she had depicted the lives and morals of her colleagues with terrible truth. She had told of her first loves and had actually mentioned her first lover by name. Karol would have wished that the mere idea of evil should not occur to her, that she should be unaware of the existence of evil on earth or that she should not remember it when speaking to him. In short, in order to complete the total sum of his fantastic requirements he would have wished that without ceasing to be the kind, tender, devoted, voluptuous and maternal Lucrezia, she should also be the pale, innocent, severe and virginal Lucie. This was all that our sad lover of the impossible asked for!

19.

After his sleep in the shade of the trees Salvator had just awakened full of a sense of well-being and cheerfulness. When we feel well and overflowing with good spirits our senses are not as delicate as usual in observing or guessing the sufferings of others. So it was that Karol's pallor and dejection escaped the eyes of his friend; and Lucrezia, attributing them to exhaustion, when love and emotion had made him weep at the sight of her portrait, did not dream of being distressed about it.

When, as children, we suffer from a secret sorrow, it is our wish that everything we do to conceal it should be of no avail before the shrewd, benevolent penetration of those who love us; and as at the same time we remain proudly silent we are unjust enough to believe that they are indifferent, because they are not importunate. Many men remain children on this point and Karol was particularly so. Consequently the energetic and noisy gaiety of Salvator depressed him more and more and Lucrezia's serenity, which had hitherto communicated itself to him through a kind of sympathy, now lost its benign influence for the first time.

For the first time, too, the noise and perpetual activity of the children tired him. They were usually calm under their mother's eyes, but during dinner they were so delighted and excited by Salvator's friendly teasing, caresses and laughter that they set up a loud din, upset their glasses on the table-cloth and sang at the top of their voices, constantly repeating the same refrain, like those finches that are made to compete in song by Dutchmen who lay wagers on them. Celio broke his plate and his dog began to bark so loud that no one could hear himself speak.

Madame Floriani was not very strict when she intervened; she laughed in spite of herself at the silly pranks of Salvator and the amusing retorts of her youngsters wild with pleasure and quite beside themselves, as so easily happens with highly strung children when they are over-stimulated.

Every day for the past two months Karol had admired the grace and pretty ways of these cherubs and loved them tenderly for the sake of their mother. It never occurred to him that they had had fathers – and who knew what fathers! It seemed to him that they were so arrayed with the divine gifts of their mother that he thought of them as being born of the Holy Ghost.

Lucrezia was infinitely grateful to him for this affection which he expressed with so much enthusiasm and which revealed itself in acute and poetic observations on their several kinds of beauty and aptitude.

And yet the children did not like him.

They seemed to be afraid of him and one would have found difficulty in explaining why his sweet smiles and his delicate attempts to please them met with such hesitation and shyness. Even Celio's dog lay with its ears back and did not wag its tail when the prince looked at him and called him. The animal was fully aware that this man spoke of him in a kindly fashion, but that he never touched him and that a secret physical aversion made him fear even the slightest contact with any animal. If dogs have a wonderful instinct which tells them to mistrust people who mistrust them, it is not to be wondered at that children have the same inner warning at the approach of those who do not like them. Karol did not like children in general, although he had never said so, not even to himself. On the contrary, he thought he was very fond of them, because at the sight of a beautiful child he was overcome with the emotion of a poet and the ecstasy of an artist. But he was afraid of an ugly or deformed child. The pity he felt at its approach was so painful that he became genuinely ill. He could not accept the slightest physical blemish in a child any more than he could tolerate a moral deformity in a man.

As Madame Floriani's children were perfectly beautiful and healthy they charmed his eyes; but if one of them had become crippled, apart from the grief he would have felt in his soul, he would have been seized with an unconquerable uneasiness. He would never have dared touch it, carry it in his arms or fondle it. If he had had to face a stupid or wicked child every day he would have regarded it as a calamity sufficient to disgust him with life, and far from undertaking to improve the child, he would have shut himself in his room so as not to see or hear him. In other words, he liked children with his imagination and not with his heart; and whereas Salvator used to say that he would endure the boredom of marriage if only for the sake of experiencing the joys of parenthood, Karol could not think without a shudder of the possible consequences of his liaison with Lucrezia.

At dessert, Celio's gaiety had reached such a high pitch that as he was cutting some fruit he cut his hand rather badly. On seeing the blood spurt the boy was frightened and was sorely tempted to cry, but his mother, with much presence of mind, calmly took his hand, wrapped it in a napkin and said to him with a smile: "It's nothing. It isn't the first nor the last time you will hurt yourself. Go on with the beautiful story you were telling us. I'll dress your hand when you have finished."

Such a good lesson in fortitude was not wasted on Celio, who began to laugh, but Karol, who at the sight of the blood had almost fainted, did not understand how the mother could be sufficiently brave not to be anxious.

It was even worse when on leaving the table Lucrezia bathed the cut, brought the lips of the wound together and made a firm ligature, and all with a hand which did not tremble once. He could not imagine how a woman could be a surgeon to her own child and he was terrified at the sight of an energy of which he felt himself incapable. Whereas Salvator had helped Lucrezia in this small operation, Karol had gone away and stood on the steps outside the house, not wishing to look, yet observing against his will this simple and everyday scene which assumed for him the proportions of a dream.

Thus it was that here as always, in small things as in great ones, he refused to come to grips with life, and while Lucrezia, quick and courageous, grasped the monster without fear or disgust, he could not make up his mind to touch it with his finger tips.

Celio had been considerably calmed by this accidental blood-letting, but it had had little effect on the other children. The little girls, and above all Beatrice, were still like wild creatures, and little Salvator, quickly passing from joy to anger and then to grief, became so wilful and screamed so persistently and desperately that Lucrezia was obliged to intervene, threaten and finally carry him off to bed against his wishes. This was the first time that he had screamed in this way in Karol's ears or rather this was the first time that Karol was in a mood to realise that a youngster, however charming, always has tyrannical instincts, a determined will, fits of insane obstinacy and, for purposes of expediency and determination, prolonged howls of fury. The child's rage and distress, his sobs, his genuine tears which streamed down his pink cheeks like a spring shower, his beautiful little arms which fought the air and attacked his mother's hair, Lucrezia's struggle with him, her strong voice scolding him, her supple, sinewy hands which held him as if in a vice, yet without losing that velvet touch which a mother's hand always has so as not to bruise the delicate limbs – this was a colourful picture for Count Albani who looked on with a smile, unlike Karol who regarded it with the same terror and suffering as he had Celio's wound and its dressing.

"Oh God,'" he cried involuntarily, "how unhappy is childhood and how cruel it is to have to curb the violent appetites of the weak!"

"Nonsense," replid Salvator, laughing, "in five minutes he will be sound asleep and after giving him a good spanking to bring about a reaction, his mother will cover him with her kisses while he is sleeping."

"Do you think that she will lay hands on him?" asked Karol in terror.

"Oh, I haven't the slightest idea. I can only infer it because that would be the best sedative."

"My mother never struck or threatened me, I am sure."

"You don't remember, Karol. Moreover that would hardly be a reason for proving that it wasn't occasionally necessary to use extreme measures. I myself have no theories on education and as for that which concerns infants, you saw that *my* art lies not so much in repressing them as in bringing out the worst in them. I don't know how Lucrezia sets about it so as to make herself feared, but I think that the best method is the one that succeeds. I do not know if there is any need to beat children a little now and then, I shall know about it when I shall have some of my own, but it will not be part of *my* duties. I have too heavy a hand; it will be their mother's function."

"And I, if I had the misfortune of being a father," Karol retorted and his voice was strained, as if he were suffering, "I could not tolerate the discordant sound of rebellion and threats, the conflict with one's children, the bitter tears shed by a helpless creature who does not understand the laws of the impossible, the sham tempers whipped up by paternal morality, the sudden frightful upheaval of domestic calm, the storms in a tea-cup which I know are nothing, but which would perturb my soul as if they were serious events."

"In that case, dear friend, you must not perpetuate your noble race, for such storms are inevitable. Do you seriously believe that you never asked for the moon, and roared with fury before you understood that your mother could not give it to you?"

"No, I don't think so . . . I have no idea . . . I can't say."

"I am only using a metaphor, but I should be greatly surprised if something similar had not happened to you, for it seems to me that you have retained some of these longings for the impossible and that you still ask God sometimes to place the stars in the hollow of your hand."

Karol was silent and Lucrezia, having succeeded in pacifying her child, returned and suggested a trip on the lake. Little Salvator had not undergone the time-honoured punishment of a beating. His mother was well aware that the coolness of the bedroom, the darkness and softness of his cot, the undivided attention she had given him and the sound of her voice when she would sing him the air which would lull him to sleep – all this would calm him almost instantaneously. She also guessed, yet without knowing what serious proportions these trifles assumed in Karol's eyes, that all the noise must have annoyed him a little.

To create a diversion she took him on the lake with Salvator Albani, Celio, Stella and Beatrice, but they had not gone very far when they encountered old Menapace who was setting out to cast his nets. The children wanted to jump on to his boat and their mother, seeing that the old fisherman wished to give them a practical demonstration of an art which in his eyes was the greatest of all, agreed to entrust them to him.

Karol was afraid when he saw the three children, still over-excited, depart with such a cold, selfish old man whom he regarded as hardly capable of rescuing them from the water or even preventing them from falling into it.

He said as much to Lucrezia, but she did not share his anxiety.

"Children reared in the midst of danger get to know it very well," she replied, "and if one of them falls into our lake it is always a stranger who has come here on an outing and who does not know how to look after himself. Celio swims like a fish and Stella, wild as she is to-night, will watch over her little sister like a mother. Besides, we shall follow them and not lose sight of them."

Yet Karol refused to be reassured. In spite of himself he expressed the anxiety which comes from paternal concern and ever since he had seen Celio cut himself, his head had been filled with visions of unforeseen catastrophes. In short, his peace was disturbed both morally and physically as from this fatal day, a day on which nothing outstanding had occurred for the others, but when the habit and need of suffering had once more awakened in him.

And yet the excursion was very peaceful. The lake was magnificent in the reflections of the setting sun and the children had become calmer and were taking a serious pleasure in watching their grandfather cast his nets in a flowery, scent-laden creek. Salvator no longer spoke of Venice and by a fortunate chance the name of Boccaferri was not mentioned again. Lucrezia gathered some water-lilies and jumping from one boat to the other with a nimbleness and skill unexpected in a person apparently somewhat heavily built but which recalled the habits of her youth, she adorned the heads of her daughters with these beautiful flowers.

Karol was beginning to regain his inner calm. With consummate skill and coolness old Menapace was steering the boat through the rocks and tree-trunks which strewed the lake shore. None of the children seemed in danger of drowning and Karol was becoming accustomed to seeing them run from one boat to the other, handling the rudder and leaning over the side, yet not to starting with fear at every one of their movements.

The evening breeze began to rise, mild and balmy, bringing with it the fragrance of the blossoming vine and the vanilla-scented bean.

But it was written that this day would end the blissful calm of Karol and would mark for him the beginning of a series of small, indefinable sufferings. Salvator thought the water-lilies so beautiful that he insisted that Lucrezia, too, should put some in her dark hair. She refused, saying that she had had enough of wearing heavy ornaments and coiffures when she was at the theatre and that she was happy that she no longer felt the discomfort of even a single pin on her head. But Karol shared his friend's wish and she agreed to putting a few flowers in her magnificent tresses.

All was going well save the coiffure which Karol was helping to arrange, but without art or skill, so great was his fear of pulling a single hair of that precious head.

Salvator had the unfortunate idea of lending a hand. He undid the prince's work, took Lucrezia's rich hair in both hands and, guided only by his taste, he rolled it easily and casually and twined it with rushes and flowers. He succeeded very well, for he had an aptitude for what is called "fiddling about", too familiar an expression, but difficult to replace. He possessed a good understanding of statuary from the point of view of ornamentation.

He made Lucrezia a coiffure worthy of a classical naiad, saying: "Do you remember in Milan, if I happened to be there when you were dressing before going on the stage, how I always gave the final touch to your costume?"

"It is quite true," she replied. "I had forgotten. You had a particular gift for adding character to ornaments and for matching colours aptly. I often asked for your advice."

"She did, Karol." Salvator turned to his friend who had winced as if pierced by a needle. "Look at her, how beautiful she is! You would never have discovered, as I did, what suited the line of her brow, the volume of her head and the strength of the nape of her neck. You did not make sufficient of her personality. She looked like a Madonna with your coiffure, which is not at all the character of her beauty. She is a goddess. Let us feeble mortals prostrate ourselves and adore the nymph of the lake!"

As he spoke Salvator imprinted a heavy kiss on Lucrezia's knees and Karol shuddered like a man stabbed with a dagger.

20.

The poor boy had forgotten that in his own way Salvator was as much in love with Lucrezia as he was, that he had magnanimously surrendered his claims on her, but not without effort or regret. As this kind of love was incomprehensible to Karol he had not realised the suffering his friend must have undergone on seeing him become the owner of the being he coveted. He had told himself that the first beautiful woman Salvator encountered would make him forget his insane desire.

Or rather, he had told himself nothing. He would not have had the courage to examine the indelicate side of such a situation. He had thrust away the memory of the first night spent at the Villa Floriani, the temptations and advances of Salvator and even the embraces of the following morning when he had thought he was saying a last farewell to Lucrezia. The crisis of the illness and the ensuing miracle of bliss had effaced everything from the prince's mind. In one day, in one instant he had grown accustomed to ceasing to form judgements on anything, or understanding anything; and in the same way, in one day, he was now beginning to judge too much and understand too much, that is, to comment on everything to excess and suffer on account of everything.

To be sure, Salvator Albani had acted in good faith when he decided that henceforth he would only look at Lucrezia with the eyes of a brother. But he possessed a fund of Italian sensuality which prevented him from ever achieving the chastity of a monk. If he had had two sisters, one beautiful and the other ugly, he probably and without being aware of his own instinct would have preferred the beautiful one, even if she had been less pleasant and kind than the other one. And of two sisters equally beautiful, if one had known love and the other only virtue, he would have been the greater friend of the one who had a better understanding of frailty and passion.

Love was his god and every beautiful woman who was kindhearted was his priestess. He could love her unselfishly, but he could not look at her without emotion. Consequently Lucrezia's love for his friend did not disturb him in his admiration and pleasure when he regarded her and breathed her atmosphere. He loved to touch her arms, her hair and even her clothes just as much as he had done in the past, and one can understand that Karol was jealous of these things, almost as much as of his mistress' heart.

Difficult as it may be to believe, Lucrezia's nature was as innocent as the soul of a child. I agree that this is very strange, on the part of a woman who had loved greatly and whose spontaneity had been such that she could not give herself in any other way but wholly, to the objects of her passion. Undeniably she was a creature endowed with very strong senses, although she could appear cold to men she disliked. The fact is that outside her love in which she was utterly submerged she saw nothing, imagined nothing and felt nothing. During the rare intervals in which her heart had been calm her senses had been idle; and if she had been separated for ever from the sight of the opposite sex, she would have been an excellent nun, tranquil and bright. In other words there was nothing purer than her thoughts when she lived in solitude, and when she loved she felt that everything which was not her lover was solitude, emptiness, nothing.

Salvator might kiss her, tell her that she was beautiful, and tremble a little as he pressed her arm against his; she was aware of it even less than on the day when, not realising that Karol loved her already, he had been driven to speak to her clearly and boldly in order to make her understand his desires.

Yet every woman fully understands the look and inflexion of voice which speaks indirectly of love. Women of the world have an insight in these matters which often goes far beyond the truth, and often, too, their eagerness to defend themselves even before they are attacked is a provocation on their part and an encouragement to boldness. Lucrezia, however, in her well-meaning kindness, put everything down to the sympathy she had aroused as an artist or the warmth she inspired as a woman. She was abrupt and bored with men who roused mistrust and suspicion in her; but with those she esteemed she wore her heart on her sleeve – she would have believed she was betraying the sanctity of friendship by being too much on her guard. She knew quite well that an occasional evil thought could pass through their heads. But she had made it a rule not to notice it and as long as she was not driven to show herself severe, she was gentle and relaxed. She thought that men were like children with whom one must often divert the conversation and distract the imagination rather than answer and discuss delicate and dangerous subjects.

Yet Karol who should have been aware of the stability of this simple, straightforward character, did not really understand it. His madness had committed the gigantic mistake of imagining that with all men other than himself she should have the austerity and the icy demeanour of a virgin. He refused to yield, he refused to understand the reality of this nature and to love her for what she was. Because he had set her too high in the fantasies of his mind he was now fully prepared to place her too low and to believe that between the invincible sensuality of Salvator and the secret instincts of Lucrezia there were fatal and terrifying affinities.

During the journey back to the villa the evening star rose like a huge white diamond in a sky still flushed with pink. They were gliding over the limpid surface of the lake that Lucrezia loved so much and which Karol was beginning to hate once more. He did not speak. Beatrice had fallen asleep in her mother's arms, Celio was handling Menapace's boat and the old man sat in silent contemplation. Stella, slim and white, was dreaming of the stars from which she derived her name and Salvator Albani was singing in a fine, fresh voice, which the sonority of the waves carried far into the distance. No one else save Karol, the purest and most irreproachable of them all, was thinking of evil. He sat with his back turned to them so as not to see something which did not exist, something which no one was thinking about; and instead of the Undines of the lake he felt he was being driven by the Eumenides.

Hadn't he been betrayed? Hadn't Salvator been mocking him outrageously when he said that he had never been Lucrezia's lover? With all the beautiful and plausible arguments he had heard him advance so often on the subject of friendship with women and which, according to Salvator, always contained some element of love, suppressed or disguised; – with all the subtle reservations of which Karol supposed him capable to enable him to enjoy happiness without having a lie on his conscience, he might well have been made happy on the night of their arrival and coolly denied it a moment later. In that case Lucrezia owed him nothing and Karol felt he was being very generous as he resolved never to question her on the matter.

Again, assuming that she had resisted on that occasion, was it likely that in her earlier life, abandoned to every emotion, when Salvator was present in her dressing room as she changed and when he laid hands on her costume, when, with her heart throbbing wildly after the fatigues and triumphs of the stage she came and flung herself on the couch near him, maybe alone with him . . . was it possible that he had not attempted to take advantage of a moment of mental confusion and nervous over-excitement? Salvator was so passionate and so bold with women! Hadn't he incurred the displeasure of Princess Lucie by daring to tell her that she had beautiful hands? And if this man had not remained speechless and trembling before Lucie, what was he not capable of with Lucrezia?

And now the terrible parallel which had been for so long thrust aside began to take a hold on the prince's mind: on the one hand a princess, a virgin, an angel; on the other hand an actress, a woman without morals, a mother of four children by three men, without ever being married and without knowing where these men were now!

The fearful reality rose before his terrified eyes like a Gorgon about to devour him. An uncontrollable trembling shook his limbs, his head threatened to burst. He thought he could see poisonous snakes crawling at his feet on the boards of the boat and he thought he could see his mother rising towards the stars, her horror-stricken face averted from him.

Lucrezia was half asleep in her dream of eternal happiness and when she took his hand to step on to the shore she merely noticed that he was cold, although the evening was mild.

She was slightly worried when she saw him under the lights of the villa, but he made great efforts to seem gay. Lucrezia had never seen him gay, she did not even know if with his high and poetic intelligence he had any talent in the direction of wittiness. She now realised that he had it to a considerable extent. It was subtly, mockingly delicate, fundamentally not at all good-natured, but as she was utterly infatuated with him she marvelled on discovering in him an additional charm. Salvator knew quite well that this thin, affected, ironical gaiety on the part of his friend was no indication of great contentment. But in the circumstances he was at a loss what to think. Perhaps love had entirely changed the prince's character; perhaps he was taking life henceforth less austerely and less gloomily. Salvator seized the opportunity to be gay and free with him, yet he thought he occasionally saw something harsh and bitter behind his brightest repartees.

Karol could not sleep, yet he was not ill. In his long and cruel insomnia he realised that he had a greater capacity for suffering than he had ever thought possible. The torpor of a slow fever did not come, as it had done once, to deaden his anxious thoughts. He rose next morning as he had gone to bed, a prey to a horrible lucidity, yet without feeling any physical discomfort and obsessed with the fixed idea that Salvator was betraying him now, had betrayed him in the past and was thinking of betraying him in the future.

"But I must come to a decision," he said to himself. "I must break away or dominate, throw up the game or pursue the enemy. Shall I be strong enough for the struggle? No, no, it is horrible! It is better to flee."

He went out as day broke, not knowing where he was going, but unable to resist the need to walk quickly. The path in the park which he was following mechanically was the most direct and most frequented, but when he realised that it led to the fisherman's cottage he decided to leave it. At that moment he heard his name uttered. He stopped. The word "prince" was repeated several times. Karol, under cover of the drooping branches of the old willows, approached and listened.

"A prince! A prince! Nonsense!" old Menapace was saying in his dialect which Karol by now had learnt to understand thoroughly. "He doesn't look like one. I saw Prince Murat when I was young. He was stout, strong, healthy-looking and wore magnificent clothes, gold and plumes. *That* was a prince! But this one looks like nothing at all and I wouldn't even trust him with my oars."

"I assure you that he is a real prince, Master Menapace," Biffi replied. "I heard his servant call him 'prince', and he didn't know I was there."

"I tell you that he is as much a prince as my daughter was a princess, out there . . . They all give themselves names like that in the theatre. The other fellow, Albani, is the one who used to play the count on the stage, but he is a singer, that's all he is."

"It is true that he sings all day," said Biffi. "So they are the signora's old comrades? Are they going to stay here long?"

"That is what I ask myself. It seems to me that the prince, as they call him, is enjoying his free board and lodging greatly. And if the other one also stays and does nothing but eat, sleep and go for quiet little walks by the water's edge, this isn't the end of it yet."

"But surely it does not affect *us*. It is not *our* concern."

"It affects *me!*" said Menapace, raising his voice. "I do not like to see idlers and pushers eating up the assets of my grandchildren. You can see very clearly that they are nothing but out of work play-actors with no feelings, who have come here to recuperate. My daughter, who is kind, is sorry for them. But if she takes all her former friends in like that, we can look out for trouble. Poor little Celio! Poor children! If I gave no thought for them they would share the fate of these so-called lords one day! Come, Biffi, are you ready? Untie the boat and let's go."

If Salvator had heard this ridiculous conversation it would have kept him roaring with laughter for a full week. He would have even devised some crazy hoax to add to the charitable suspicions of the fisherman. But Karol was cut to the heart. The idea of such a thing happening to *him* would have seemed impossible. To be taken for a play-actor, a beggar, and to be despised by this old miser! He felt as if he were walking in filth, he who found only the clouds soft and pure enough to bear him!

One would have to be very strong or very carefree not to be prostrated by an absurd role and only see its ludicrous side. Moreover, one never or almost never laughs at oneself, and Karol was so beside himself that he left the park just as he was, without even any money on him, and fled at random into the open country, determined, or at least believing he was determined, never to set foot again in Madame Floriani's house.

Although after his illness his health had been better than it had ever been before, he was still not a very good walker, and when he had gone half a league he was obliged to reduce his pace. Then it was that the burden of his thoughts overwhelmed him and he could only drag himself with great effort in the aimless direction which he had taken.

If my conception of the novel were in accordance with modern rules and I ended the chapter at this point, I would leave my reader in suspense until to-morrow, assuming that instead of sleeping you would be asking yourself all night: "Will Prince Karol depart or will he not depart?" But the high opinion I always have of your perception forbids me to have recourse to this clever ruse and I will spare you all agony. You know full well that my novel is not sufficiently advanced for my hero to put an end to the matter so abruptly and against my will. Moreover, his flight would be very unrealistic and you would never believe that one can break the chains of a violent love at the first blow.

Set your mind at rest then, attend to your occupations, and may sleep strew its red and white poppies over your eyes! We have not reached the dénouement yet.

21.

Karol too was asking himself the same question. "Shall I depart? Shall I be able to depart? A quarter of an hour from now, won't I be compelled to go back? Since this is inevitable, why tire myself making a useless journey?"

"I shall depart," he cried as he flung himself on the grass that was still wet with dew. His indignation was rekindled and his strength came back to him. He set off again but fatigue soon came and with it the return of doubt and dejection.

Bitter regrets brought tears to his eyes wearied by the brightness of the sun which seemed to be coming towards him and saying: "We are travelling in opposite directions. Are you going to flee from me and enter eternal darkness?" His thoughts went back to his happiness of the previous day when, at this same hour, he had seen Lucrezia come into his bedroom, open his window to allow him to hear the song of the birds and breathe the scent of the honeysuckle, pause near his bed to smile at him and before giving him his first kiss, embrace him with that ineffable look of love and adoration which is more eloquent than all words, more passionate than all caresses. Oh, how happy he still was at that moment! The sun had merely to traverse the horizon and everything was destroyed! He would never again see this tender woman intoxicate him with her deep look and replace the visions of his dreams by her calm and radiant image! That hand which, as it passed softly through his hair, seemed to give him new life; that heart whose fire had never become exhausted as it fed his;

that spirit whose strength maintained in him a hitherto unknown serenity; those sweet attentions at all moments, that constant solicitude, more assiduous and more inventive even than his mother's had been; that bright and happy home where the atmosphere seemed relaxed and warmed by a magnetic influence; that silence of the park, those flowers in the garden, those children with their melodious voices who sang with the birds, everything including Celio's dog which ran so gracefully through the grass chasing the butterflies so as to imitate his young friend – in short, the combination of all these things which he was now picturing and detailing for the first time as he was about to be separated from them, was at an end for him!

And just as he was thinking of Celio's dog, the noble creature itself rushed towards him and for the first time caressed him tenderly. Yet he had not come in pursuit of Karol, and the latter thought at first that Celio was not far away. But when he did not see him appear he remembered that on the previous evening Laertes (this was the dog's name) had run ahead along the bank where the boats had stopped, that they had tried calling him back, but to no avail, and that when they had returned home Celio had been anxious on discovering that he was not there. They had whistled and called again, in the belief that he had skirted the lake and returned by way of the meadows; but they had gone to bed and he was still missing. Lucrezia had comforted her son by reminding him that the dog had already spent the night outside on several occasions and that he was far too intelligent not to be able to find his way back home as soon as he wished.

The fact was that Laertes, lured by a passion for the chase, had marked down and pursued a hare till daybreak. It is not clear whether he lost its trail or succeeded in reaching the hare and devouring it, but at this moment he was thinking of Celio who played with him, Madame Floriani who fed him herself, little Salvator who pulled his ears, his cool cushion and his breakfast. He was fully aware of the time and told himself that he must be going home now so as not to be scolded for his excessive absence. It is even possible that he was cunning enough to imagine that it hadn't been noticed.

On seeing Karol he could only think that he had come to look for him and feeling guilty and not wishing to add to his crimes he came towards him with an affectionate and modest look, sweeping the ground with his long, silky tail and giving himself all kinds of graces in order to win forgiveness for his escapade.

The prince could not resist his advances and resolved to pat him a little on the head. "You too," he thought, "wanted to break your chain and taste freedom. And there you are, hesitating between the servitude of yesterday and the fear of to-day."

Karol could only envisage the solitude of the days before Lucrezia with the greatest of terror. He told himself that it was better to suffer the tortures of love perturbed by doubt and shame than to live an empty life. What would he return to if he sank back into isolation? Henceforth the image of his mother or Lucie would only appear to him in order to reproach him bitterly. He tried to evoke them now, but they no longer obeyed his summons. He had never been able to convince himself in the past that his mother was dead, but he felt it now: the grave no longer yielded its prey. The features of Lucie were so effaced from his memory that he strove in vain to picture them. They were covered by a thick cloud. Now that Karol had drunk of the cup of life, the company of these shades terrified him instead of pleasing him. Must he live then? Must he go on living against his will? Must he love life even while despising it and plunge into it despite the fear and disgust it inspired? Was it the will of God or the temptation of a spirit of confusion and darkness?

"But is it life that I shall find with Lucrezia? Will it not be death – this attachment whose circumstances make me blush and in which doubt will poison everything? If I am to choose between two kinds of self-annihilation would it not be preferable to languish and waste away with the feeling of my own courage rather than in indignity?"

He found no way out of his uncertainty. He rose, walked one step towards exile and looked behind him. His heart was breaking and was being rent at the thought that he would never see his mistress again and he could feel that heart physically dying, as if the woman was its sole driving force.

By now he was almost conquered and was looking round for some omen, some heaven-sent chance – the last resort of weakness – which would show him the path to follow. Laertes came to his rescue. Laertes was resolved to go back home. When Karol turned away from the villa, the dog stopped and looked at him in surprise; then, when the prince came back towards him, he leapt with joy and his eyes, bright with expression and intelligence seemed to say: "This is the right way. You were wrong. Just follow me!"

Karol thought of a subterfuge which would have been worthy of a child. He told himself that Lucrezia valued this dog highly, that Celio was capable of weeping a whole day if he did not recover it; that the animal was very young and high-spirited and would perhaps allow itself to be tempted by some other prey before returning home; finally it could get lost or be lured away by some huntsman and his, Karol's, duty was to take it back to its home.

So he called Laertes, kept a feeble eye on him and reached the Villa Floriani without actually losing sight of him. Yet one can say that never was a blind man more literally led by a dog!

On seeing the park gate open, Laertes began to run and in his delight to be home outstripped Karol, reached the house and Celio's room where he curled up under the bed and waited for him to wake up. Thus Karol's excuse about returning the dog was rendered ineffective. He was not obliged to go through the park gate and yet he was about to do so when his eyes encountered an inscription painted on a stone in the wall. They were the famous lines of Dante.

> *Per mi si va nella citta dolente,*
> *Per mi si va nell' eterno dolore,*
> *Per mi si va tra la perduta gente . . .*
> *. . . Lasciate ogni speranzo, voi ch'entrate!*

And underneath: Visitors, take heed! – Celio Floriani.

Karol remembered that a few days earlier Celio, who had just learned this famous passage of the *Divina Commedia* by heart and repeated it at every turn with that mixture of admiration and parody typical of children, had amused himself by writing it on the gate post in the park and had added a facetious warning to passers by. As the villa did not stand on any public thoroughfare there was no harm in allowing Celio's inscription to remain until the next downpour would wash it away. Lucrezia had merely laughed and Karol for whom these gloomy lines had no meaning at the time was in no way alarmed by them. He had passed through this gate several times since, without paying attention to the words, and he would never have given any thought to them if not for the revolution which had taken place inside him. At first sight, the words *perduta gente* struck him as a hideous allusion and possibly true in part, for he hastened to erase them. Then, on re-reading the last verse, as if against his will, he was seized by a superstitious terror at the thought that children often prophesy without realising it and even as they laugh, utter frightful truths. He picked up a handful of grass and rubbed the wall with it, but by a very ordinary chance the last verse, because it was painted on a stone which was not as smooth as the others, was not entirely erased and remained visible in spite of Karol's every effort.

"Well," said he, rushing forward into the park, "thus it is written in the book of my fate. Why should my eyes be offended thereby? Oh, Lucrezia, you gave me nothing but happiness. Now that I am going to suffer through you and for you, I see how much I love you."

Lucrezia was already extremely anxious. She had sought Karol everywhere in the park and could not imagine that, contrary to his habits, he would have risen before her and gone for a walk without her. She was in the fisherman's cottage when she saw the prince efface the inscription and hurry towards the house as if, like Laertes, he was afraid of being scolded. She ran after him and clasping him in her arms she said: "Don't you think that it is a wicked lie?"

Karol's mind was hardly on the subject. He could not imagine that she might have seen him erase Dante's lines. His thoughts were no longer on the verses, but rather on Salvator's possible betrayal. He believed that she was answering his secret thoughts, that she had guessed his anxiety, had watched his attempts to flee. The most unlikely things came to his mind and he replied with a scared look: "Be your own judge, it is not for me to answer for you."

Lucrezia was a little surprised and began to fear one of those attacks when he behaved in an unaccountable manner. Salvator had warned her of them more than once before she had given her heart to the prince. But she had refused to believe him because since his illness Karol had always lived in the seventh heaven of delight and had never caused her a moment's fear. She now wondered if he was completely cured, if he was not threatened with an imminent relapse or indeed if his brain was really deranged and tortured with fantastic ideas. She questioned him. He refused to reply, but kissed her hand repeatedly and begged her forgiveness. But forgiveness for what? That was something Lucrezia could not learn despite all tender inquiries. Just as his appearance and speech had changed, so had his manner. He had told himself that if he decided to return to Lucrezia, he must never question or reproach her, never debase his own love by hurtful words; in short, he hid behind a cult of chivalry and excess of outer respect, as if in that way he could repair the wrong he had done her in his heart by suspecting her.

Lucrezia had always been deeply touched by the respect he showed her in the presence of her children and her servants. Nothing in him recalled the offensive over-familiarity and the impertinent lack of restraint of successful lovers. But when they were alone she was not accustomed to seeing him turn his face away from her lips and greet her by kissing her hand, like an abbé paying his respects to a dowager. She attempted to put an end to this cold atmosphere; she reproached him tenderly, she poked gentle fun at him: it was all in vain.

He hurried on towards the house, for he felt that his suffering was not sufficiently calmed for him to assume a happy appearance.

Salvator was not especially surprised to see his friend silent and gloomy on that day. He had seen him so, so often before!

"I am worried this morning," Lucrezia murmured to him. "Karol is so pale and sad!"

"You should be used to him waking up entirely different from what he was when he went to sleep," replied Salvator.

"Isn't he as unstable and changeable as the clouds?"

"No, Salvator, he is not at all like that. For two months he has been a pure, glowing sky, without a single cloud, without the slightest shadow."

"Really? What miracle is this you are telling me? I can hardly believe you."

"I swear it. What can the matter be with him to-day?"

"Nothing. He will have had a bad dream."

"But that is all gone now. He has been dreaming none but beautiful dreams."

"Well, it was a lucky chance or a sheer miracle. I have never seen him for one week – no, one whole day, when he hasn't succumbed to some fit of melancholy."

"And why did it happen so frequently?"

"You are asking me something I could never get him to tell. Isn't Karol a walking hieroglyph, a personified myth?"

"He has not been so far for me until this hour; and seeing that without my knowledge I had found the way to make him happy and secure, it must be that since yesterday I have displeased him in some way."

"Did you quarrel last night?"

"Quarrel? What a word!"

"Oh, you have become *sublime* like him, I see, and we must create a vocabulary specially selected for you two... Come now, when you were chatting last night, didn't you touch on some painful spot of your or his life?"

"Last night, like every other night, I did not leave my children. We retire early. I get up with the dawn and while the little ones are still dozing or prattling with their nurse before they get up I go and waken Karol gently and we chat together. Most often we look at each other and adore each other without exchanging a word. These are two hours of bliss, in which no painful word, no positive reflection or memory of the troubles and ills of the real world have found a place. This morning I went to open the window as usual, as I have always done since he was ill.

"He had already gone out, a thing he had never done before. He remained absent for two hours. When he returned he looked distraught; he spoke words I do not understand, his manner was peculiar. He almost frightened me and now his despondency and the care he takes to avoid us hurt me. You who know him, try to make him say what ails him!"

"I who know him can tell you nothing save that he was cheerful last night, which was a sure sign that he would be sad this morning. He has never been able to expand for a single hour in his life without paying for it later by reserve and taciturnity. There are certainly moral causes for it, but they are too slight or too subtle to be perceptible to the naked eye. You would require a microscope to read a soul which is penetrated to so slight an extent by the light which is used by ordinary mortals."

"Salvator, you do not know your friend. That is not at all how he is constituted. A sun purer and brighter than ours shines in his passionate and noble soul."

"As you wish," Salvator smiled. "Well, try and see what you can make of it, but don't ask me to hold the taper."

"You are laughing, my friend," said Lucrezia, sadly. "But I am in agony. I keep on questioning myself, but in vain. I cannot see how I have been able to grieve the heart of my dear love. Yet his icy look freezes me to the very marrow and when I see him thus it seems to me that I am about to die."

22.

A few words of frank explanation would have cured the suffering of Lucrezia and her lover; but in asking to know the truth, Karol would have needed to have faith in the honesty of the reply; and when one has allowed oneself to be dominated by an unjust suspicion, one loses too much of one's own frankness to rely on that of other people. Moreover, the unhappy young man was not in full control of his reason and he only retained just sufficient of it to know that reason would not convince him.

Fortunately these natures, quick to be perturbed and extravagant in their fears, recover quickly and forget. They themselves feel that their anxiety eludes the help of those who love them and that it can only end by self-exhaustion. And this is what happened to Karol. On the evening of that dismal day he was already weary of suffering and he was bored with solitude. At night, as he had not slept for a long time, he was overcome by a torpor which brought him some hours' rest. The following day he once more found happiness in Lucrezia's arms, but he offered no explanation on what had made him so different from his usual self the previous day and she was obliged to be content with evasive replies. It remained in him like a sore which closes but which must open again, because the germ of the disease has not been destroyed.

Lucrezia did not forget so quickly what her lover had suffered. Although she was far from penetrating its cause, she felt its after-effects. With her it was not a sudden pain, violent and fleeting. It was a secret anxiety, deep and continual. Despite Salvator, she persisted in believing that there is no suffering without a reason, but as her self-searching was of no avail and her conscience was clear, she was reduced to thinking that Karol had felt stirring in him either the memory of his mother or the regret of having been unfaithful to Lucie.

Thus Karol had regained his calm and sense of security even before Lucrezia had found consolation on seeing him unhappy; but as she was finally becoming reassured and was beginning to forget the dread which this cloud had caused, an incident occurred to reawaken Karol's suffering. And what an incident! We hardly dare repeat it, it was so absurd and childish. While Lucrezia was playing with Laertes, she was so touched by his grace and affectionate look, that she kissed him on the head. Karol regarded this as a profanation and declared that Lucrezia's mouth ought not to brush the head of a dog. He could not refrain from expressing his opinion with some heat, which betrayed his aversion for animals. Lucrezia, astonished to see him take such a thing seriously, could not help laughing and Karol was deeply hurt.

"Come now, my dear," she said, "would you prefer a formal discussion on the subject of a kiss given to my dog? As far as I am concerned, I would not care to disagree with you on anything, but as I don't find the matter worthy of comment or careful consideration I must laugh a little at the vey oddity of the subject."

"Ah, I know I am ridiculous," said Karol, "and it is a fatal thing for me that you are beginning to realise it. Couldn't you answer in any other manner than by a burst of laughter?"

"I could not think of anything to say in answer, I tell you," retorted Lucrezia, somewhat impatiently. "When you make a remark to me, must I bow my head in silence even if I am not convinced that it was worth making?"

"It is evident that we must become strangers to one another on anything which concerns the real world," said Karol, with a sigh. "We would agree so little on this point that I must apparently be silent or only open my mouth to make others laugh."

He sulked for two hours about this, after which he gave it no further thought and once more became as agreeable as usual. But Lucrezia was sad for four hours without sulking or revealing her sadness.

The following day it was something else, something even more trivial, and the day after they were both sad for no apparent reason.

Salvator had of course seen nothing of the dazzling purity of the happiness of the two lovers during his absence. On the contrary, all he saw on his arrival was the return of Karol to his old hyper-sensitiveness. At times he found him full of affection for him, at others very cool. This did not surprise him as it was nothing new, but he told himself sadly that the cure was by no means complete and he came back to the conviction that these two beings were certainly not made for each other.

After several days of observation and reflection on the matter he resolved to have it out with his friend and to induce him, even if unwillingly, to explain himself. He knew that this was not easy, but he equally knew how he must set about it.

"Dear child," he said to him a week or so after his return to the Villa Floriani, "if it is at all possible I would like to have your answer to the following question: Are we going to stay here much longer?"

"I don't know," answered Karol, curtly. The question seemed to annoy him, but a moment later his eyes filled with tears and from the way in which he looked at Salvator he apparently foresaw that their separation was inevitable.

"Please, Karol," Count Albani went on, taking hold of his hand, "for once in your life try to form your own idea about the future. Do it to please me, because I cannot remain eternally dependent on the turn of events. In the past, that is before you came here, you always fell back on the state of your health which would not permit you to make any plans. 'Do with me as you wish,' you said. 'I have no will, no desire.' Now the roles are changed and your health can no longer serve as a pretext: you are very well, you have grown stronger. Don't shake your head. I know nothing about your moral state, but I can clearly see that your physical condition is excellent. You are no longer like your old self, your face has changed in colour and expression, you walk, eat and sleep like everyone else.

Love and Lucrezia have performed this miracle. You are no longer bored with life. Apparently you have no more doubts. It is my turn now to be uncertain and unable to see where I am going. Come now, you want to stay here, don't you?"

"I don't know if I would be able to go away, even if I wished," answered Karol, who was extremely unhappy at being compelled to reply clearly. "I believe I wouldn't have the strength to do so and yet I ought to."

"You ought to because . . . "

"Don't ask. You can guess the reason yourself."

"So you are still as mentally reluctant as ever when it is a matter of dealing with the dull subject of real life?"

"Yes, all the more reluctant as I have been further away from it for some time."

"So you want me to do as I always do: that I should think for you, that I should discuss things with myself as if it were with you, and that I should find good reasons for proving to you that it is right for you to do what you wish to do."

"Well, yes," replied the prince, with the serious look of a spoilt child. Not that in the present situation he needed the advice of another person so as to know the strength of his love; but he was very pleased to hear Salvator judge of his condition, for it would enable him to read into his friend's secret feelings.

"Very well," said Salvator, gaily, suspecting no trap because he had no ulterior motive. "I will try, though it is not so simple now. Everything about you has changed: it is no longer a question of knowing if the climate of this country is healthy, if you are enjoying your stay, if the inn is well kept and if the heat or cold will force you to leave. The summer of your passion would warm you even if the June sunshine were not sending its beams down upon you. This country house is beautiful and our hostess is not unpleasant . . . Come, aren't you even going to smile at my wit?"

"No my friend, I can't. Speak seriously."

"By all means. Well, I shall be brief. You are happy here and you feel intoxicated with love. You cannot foresee how long it will be before it becomes clouded and dark. You wish to enjoy your happiness as long as God will allow. And after that? I repeat, after that? Answer! Hitherto I have stated things as they are. It is what will happen afterwards that I am anxious to know."

"Afterwards, afterwards, Salvator? After the light there is nothing but darkness."

"Excuse me, there is twilight. You will tell me that that is still light of sorts and that you will enjoy it until the final extinction. But when night falls, you will have to turn towards some other sun, won't you? Whether it is art, politics, travel or marriage remains to be seen. But tell me, when we have reached that stage, where shall we meet? To which island in the ocean of life must I go and wait for you?"

"Salvator," cried the prince in terror, forgetting for the moment the sad suspicions that haunted him, "don't speak to me of the future. I tell you now that I am more incapable then ever of foreseeing anything in the future. You predict the end of my love or hers, don't you? Well, speak to me of death; that is the only thought I can associate with the one you suggest to me."

"Yes, yes, I understand. Well, let's say no more about it, since you are still in that paroxysm when one cannot think of either putting an end to happiness or making it endure. Perhaps it is unfortunate that some measure of attention and foresight is not possible at such times; for every ideal rests on earthly foundations and a little planning could contribute to the stability or at least the prolongation of happiness."

"You are right, my friend. Help me then! What must I do? Is there anything possible in the strange situation in which I find myself? I thought that that woman would love me forever!"

"And you no longer believe it?"

"I no longer know anything. I no longer see anything clearly."

"I must see for you then. Lucrezia will always love you if you can arrange to go and live on Jupiter or Saturn."

"Heavens! Why do you jest?"

"No, I do not. I am talking sense. I know of no heart more passionate, more loyal or more devoted than that of Lucrezia. But I know of no love which can preserve its intensity and exultation beyond a certain time on this earth of ours."

"Leave me alone . . . Leave me alone," said Karol bitterly.

"You do nothing but hurt me."

"My object is not to attack love," continued Salvator calmly. "Nor do I purpose to prove that your love is ordinary and that it cannot resist better than any other man's the laws of its own destruction. On this subject you know more than I do and you know Lucrezia from an angle which I have only been able to surmise and guess. But what I know possibly better than both of you – in spite of all the experience of that adorable wild creature of a Lucrezia – is that the environment in which lovers live affects their passion in spite of them and in spite of everything. You may have heaven in your heart, but it is to no avail: if a tree falls on your head I defy you not to feel the effects of it. Well, if outer circumstances help and protect you, you can continue loving one another for a long time, possibly for ever! – until old age comes to teach you that the 'for ever' of lovers is just an idea. . . . If on the other hand, without anticipating or analysing anything, you allow evil influences to approach and reach you, you will ultimately succumb to the common fate, that is, you will see troubles come to confuse and destroy you."

"I am listening. Go on. What must I fear and anticipate? What can I prevent?"

"Madame Floriani is as free as the air, she is rich, independent of all former associations, and it seems that she had a foreknowledge of what suited her happiness when she broke with the world even before she met you and came to bury herself in this solitude. These are excellent conditions for the present, but will they last for ever?"

"Do you believe that she feels the need to return to the world? Oh God, if that happens . . . Heaven help me!"

"No, no, dear child," said Salvator, stricken by the despair and terror of his friend. "I don't mean that, I don't believe it. But the world can come and seek her here and beset her in spite of herself. If I had not been as silent as the grave in Venice with all those people who spoke to me about her, if I hadn't said evasively to those who actually knew she was here, 'She is possibly planning to settle there, but nothing is definite, she is going away, maybe to France . . . ' everything that Lucrezia herself had suggested I say in answer to indiscreet questions –

if I had not done so, believe me, you would already be flooded with visitors. One cannot postpone things for ever. The day may come when you two will no longer be alone here. What will be your attitude towards the former friends of your mistress?"

"Oh horrible, horrible!" cried Karol, striking his breast.

"You take everything in too tragic a manner, my dear prince. It is not a question of giving way to despair over it, but to expect it and be prepared to strike tent when the necessity arises. Thus this disaster would not be without its remedy. You could depart and go and seek some other temporary solitude. There is a certain art by which one can utterly discourage visitors, and that is never to allow them to be certain of meeting you. Lucrezia understands this art very well. She will help you out of your plight. So calm yourself!"

"Are there no other dangers then?" said Karol who, as changeable as ever, was moving from exaggerated panic to easy over-confidence.

"Yes, my child, there are other dangers," replied Salvator, "but you are going to excite yourself again, more than I would like, and maybe you will tell me to go to the devil."

"Keep on talking."

"When you have surrounded yourselves with solitude there will be the danger of satiety."

"That is true," said Karol, overcome by this thought. "Perhaps you already sense it on her part, and rightly, too. Oh yes, I have been ill and morose these last few days. She must have become tired of me and bored. Has she told you so?"

"No, she has not told me so. She has not thought it and I don't believe that she will grow tired first. It is for you much more than for her that I fear emotional lassitude."

"For me, you say?"

"Yes. I know that you are an exceptional being, I know of your perseverance in loving a woman whom you did not know intimately. (Allow me to say so now.) I also know in what exclusive and admirable manner you loved your mother. But all that was not love. Love wears away and because yours is so utterly incapable of enduring the attacks of reality it will wear away quickly."

"You lie!" cried Karol with an ecstatic smile which was both sublime and naïve.

"My child, I admire you, but I pity you. The present is radiant, but the future is veiled."

"Spare me your commonplaces."

"Please listen to one only. Consider your noble family, your former friends, that very restricted and therefore highly selective and rigid section of high society which has been your milieu and even, if I may say so, the very air you breathed. What part will you play in it?"

"I renounce it forever! I have thought about it, Salvator, and its consideration has weighed less than a straw in the scale of my love."

"Very good. When you return to your noble relatives they will undoubtedly absolve you. But that will not prevent them from saying that it was wrong of you to have been the lover of an actress for so long a time and so seriously. These virtuous friends would forgive you more readily for having a hundred casual pleasures than one love."

"I don't believe you. But even if it were so, that is all the more reason for breaking without regret with my family and all my old ties."

"Splendid. Noble relatives are admirable people but also great bores; I have been allowing mine to talk for a long time without interrupting them. If you wish to be refractory too, it is very unexpected, very amusing... and upon my soul, it pleases me greatly! And yet, dear Karol, there is another family which you have not thought about. It is Madame Floriani's and they are witnesses of your love and hers."

"Ah, at last you are touching the painful spot," cried the prince, shuddering as if bitten by a snake. "Her father, yes, that wretch, the one who takes us for starving play-actors who are receiving charity here in the form of board and lodging! It is hideous and I nearly left when I heard him say so to Biffi."

"Does old Menapace do us such an honour?" replied Salvator, bursting out laughing. But seeing how seriously Karol took the ridiculous incident he attempted to calm him down.

"If you had told Lucrezia of this farcical adventure," he

went on, "her answer would have comforted you, and this is what that wonderful woman would have said:

'My child, all my lovers were paupers – so terrified was I to be regarded as a kept woman. You have millions, people may think that you render me great services, but I love you so much that I have never given it a thought nor do I give a rap for what people think. So forget my father's and Biffi's nonsense, as I forget the whole world for you.'

"You see, Karol, you ought to be grateful to her for not being so sensitive on the subject of public opinion. But let us speak of her children. Have you given any thought to them, my friend?"

"Don't I love them?" cried the prince. "Would I wish to separate them from her for a single moment?"

"But won't they grow up one day? Will they never understand? I know that they are all illegitimate, that they do not remember their fathers and that they are still at that innocent age when they can be persuaded that in order to be born only a mother is necessary. How she will one day extricate herself from this quandary in relation to them, and what sublime or lamentable drama will be enacted in the bosom of this family concerns neither you nor me. I have faith in the wonderful instincts of Madame Floriani to find a solution with honour. But that is no reason why you should complicate the situation by your continued presence. You will never be able nor will you ever wish to lie. How will you deal with the problem?"

Karol who was unable to express his emotions in a flood of words when he was in the depths of despair now hid his face in his hands and did not reply. He had already had a premonition of this horrible problem. It was the day when the children's laughter and cries had caused him such physical pain and a vision of the future had passed vaguely before his eyes. The idea that one day he would become the natural enemy and the unintentional bane of these adored children had naturally associated itself with the first moment of boredom and displeasure they had caused him.

At last he spoke. "You have torn open the heart of truth and flung its bleeding fragments in my face. So you wish me to renounce my love and die? Then kill me now. Let us depart!"

23.

Salvator was astonished at the violence of the feeling which still dominated Karol. He was far from anticipating that instead of diminishing, this violence would increase in proportion to the suffering. Salvator sought happiness in love and when he no longer found it there, his love gently departed. In this he was like everyone else. But Karol loved for the sake of loving; no suffering could discourage him. After exhausting the phase of intoxication, he was entering on a new phase, that of pain. But he would never experience the phase of cooling off. Instead it would be that of physical agony, for his love had become his life and whether sweet or bitter, it was beyond his power to escape it for a single moment.

Salvator who knew his character so well but did not understand its basis, was convinced that the fulfilment of his prophecy would only be a matter of time.

"My friend," he said, "you do not understand me or rather you are thinking of something else, something we are not talking about. Heaven forbid that I should wish to tear you away from the first moments of a passion which is far from approaching its exhaustion. On the contrary, my advice is that you should not resist happiness and that for the first time you should yield entirely to the gentle caprice of fate. But what I have to say next is that when happiness retreats you must not persist in attempts to force it. A day will come, sooner or later, when you will notice some failing of light in the star which is pouring its rays down upon you to-day. When that happens you must not wait for disgust and boredom before you leave your love. You will have to flee resolutely – so as to return, you understand, when you once again feel the need to rekindle the torch of your life from hers. As you see, I accept that your constancy will be eternal, which is all the more reason for lightening the yoke which binds you. This can be achieved by avoiding the overwhelming pressure of being perpetually and wholly alone together. Everything which has begun to offend you here will disappear when you are away from it and when you come to face it again on your return you will see that the mountains are grains of sand. All the real dangers of a situation which you have just realised will vanish when once you are no longer the sole and exclusive guest of the family. The children will have no cause to reproach you, for if people suspect their mother's preference for you, they will be unable to prove it. You will no longer give the impression of defying public opinion, but of maintaining a noble and lasting friendship by frequent meetings. Even if you were merely the friend and brother of Lucrezia, like me, for example, it would still be wrong and dangerous to live for ever under the same roof. But as you are her lover, you owe it even still more to her dignity and to yours to hide the passion somewhat from the eyes of others. You possibly think that I am taking great care of the reputation of a woman who has taken none herself. But you would hardly be the one who would doubt the sincerity with which she had resolved to rehabilitate herself beforehand for the sake of the future honour of her daughters, by leaving the world and breaking all previous ties. Nor would you be the one to wish to make her lose the price of the sacrifice she had just made, the good resolutions which were already beginning to make her so happy and above all to prevent her from being a virtuous mother, something on which she prided herself in all solemnity on the day we knocked at her door. That door was closed, remember! I would have it eternally on my conscience that I forced my way in and then almost flung you into the arms of that trusting, generous woman if, one day, she came to curse the fatal hour when I destroyed her repose and shattered her dreams of calm and peace."

"You are right," cried the prince, flinging himself into the arms of his friend, "and this is the way you should have spoken to me right from the beginning. Of all reality there is only one thing which I can understand, and that is the respect I owe to the object of love, the care I must take of her honour, her repose, her domestic happiness. Ah! if in order to prove my blind devotion and my idolatry I must leave her this very minute, I am ready. Doubtless it is she who has charged you with suggesting to me the reflections which you have made. When she saw that I was giving no thought to anything, that I was lulled by happiness, she told herself that I must be awakened. She has done well. Go and beg her pardon for my short-sighted selfishness. On the day of my departure she herself will fix the duration of my absence – and will perhaps also fix the day of my return."

"Dear child," replied Salvator smiling, "I would be wronging Lucrezia if I thought her more reasonable and prudent than you. It was of my own accord and without her knowledge that I spoke to you as I did, at the risk of breaking your heart. If I had asked her permission, she would have refused, for a lover like Lucrezia has all the weaknesses of a mother and if we say a word about departure, not only will she not approve, but we shall have a battle on our hands. But we shall speak to her about her children and then she will yield. She will understand that a lover must not behave like a husband and settle in her home like the keeper of a fortress."

"A husband . . ." said Karol, as he stared at Salvator. "Suppose she got married?"

"Oh, don't worry about that," replied Salvator. "There is no danger of her being unfaithful to you in that way." He was amazed at the effect the casual mention of the word "husband" had had on the prince.

"You said a husband," continued Karol, persisting in this sudden thought. "A husband would be the rehabilitation of her whole life. Instead of being the enemy and the bane of her children, if he were rich and worthy he would become their natural support, their best friend, their adopted father. It would be a noble duty that he was accepting, and how well he would be rewarded! He would never leave this adorable wife, he would be a rampart between her and the world, he would beat off calumny and defamation, he would watch over his treasure and not waste a single day of his happiness through cruel and tiresome conventions. Be her husband! Yes, you are right! Without you I would never have thought of it. You can see that I am stricken by a kind of idiocy in everything which concerns the conduct of social life. But now my eyes are opened: love and friendship will have done me the service of making a man of me instead of the child and madman I used to be. Yes, yes, Salvator, to be her husband – that is the solution to the problem! With this sacred title I shall never leave her and I shall serve her instead of harming her."

"That certainly is a brilliant idea!" Salvator laughed. "You take my breath away. What an amazing thought! Do you realise what you are saying, Karol? You, marry Lucrezia?"

"Your doubts are offensive. Spare me your surprise. I am resolved on it. So come with me to plead my cause and obtain her consent."

"Never," exclaimed Salvator, "unless you come to me ten years from this day and make the same request then. Oh, Karol, despite all the days I have spent close to you I still don't know you. You who used to refrain from living through an excess of austerity, mistrust and pride, are now ready to fling yourself into the opposite excess and grapple with life with the frenzy of a madman. I who have been obliged to endure so many sermons and remonstrances from you, now see myself playing the role of mentor to save you from yourself."

Salvator then enumerated to his friend all the impossibilities of such a union. He spoke to him firmly and simply. He admitted that in herself Lucrezia was worthy of so much love and devotion and that if he, Salvator, were ten years older and could accept the bonds of marriage he would prefer her to all the duchesses in the world. But he proved to the young prince that the harmony of tastes, opinions, character and inclinations which are the basis of conjugal calm, could never exist between a man of his, Karol's age, rank and nature and a peasant's daughter who had become an actress, was six years older than he, a mother, a democrat in her instincts and early background, etc, etc. It is not even necessary to tell the reader everything that Salvator felt obliged to say on the subject. But the influence he had gained over his friend during the first part of this conversation, failed completely in face of his obstinacy. Karol had understood of life everything he was capable of understanding of it: absolute devotion. Everything which was prudent and advantageous as far as his own existence was concerned, was a closed book to him.

I hope that the reader will excuse him for his puerilities, his jealousy and his caprices. They were not so to him and it is in such circumstances that the grandeur and strength of his soul compensated for these failings. The more Salvator pointed out to him the disadvantages of his plan, the more ardent grew his love. If Salvator could have transformed this marriage into an incessant martyrdom in which Karol was to suffer all kinds of torture for the benefit of Lucrezia and her children, Karol would have thanked him for drawing a picture of a life so consistent with his ambition and his need for self-sacrifice. He would have accomplished this sacrifice with fervour. He would still have been capable of making Lucrezia out to be a criminal if in his presence she uttered a name which offended his ear, allowed Salvator to embrace her knees, threatened to beat her child or caress her dog excessively, but he would never have thought of reproaching her for accepting the sacrifice of his whole life.

Fortunately – am I right to say "fortunately"? but no matter – Madame Floriani, on receiving this unexpected proposal, won a victory for Count Albani's arguments by refusing it. She was moved to tears by the prince's love, but she was not surprised by it and Karol was grateful to her for believing in his sincerity. As for her consent, she said that even if the lives of her children depended on it, she would not give it.

Thus ended a battle of delicacy and nobility which lasted for more than a week. The idea of this marriage hurt Lucrezia's invincible pride. Perhaps in the very interest of her children she was making a mistake. But this resistance was in keeping with the kind of pride which had made her so great, so kind and so unhappy. Once in her life, at the age of fifteen, she had judged it as very natural to accept the innocent offer of a marriage which was apparently unsuitable. However, Ranieri was neither noble nor very rich and at that time the daughter of Menapace had brought as her marriage portion her innocence and her beauty in all its splendour. But he had been unable to keep his word to her and Lucrezia herself had quickly released him from it because of her accurate knowledge of society and the thought of the suffering to which her lover, cursed by his father and persecuted by his family, would have been condemned for her sake. Since then she had made an oath, not to renounce marriage, but never to marry anyone but a man of her own condition and for whom this union would be not a shame but an honour.

She felt this so deeply that nothing was able to shake her and the prince's persistence distressed her greatly. What any other woman in her place would have regarded as heady flattery, to her appeared almost as a humiliating presumption, and if she had not known that Karol was utterly ignorant of all the deliberate calculations of social life, she would have been annoyed by his hopes of moving her.

Ever since the time when she had become the mother of four children and had experienced the outbursts of retrospective jealousy on the part of her lovers at the sight of this family, she had resolved never to marry. She did not fear anything similar from Karol as yet, nor did she anticipate that he would very soon endure the same tortures as the others in this connection. But she told herself that she would be forced to make sacrifices to the position and interests of any man she married, and these sacrifices would affect her intimacy with her children. Moreover this husband would inevitably have to blush before the world when he appeared with them and patronised them. And finally Karol would lose his esteem and recognition as a sensible man in the cold and cruel opinion of the world by accepting all the consequences of his romantic devotion.

Therefore she had no need to gain support from Count Albani in order to remain resolute. As long as he hoped to sway her, Karol was full of persuasive charm. But when Lucrezia saw that by continually urging consideration for the prince and the feelings of his noble family she was in danger of apparently acting like those women who offer a hypocritical resistance in order to ensnare their prey even more, she cut short his entreaties by a clear and rather abrupt refusal. She was also greatly terrified of allowing herself to weaken, for although she listened to nothing but her maternal love for the moment, she would have ultimately yielded to his prayers and tears. She was therefore compelled to pretend a little and to proclaim a kind of systematic hatred for marriage, although she would never have dreamed otherwise of opposing marriage in general.

When the prince was finally convinced of the futility of his pleading he fell into a deep sorrow. The tears tenderly dried by Lucrezia were followed by a need to dream, to be alone, to lose himself in conjectures about that real life which he had wished to enter and which despite his efforts he failed to understand. Then followed the return of the phantoms of the imagination, the suspicions of a mind unable to appreciate any material fact at its correct value, and jealousy, the inevitable torture of a dominating love disappointed in its hopes of absolute possession.

The idea occurred to him that Salvator had prearranged with Lucrezia all their long conversations; Salvator's apparent inspirations, the seemingly spontaneous and natural speeches during which Karol's spirit had been utterly exhausted – all this was planned in advance. He thought that Salvator had not renounced the idea of being Lucrezia's lover after him and that, treating him as a spoilt child, he had permitted him to precede him so as to claim his rights in secret as soon as he saw him satiated. It was for that reason, he thought, that he had urged him so much to go away from time to time, in order not to allow Lucrezia's love to become too serious and to be able to persuade her to listen to him during some suitable interval.

Or else (a supposition even more groundless and insane) Karol told himself that Salvator had thought of marrying Lucrezia even before he had had the same idea and that by mutual consent she and he, tied by an affection consistent with their characters, had agreed to be united one day when they had enjoyed their respective freedom for some time longer.

Karol recognised the fact that Lucrezia's love for him had been innocent and spontaneous, but he feared to see it end as quickly as it had been kindled and like all men in such circumstances he was alarmed by this emotion which he had once so greatly admired and blessed.

And then, when the inner conscience of the unhappy lover justified his mistress in face of the fancies of his sick mind, he told himself that for the first time in her life Lucrezia had in him a lover worthy of her, and that she would cling to him naturally and for ever, if alien contrivances did not come and entice her away from him. Then his mind turned to Count Albani and he accused him of wishing to seduce Lucrezia by arguments of epicurean philosophy and the shameless fascination of his ill-stifled desires. He indicted the smallest word, the slightest gesture. Salvator was vile, Lucrezia was weak and abandoned.

Then he would weep when those two friends, who in all their conversations spoke only of him and lived only for his happiness, came to wrench him away from his solitary meditations and overwhelmed him with open caresses and gentle reproaches. He would weep in Salvator's arms, he would weep at Lucrezia's feet. He did not confess his madness and a moment later he was obsessed by it all the more.

24.

"She does not love me, she has never loved me." These were his words to Salvator at moments when the idea that Salvator was still his friend became lucid to him once more.

"That soul so cold and so strong does not even understand love when in order to dissuade me from marrying her she invokes personal considerations – that is, personal to me! Doesn't she know then that nothing can impair the joy of a heart filled with love when it has sacrificed everything to the possession of the object of its love? Why does she speak to me of preserving my liberty for me? On the contrary I understand that it is she who is afraid of losing hers. But what does the word 'liberty' mean in connection with love? Can one imagine any other but that of belonging to each other without any obstacle? If on the other hand it is a door left open to distractions and the cooling of affection, that is, to infidelity, there is not, nor has there ever been any love in a heart which defends itself thus!"

Salvator tried to justify Lucrezia against these cruel suspicions, but it was useless. Karol was too unhappy to be just. Sometimes he would come and ask his friend for comfort and help against his own weakness, at others, convinced that he was the principal enemy of his happiness, he avoided him.

This situation became more gloomy and more painful every day and Count Albani, bringing good advice and affectionate words to both lovers in turn, could, in spite of everything, see the wound festering and their happiness becoming torment. He would have liked to put an abrupt end to the situation by carrying his friend off, but it was impossible. His own life was hardly enviable in this perpetual conflict and he would have wished to go, yet he dared not abandon his friend in the midst of such a crisis.

Lucrezia had hoped that Karol would grow calmer and become reconciled to the idea of being no more than her lover. On seeing his suffering continue and becoming more frenzied, she was suddenly overcome by utter lassitude. When a mother sees her child, who is condemned to a diet by the doctor, suffer, weep and ask for food with desperate earnestness, she is perplexed, she hesitates and wonders if she should heed the strict regime of science or rely on the instincts of nature. Lucrezia proceeded rather similarly with respect to her lover. She asked herself if it were not preferable to administer to him the dangerous but possibly sovereign remedy of yielding to his will rather than condemn him, out of prudence, to a lingering death. She summoned Salvator, spoke to him and confessed that she was almost beaten. She also admitted that she felt that this marriage would be her own destruction, but that she could no longer endure the sight of a grief like Karol's and that she did not wish to deny him this proof of love and devotion.

Salvator felt almost as shaken as Lucrezia. Yet he hardened himself against compassion and continued to fight in order to save these two lovers from the temptations of an irreparable madness.

Karol who spied on all their movements more than they thought and could guess without hearing all that was said around him, saw Lucrezia's indecision and the Count's persistence. It seemed to him that the latter was playing an odious role. There were moments when he felt nothing but a deep hatred for him.

Things had reached this stage and Karol would have triumphed, if not for an event which revived the full force of Lucrezia's argument.

Karol was strolling along the sand on the lakeside at the lower end of the park which was part of the estate and was closed day and night to strangers. However, as the water was shallow as the result of drought, a dry strip of sandy shore became exposed and this enabled people from outside to enter the enclosure if they felt inclined to do so. The instinctive jealousy of the prince had drawn his attention to the situation, and on several occasions he had ventured to observe aloud that a few stakes interwoven with branches would form an easily constructed and effective barrier against the few yards of exposed beach. Lucrezia had promised to have this done, but being preoccupied with more important thoughts, she had forgotten about it. At this moment she was in her boudoir with Salvator and was telling him that she had reached the end of her courage and that to see the endless suffering – through her own fault – of the being for whom she would be willing to give her life, had become an undertaking beyond her strength.

Meanwhile Karol was walking on the beach, a prey to his usual agitation and seeing nothing of external objects save what was calculated to irritate his suffering and add to his anxieties. This strip of ground which was so badly protected made him particularly impatient each time he saw its inadequacy.

Although nature around him lay there in all its splendour, he saw nothing of it. The rays of the setting sun turned the sky to crimson, the nightingales sang, and in a skiff moored a few yards away from the prince, Stella was rocking little Salvator who was playing with some shells.

The two children formed an admirable group, the one absorbed by that mysterious intenseness which children apply to their games, the other lost in a no less mysterious reverie, making the light craft sway with her small feet and in a voice as light as the murmur of water singing a slow and monotonous refrain. As she sang thus on the boat tied up to a willow, Stella imagined she was going for a long voyage on the lake; she was launched on an endless poem peopled with the happiest creations. And as little Salvator examined, arranged and re-arranged his shells and pebbles on the seat of the boat, he had the serious and profound look of a philosopher solving a deep problem.

Antonia, the handsome peasant girl who was watching them, was sitting some distance away and was spinning gracefully. Karol had no eyes for these things. He did not even suspect the presence of the two children. All he saw was Biffi engaged in cutting stakes, and rather too slowly for his liking, for night would soon fall and he would not have even begun to plant them by that time.

All at once Biffi gathered up his stakes, slung them on to his shoulder and made as if to take them in the direction of the fisherman's cottage.

The prince would have regarded it as a crime if he had ever given an order in Madame Floriani's house; for a slight indiscretion, the least offence against good breeding, is a veritable crime in the eyes of people of his class. But at that moment, seized by uncontrollable impatience, he asked Biffi in an authoritative tone why he was giving up his task by removing the materials.

Like all his compatriots, Biffi had a gentle, mocking nature. At first, probably thinking that the actor was playing at being a prince to try him out, he pretended to be deaf. Then surprised on seeing that Karol was really angry, he stopped and deigned to reply that these stakes were meant for old Menapace's garden and he was about to fix them there.

"Hasn't the mistress ordered you," said Karol, trembling in every limb with inexplicable rage, "to put them here to cut this beach off?"

"She said nothing to me," replied Biffi, "and I see nothing to cut off here, seeing that when it rains again the water will rise as far as the outer wall."

"That does not concern you," retorted Karol. "If the signora gives an order, it seems to me that it should be obeyed."

"So be it," replied Biffi. "I am quite agreeable. But if old man Menapace sees me using on this job the wood he needed to support his vines, he will be angry."

"No matter," said Karol, quite beside himself. "You must obey the signora."

"I agree," said Biffi, hesitating and half dropping his burden; "she is the one who pays me, but it is her father who grumbles at me."

Karol insisted. He saw or thought he saw in the distance a man following the side of the lake and stopping at intervals as if trying to make his way in the direction of the Villa Floriani.

Biffi's slowness and disobedience exasperated the prince. He put his hand on the youth's shoulder in a commanding way and with a look of indignation which was so foreign to the customary gentleness of his expression that Biffi was afraid and hastened to obey.

"Well now, Your Highness," he said, in a half wheedling, half mocking tone which the prince thought more offensive than it was, "show me the place and command me, seeing that you know what's to be done. For *I* know nothing about it. Nobody told me anything, I swear it."

Karol did something of which he had never in his life thought himself capable. He stooped to the execution of a material thing, even as far as to draw with his stick on the sand the line of the fence which Biffi must follow, and to show him the spot where he must drive the stakes, and he did it with all the more accuracy and zeal as for once he was not mistaken, because the stranger he had seen in the distance was approaching visibly and, still walking on the beach, was making his way towards him without hesitation.

"Hurry," said the prince to Biffi. "If you haven't the time to intertwine the branches in the fence to-night, at least let your stakes be fixed so that strollers may respect this indication."

"I will do everything Your Excellency wishes," Biffi replied with his sly humility. "But don't worry, there are no bandits in these parts and none has ever entered this way."

"Keep on all the same; hurry," said the prince, a prey to a consuming and completely morbid anxiety. And he rolled a gold coin in his hand to show Biffi that he would be handsomely rewarded.

"Your Excellency is going to lose that fine sequin," said the cunning peasant as he cast a covetous glance at the trembling careless hand of Karol.

"Master Biffi," replied the prince, "I know the custom. I have trespassed on your services. I owe you a tip. It is all ready for when you have finished."

"Your Excellency is too kind!" cried Biffi, suddenly electrified. "Of course he is a real prince," he thought. "I see it now, but I won't tell old Menapace. He would only keep my sequin for me, to prevent me, as he would say, from spending it to a bad purpose." And he began to work with speed and athletic vigour, fully determined, if the fisherman came and interrupted him, to tell him coolly that he was acting on the direct orders of the signora.

All the posts were driven in when the persistent individual whose approach brought a cold sweat to the prince's brow, arrived at this boundary line and stopped, with arms folded across his breast, his eyes staring ahead in the direction of the expanse of the beach, and yet without apparently paying any attention to the prince or Biffi.

This preoccupation was odd, to say the least of it, for he was only separated from them by a few stakes. Yet he did not seem to think of crossing this recently made boundary. He was a young man of medium height and fairly elegant, but not very tasteful dress. His face was remarkably handsome, but his stare and distracted manner indicated some kind of madman or at least a crank, unless this was the kind of impression he deliberately wished to make.

At first the prince, shocked by his audacity, was beginning to think that the man did not really know where he was nor where he meant to go, when the stranger, addressing Biffi, said in a booming voice: "My friend, isn't that the Villa Floriani?"

"Yes, sir," replied the young man without interrupting his work.

The prince flashed the stranger the look of a lion defending his prey. The stranger cast him a mildly curious glance and without worrying in the slightest at the expression on his distraught face he began to gaze once more at the beach behind Karol's back.

Karol turned quickly, thinking that Lucrezia might be coming from that direction and that it was her approach which was fascinating the traveller in this way, but all that was to be seen on the beach was the children and their maid.

At that moment Stella was coming out of the boat and, lifting her little brother in her arms, she was saying: "Come along, Salvator, let me help you or you will fall into the water."

At the idea that the child might fall into the water before the maid had joined them Karol, whose sad spirit always anticipated some disaster, forgot the stranger and ran towards the boat to help Stella; but the two children were already safe on the sand and Karol, hearing footsteps close behind him, turned round and saw the stranger there.

Without ado he had crossed the fatal line and without deigning to look at the prince he passed him, leaped towards the children and picked little Salvator up in his arms as if meaning to carry him off.

In a spontaneous movement Karol and Antonia rushed upon the stranger. Karol seized him by the arm with a strength increased tenfold by indignation, and Biffi, armed with his billhook, came nearer, with a view to offering assistance against the stranger if the need arose.

The latter only replied with a scornful smile. But Stella was the only one who did not show any sign of fear.

"You are all mad," she exclaimed, laughing. "I know this gentleman well. He doesn't mean any harm to Salvator for he loves him very much. I am going to tell Mama that you are here," she added, addressing the stranger.

"No, my child," replied the latter, "there's no need at all. Salvator does not recognise me and I have frightened everybody here. They think I want to carry him off. Here," he added, returning her the child, "don't trouble. I only want one thing, and that is to look at you both a little longer, then I'll go."

"Mama won't let you go without saying good-day to you," the little girl went on.

"No, no. I have no time to stop," said the stranger, visibly moved. "Give your mother my kind regards. Is she well?"

"Very well. She is in the house. Hasn't Salvator grown tall?"

"Yes, and beautiful," said the stranger. "He is an angel. Ah! if he would just let me kiss him! But he is afraid of me and I don't want to make him cry."

"Salvator," said the little girl, "give the gentleman a kiss. He is a good friend and you have forgotten him. Come, put your arms round his neck. You shall have a sweet and I'll tell Mama that you have been good."

The child agreed and after kissing the stranger he asked for his shells and pebbles again and returned to his playing on the sand.

The stranger was now leaning against the boat. With eyes full of tears he was still looking at the child. The prince, the maid and Biffi who were watching him closely seemed invisible to him.

However, after a few moments, he seemed to become aware of their presence and he smiled at the anxiety which was visible on their faces. Karol's look drew his attention particularly and he made a movement as if to approach him.

"Sir," said he, "it is Prince de Roswald whom I have the honour of addressing, isn't it?"

And when the prince nodded he added: "You give orders here, whereas all I probably know of this house is the children and their mother. Have the goodness to tell these worthy people," and he looked at the servants, "to step aside so that I may have the honour of saying a few words to you."

"Sir," said the prince, taking him a few yards apart, "it seems simpler for *us* to move away, for I do not give orders here, as you assume, and I have only the rights of a friend. But they are sufficient for me to regard it as a duty to draw your attention to a certain matter. You did not enter here in a proper manner and you cannot remain here any longer without the permission of the mistress of the house. You have crossed a fence – incomplete, it is true – but which propriety ordered you to respect. Be good enough to withdraw the way you came and present yourself with your name to the park gate. If Signora Floriani thinks fit to receive you, you will no longer run the risk of meeting people there disposed to make you leave."

"Drop the part you are playing, sir," replied the stranger haughtily, "it is ridiculous." And seeing the prince's eyes glitter, he added in a mocking, yet gentle voice: "This role would be unworthy of a man as magnanimous as you, if you knew who I am. Listen to me and I will convince you."

25.

"My name," continued the stranger, lowering his voice, "is Onorio Vandoni and I am the father of that beautiful child whose guardian you will be appointed as from now. But you haven't the right to prevent me from kissing my own son. It would be useless for you to claim this right, for if persuasion were not enough I would refuse it by force. You probably believe that when Signora Floriani thought she must break the bonds which united us it would have been easy for me to claim or at least contest the possession of my child. But God forbid that I should wish to deprive him at so tender an age of the caress of a woman whose maternal devotion is beyond comparison. I submitted silently to the verdict which separated me from him, I consulted only his interests and his happiness. But do not think that I agreed ever to lose sight of him. From afar as from near I have always watched over him and I shall always do so. As long as he lives with his mother I know he will be happy. But if he lost her or if some unforeseen circumstance required the signora to separate from him, I would reappear with the zeal and authority of my role as a father. We are not at that stage yet. I know what is happening here. A combination of chance and a little shrewdness on my part told me that you were the fortunate lover of Lucrezia. I pity you for your happiness, sir! For she is not a woman whom one can love by halves and for whose loss one can console oneself. But that is not the point. It is only the child that matters. I know that I have no right to speak about the mother.

I have therefore made certain about your feelings towards the child, the gentleness and dignity of your character. I know ... and this is going to surprise you, for you think your secrets well kept in this retreat which you guard jealously and which you were in the process of fencing off when I dared to stride over your fortifications. Well, know that there is no family secret which escapes the eye of servants! I know that you wish to marry Lucrezia Floriani and that Lucrezia Floriani has not yet accepted your devotion. I know that you would have gladly served as a father to her children. I thank you for it on my account, but I would have freed you of this trouble as far as my son is concerned, and if the signora happens to allow herself to be persuaded by your entreaties you can always count on three children, not four.

"What I am telling you now, sir, is not to be repeated to Lucrezia. It would sound like a threat on my part, a cowardly attempt to oppose the success of your enterprise. But if I avoid the sight of her, if I do not go and seek the painful and dangerous pleasure of seeing her, I do not wish you to be mistaken about the motives of my prudence. On the contrary, it is good for you to know them. You see that in spite of your entrenchments it was very easy for me to penetrate here, see my son and even carry him off. If I had come with such a resolution I would have made use of more audacity or more skill. I did not expect to have the pleasure of conversing with you when I approached this house and allowing myself to be fascinated by the sight of my child whom I recognised ... ah, almost a league away and when he only appeared to me as a black speck on the beach! Dear child! I shall not say: Poor child! He is happy, he is loved! But as I go away I say to myself: Poor father! Why couldn't *you* be loved too? Farewell, sir! I am delighted to have made your acquaintance and I leave to you the decision to relate this strange interview as you think fit. I did not provoke it, I do not regret it. I feel no hatred for you. I like to believe that you deserve your happiness more than I deserved my misfortune. Fate is a fickle woman whom one curses at times, but whom one always invokes."

Vandoni went on speaking for some time with more facility than coherence and with more frankness than warmth. Yet when he had embraced his son for the last time in silence, he appeared deeply moved.

But immediately afterwards he took leave of the prince with the obsequious mocking self-assurance of the actor and he went on, without turning round, as far as the fence where Biffi had begun to work again. There he stopped once more for quite a long time to look at the child, then at last he waved a final farewell to the prince and set off once more.

Apart from the feeling of annoyance and the intolerable unpleasantness of such an encounter, the face, voice, figure and speech of this man, although indicating natural kindness and loyalty, aroused in Karol nothing but definite antipathy. Vandoni was handsome, fairly well educated and unfailingly honest. But everything about him smacked of the theatre, and it required Lucrezia's habit of frequenting actors even more affected and more bombastic for her never to have noticed what shocked the prince so much at first sight, namely the affectation of solemnity which betrayed study at every step and every word. Vandoni was a mixture of bombast and naivety rather difficult to define. Nature had made him what he wished to appear, but as happens with second rate artists, art had become second nature to him. He was sincerely generous and sensitive, but he could no longer be satisfied with being so in fact; he required to say so and to confide his feelings in the same way as he recited a monologue on the stage. Whereas great actors carry their souls into their parts, those who only have mediocre inspiration transfer their parts into their private life and act it, unconsciously, at all moments of the day.

Because of this weakness poor Vandoni appeared less serious than his feelings and he deprived his words of the importance they would have had in themselves if he had not delivered them with excessively deliberate care.

Whereas Madame Floriani's correct inflections and clear pronunciation came from herself and from her alone, the clear pronunciation and correct inflections of Vandoni smacked of the elocution class. It was the same with his walk, his gestures and his facial expression: all told of hours before the mirror. True, practice had become part of his being and his blood, and he could say extempore what once he had made it his painful study to say well. But the first model of his speech and attitude always reappeared and whereas good taste in conversation consists in toning down the form in order to lend more force to the content, *his* good taste consisted of emphasising everything and leaving nothing in shadow.

Thus in speaking of his paternal love there was too much play of emotion; in asserting his love as a father and speaking nobly of his rival he overposed as the hero of a drama; in wishing to appear reconciled to the faithlessness of his mistress he overplayed his part and almost assumed the appearance of a roué, which was far beyond his natural audacity. Add to all this a secret embarrassment of which mediocre artists least rid themselves when they are striving for ease and you will understand that vague smile which Karol took for the height of impertinence, that occasionally blurred look which he attributed to the stupefaction of debauchery, and finally those smooth gestures which made Karol's fingers itch to box his ears.

Yet the personal impression of the prince in contact with the actor was entirely relative. The faults of both men were so opposite that in seeing them together it would have been necessary to condemn in turn two characters which one would have accepted separately. Karol sinned through excess of reserve and because he hated everything which, in form, could be accused of the slightest exaggeration; he had at times an icy, ungracious inflexibility. Vandoni on the other hand did not wish to pass anyone without leaving behind a certain opinion of his merit. His eyes did not try, as did the prince's, to avoid the insult of an inquisitive look; they sought out this look and questioned it to judge of the effect produced. When the effect seemed to have failed he became obstinate and tried to find a better one; but as he did not possess the readiness of mind of the great actor, the great lawyer and the great conversationalist, which enables them to create the occasion to display and develop themselves, he often failed to produce his effect.

Yet he was nothing like what the prince would have him be, to judge from his manner and behaviour. He was neither narrow-minded, nor boastful, nor debauched, nor insolent. His was rather a nature which was kindly, although rather self-centred, sincere yet vain, temperate and mild although inclined on ocasion to pride itself on being the exact opposite. He had had the misfortune of always aspiring to more fame than he was capable of. His passion was to play leading parts, but he had never achieved this. So, wishing to make the best of the small parts which were entrusted to him he had played too intensely the role of noble father, druid, confidant or captain of the guard. It is a great mistake to wish to draw too much attention to the parts of a play to which the author has given a secondary place. And so it happened that if there was a weak spot or even a platitude in his part, Vandoni emphasised it pitilessly and then wondered why the dramatist had been hissed when he himself had tried so hard and had given of his best.

Moreover he was small and wanted to appear tall. He had one of those beautiful basso profundo voices which cannot vary their inflexions and which nature has condemned to a monotonous sonority. He took an empty pride in having a more beautiful timbre than such and such a famous actor and did not tell himself that a harsh voice used with talent is more sympathetic and more effective than a powerful instrument handled crudely. Poor Vandoni! He went off convinced that he had used much delicacy, restraint and dignity in putting in its place the jealous pride of young Prince de Roswald. And Prince de Roswald shrugged his shoulders as he saw him go, wondering with profound sorrow how Lucrezia had been able to endure even for a single day the intimacy of so ridiculous and mediocre a man.

Alas! Karol was not at the end of his sufferings as far as Vandoni was concerned, for the latter was retiring, not fully satisfied with the dramatic effect he was making. He regretted that he had not met Lucrezia, in order to show her the philosophical detachment or the magnanimous pride which he had been unable to feign at the moment of their rupture. He regretted that he had left this strong woman with the impression that he was not as strong as she and he wished to wipe out the memory of the naïvety and weakness of his tears and anger by some scene of false nobility and generosity which he considered more elevated in style.

So, as he walked further away more and more slowly, fully aware that one must always lend a helping hand to chance, the most obvious form that chance could take now came to his aid: he was still in sight when Lucrezia came down to the beach.

And what was she doing on this beach, when she should have been in her boudoir still talking to Count Albani? The fact is that she had finished talking, she had triumphed over Salvator's resistance, and she was on her way to say to the prince: "You have won. I love you too much to persist in making you suffer. Be my husband. I am exposing my maternal love to harsh conflicts, I am defying the future, I am silencing the voice of my conscience, but I will incur damnation for you if I must."

But just as one breaks one's hands and head while running eagerly towards a door which one intends to go through but which turns out to be locked, so was Lucrezia halted and as if felled by the sight of the cold, troubled face of her lover.

He greeted her with the respect which had become nothing more than a formality, but his look seemed to say: 'Woman, what is there in common between you and me?'

Never before had she seen him so sad; and because, as happens with all unyielding natures, sadness assumes the appearance of disdain, she was terrified by the expression on his face. She looked around her as if to ask external objects for the cause of this fatal change. She saw Vandoni in the distance. Her thoughts were so remote from him that she failed to recognise him, but Stella came running up and pointed him out to her. "Signor Vandoni is going away, he didn't want me to call you, he says he hasn't the time to stop. Most likely he will come back. He asked how you were. He kissed Salvator and he cried. He seemed to be very sad. And he chatted with the prince who'll tell you all about it. I don't know any more."

And the child went back to play with her brother.

Lucrezia looked alternately at the prince and Vandoni. The actor had turned round and he saw her, but he pretended to be still absorbed by the sight of his son. The prince had turned away with a kind of disgust at the idea that Lucrezia would detain her former lover and possibly introduce him.

She fully understood what was happening and was no longer surprised at Karol's agony. But she knew or at least she thought that with a single word she could bring that suffering to an end, and Vandoni would doubtless depart humiliated and broken. She thought she could see him moving away discreetly, without having had the time to recognise and caress his son. She imagined that he was suffering dreadfully, whereas at that particular moment he was not really suffering at all. He certainly had paternal feelings and when he was alone and thought of little Salvator he wept sincerely. But in the presence of his rival and his faithless mistress he had a role to sustain and as always happens with actors on the stage, reality disappears before the emotion of the fictitious world.

Madame Floriani was too genuine, too affectionate and too warm-hearted to realise what he was experiencing at that moment. All she felt was an immense compassion, and a horror of imposing unhappiness and shame on a man who had loved her greatly and whom she too had striven to love. She understood that what she was about to do would annoy Karol very much, but she told herself that after reflection not only would he forgive her, but he would even approve of her gesture. The heart argues quickly and when it is urged on by conscience it overcomes all repugnance and all self-interest. She ran towards the fence, called Vandoni in a calm tone and when he had turned round so as to come to her she went forward a few steps, held out her hand and kissed him cordially.

Vandoni was certainly touched by so generous and bold an impulse. He had hoped to extract a little vengeance from Lucrezia's confusion in the presence of her latest lover. He had not expected her to call him back; that is why he had been very happy to remain there as long as possible to prolong his rival's suffering. But the heart of Lucrezia was above such pettiness and one cannot embarrass a deeply sincere and courageous woman.

Vandoni forgot his role and covered his faithless one's hands with kisses and tears. He was no longer play-acting, he was defeated.

"I will not allow you to leave us thus," said Lucrezia, calm and affectionate, yet firm. "I don't know where you come from, but tired or no, you must rest here and see Salvator whenever you please. We shall talk about him together and we shall leave one another this time more calmly and better friends than before. You do want that, don't you, my friend? We used to be like brother and sister. Now is the time to become so again."

"But what about Prince de Roswald?" said Vandoni, lowering his voice.

"Do you think he will be jealous? Don't be fatuous, Vandoni! He will not be. And you will see that he has not heard anyone here speak ill of you and you have a right to his regard and esteem."

"In his place I would never tolerate a former lover to . . . "

"Apparently he is better than you," she interrupted him. "He is more trusting and more generous than you were with regard to me. Come, I want to present you to him."

"There is no need," said Vandoni, who was feeling weak and emotional and could not make up his mind to act naturally towards his rival. "I have already introduced myself to the prince. He was very polite. But do you really insist that I stay? It is madness."

Lucrezia's only reply was to point to little Salvator. He yielded, partly from affection, partly from love of mischief.

26.

If there are hardly any men who can resign themselves to confronting the one who has replaced them in their mistress' heart without wishing to revenge themselves just a little, there are hardly any women who would venture to bring these two men together without a little anxiety.

Yet Lucrezia did not experience the inner embarrassment which accompanies such encounters. Why should she have experienced it when throughout the whole of her life she had acted honestly and with the utmost candour? This was not a case of employing audacity or ingenuity in order to manoeuvre two rivals equally deceived. Here it was a matter of a lover who was acknowledged in the present and a lover acknowledged in the past. If love could be just a little philosophical the successful lover would be full of courtesy and magnanimity towards the forsaken lover; but love is not philosophical. It takes fright at a memory and here it argues very badly: for in matters of love nothing is less tempting than a return to the past, nothing is less dangerous than the sight of a being whom one has left freely and through waning passion.

Unfortunately no one was less acquainted with the human heart than Prince Karol. His own was the only one of its kind and every time he wished to compare the emotions of others with his own he was certain to make a mistake. He tried to imagine his feelings if Princess Lucie happened to appear to him, and he felt sure that if she did appear, like Banquo's ghost, at Lucrezia's table he would fall, struck down not so much with fear as with remorse and regret. From there he went on to suppose that Lucrezia could not see Vandoni again in the flesh without also experiencing the violent regret of having destroyed him and remorse at belonging to another before his very eyes.

Now there never was a supposition which could have been more unjust and more absurd than this one. Again Lucrezia saw all the little failings, all the harmless absurdities of Vandoni with eyes which she no longer scrupled to keep wide open. She compared this being of whom she had never been greatly enraptured with the one who gave her endless rapture. Moreover the comparison was so much in the prince's favour that if he had been able to read into the soul of his mistress he would have clearly seen that the presence of Vandoni increased Lucrezia's passion for himself.

He could not appreciate the triumph of his position. His jealous anxiety made him too modest on this score whilst on the other hand the indifference with which he saw fit to treat Vandoni made him so haughty that he felt humiliated to succeed such a man. He could not conceal his resentment, his anxiety and his mortal pain. While Vandoni was eating at Lucrezia's side he was unable to sit still. So as not to see or hear him he went out. Then he came in again to prevent him from initiating any move which might displease him. He did nothing but go back and forth, tormented by a terrible fever, avoiding the tender and reassuring glances of Lucrezia and disdaining the advances of poor Vandoni who, thanks to Karol, felt himself entrusted with the role of the magnanimous hero.

If, as I believe, it is pride which makes us jealous, it must be admitted that it is a very blundering and very inconsequential pride. Vandoni had originally promised himself that he would cause his rival a little anxiety by adopting an air of confidence and familiarity with Lucrezia. But he had not succeeded. In the tranquil goodness of Lucrezia there was something so frank and so dignified that all the art of the actor failed before this absence of art. But the prince made it so much a point to encourage Vandoni's longing to be impertinent that the latter found himself avenged without making the slightest effort. He was in a position to rejoice to see the suffering he was causing, and when supper was over he said to Lucrezia as his eyes followed Karol who was going out for the tenth time: "You were boasting, fair lady, you were boasting of your charming prince when you told me that he was better than I, that he was not jealous of the past and that it would not hurt him when he saw me here. On the contrary he is suffering, he is suffering too much for me to remain any longer. Farewell then! I depart with the sad truth that there are no sublime lovers and that the troubles you thought you were fleeing on leaving me will return with another. You have done nothing more than put a handsome dark face in the place of a fair face which was not bad looking. Change is always a pleasure to women! But admit now that when I was jealous of you I was not a monster, for here you see your new god, your idol, your angel, tortured by the same demon as gnawed *my* heart."

"Vandoni," replied Lucrezia, "I do not know whether the prince is jealous of you. I hope you are wrong, but as I don't wish you to accuse me of pretending with you, let us assume that it is so. What do you wish to prove? That I was wrong to leave you? Have I been making a speech for the defence to prove that I was right? No, I believe the wrong is always on the side of the one who wishes to escape from suffering. I committed this wrong. Have you not forgiven me yet?"

"Ah, who could harbour resentment against you?" said Vandoni, kissing her hand with sincere emotion. "I still love you, I would always be ready to devote my life to you if you wished to return to me, even if you did not love me any more than in the past . . . For I have no illusions: your love for me was nothing more than friendship."

"At least I have never deceived you on that point and I did my utmost not to be too ungrateful. Perhaps our affection was too old, we felt too much like brother and sister to be lovers."

"Speak for yourself, cruel one! I for my part . . . "

"You have a noble heart and if you really feel certain that you are making the prince suffer you must take your leave. But not for all the world would I care to renounce your friendship and I hope to find it there still, later, when the fires of youthful passion will have given place in the prince to the calm of a peaceful affection. Mine for you, Vandoni, is based on esteem;

it is proof against time and absence. Between us there exists an indissoluble bond; my affection for your son is your guarantee of the feeling I retain for you."

"My son! Ah yes, let us speak of my son," cried Vandoni who had suddenly grown serious again. "Well, Lucrezia, are you pleased with me? Did I ever make it clear to your other children that that one belonged to me? Ah, what a strange position you have made for me! Never to hear the word father uttered by the lips of my son!"

"Vandoni, your son can hardly speak and as yet only knows my name and his brother's. Now, if you are calm, if you have formed an important decision, speak! By what name and in what principles do you wish me to rear him?"

"Ah, Lucrezia, you know my weakness for you, my blind devotion, or should I say my cowardly submissiveness? If you are not to get married let it be as you wish. Let my son bear your name and let me be permitted merely to see him and be his best friend, after you. But if you are to become Princess de Roswald I insist that my son be restored to me. I would rather see him share my vagabond life and my precarious fate than abandon my authority and duties to a stranger."

"My friend," said Lucrezia, "there is more pride than tenderness in this decision and I shall employ only one argument to oppose it. Supposing I get married tomorrow, Salvator will still be a child for eight or ten years at least and the attentions of a woman are necessary to him. To what woman will you entrust him then? Have you a sister or a mother? No! You will only be able to entrust him to a mistress or a servant. Do you think he will be as well looked after, as well brought up and as happy as with me? Will you be able to sleep easily when, obliged to attend rehearsals all day and performances in the evening you'll leave this poor child to the mercy of an unreliable maid-servant or a hateful stepmother?"

"Of course not," said Vandoni, sighing. "You are right. Because you are rich, independent and famous you have all rights, all powers — even that of driving away the father and keeping the child."

"Vandoni, you are hurting me," exclaimed Lucrezia. "Don't speak to me in that way! Do you want me, here and now, to ensure to our child part of my fortune of which you will have the control and direction? Do you wish to supervise his education, be consulted over all its details and settle his future? I gladly consent, provided you leave him with me and you instruct me to be the executor of your wishes. I am sure that we shall agree on all points in the interest of a being who is dearer to us than life."

"No, no. No charity!" cried Vandoni. "I am no coward and I shall die in the poorhouse before accepting alms from you disguised by some other name or form. Keep the child. Keep him completely. I know full well that you will be the only one he will know and love. In vain would I come one day to claim him and tell him that he is mine and must follow me. He will never part willingly from a mother such as you! Come, the die is cast. I see that you are to be a princess."

"Nothing has been decided on that subject, my friend. I swear it and what is more, I swear it by what is most sacred, your honour and your son, that if you make it a condition of my marriage that I must part from this child, I shall never get married."

"So you are still the same, oh strange and admirable woman!" cried Vandoni, transported by her words. "You still prefer your children to glory, riches – and even love."

"Riches and glory, certainly," she replied with a calm smile. "As for love, I dare not answer you at this moment; but what is certain is that I know my duty is to sacrifice everything, even love, to these children of love. The most infatuated, the most faithful of lovers can console himself, but children can never find another mother."

"Well, I leave reassured," said Vandoni, shaking her hand, "and I exact only one promise from you. Swear to me that you will not marry the prince, who is so charming but so jealous, before a year from now. I cannot persuade myself that he is better than I and that he will always see with a calm eye these pledges of your former loves. I know your clearsightedness, your steadfastness and the promptness of your sacrifices when you feel that the fate of your children is in jeopardy. I am well aware why you were unable to endure me for long. It is because no matter what I did I loathed the resemblance between your Beatrice and the wretched Tealdo Soavi. Well, a year hence Prince de Roswald will loathe Salvator, if he doesn't do so already. Don't act suddenly or on impulse, I beg you, my dear Lucrezia, and then you will always remain free. For now that I am sensible and personally not involved in the matter I realise one thing fully, and that is that absolute freedom is the only state that suits you and the tender mother of four love children must not entrust their fate to the virtue of a husband, however reliable it may seem."

"I believe that you are right," said Lucrezia, "and it is with great pleasure that I recognise the voice of my friend of the past. Have no fear, dear brother! Your old comrade, your faithful sister, will never, in a moment of ecstatic passion, endanger the future of the children she adores."

"Farewell then," said Vandoni and clasped her to his heart with deep, sincere tenderness. "Farewell to you, being that I still love most of all! Perhaps I shall not see you again so soon. I would disturb your love and I confess that I am not strong enough to look on without suffering. If in the midst of your sublime and mad passion you find an interval for repose and freedom, summon me to you for one moment. I shall kneel at your feet, docile and submissive, happy to see you and to kiss my son, until you tell me as you have done to-day: 'Begone, I am in love and it is with another.' "

If Vandoni had left immediately after this noble effusion he would have been what God had made him, a kind, warm-hearted person. If instead of chasing the world of artifical emotions imposed upon him by his work he could have paused a while and retained this honest disposition he would have reappeared transformed on the stage, and the public would possibly have been greatly surprised to have an excellent artist to applaud instead of being obliged to smile patiently at the cold and correct declamations of yet another adequate actor.

But as one cannot avoid one's fate and as Karol suddenly reappeared, Vandoni equally suddenly returned to his old affectation. He wished to make him a farewell speech in which he would contrive to insinuate delicately the ideas and feelings under whose sway he had momentarily been. He failed completely; he could only utter tasteless, incoherent phrases and moving from sternness to tenderness, from humour to solemnity, he was in turn bombastic and trivial, pedantic and ridiculous.

It is true that the haughty and impatient attitude of the prince, his laconic replies and his ironic manner were calculated to deflate an actor even more able than Vandoni. The latter soon saw that his attempt to create an effect had misfired, so, falling back on the artificial aplomb of the actor who has been hissed off the stage, he turned to Lucrezia and losing something of his super-imposed exaggerated refinement said: "Upon my word, I believe that I am floundering and I will do well to go no further if I do not wish to sink completely and make you blush for your poor comrade. No matter, you will speak for me when I have gone and you will say that your friend is a good fellow who doesn't want to harm anybody." What an anticlimax!

With his usual kindness Salvator Albani who had spent the last two hours trying to distract Karol, hastened to erase all these miseries by being polite, good-humoured and friendly. Saying that he was delighted to have made his acquaintance he took Vandoni by the arm and told him that he would go and see him perform if they happened to be in any town in Italy at the same time, and finally, that he would keep him company by walking with him as far as Iseo where Vandoni had left his cab.

"And little Salvator?" asked Vandoni, as he was about to leave, "am I not to see him again?"

"He is asleep," replied Lucrezia. "Come and say good night to him."

"No, no," he said in a low voice, but not too low for the prince and the count not to hear, "that would make me lose the little courage I still have."

He was rather pleased with the intonation of the last sentence and the gesture he made as he tore himself away from that house. It was only a small effect, but it was correct, and not all the children in the world would have induced him to forgo a dramatic and abrupt exit at this point.

"Unless the prince is an ass," he thought, "he cannot doubt but that my character contains a certain natural heroism which makes me greatly superior to the subordinate tasks to which I am reduced by the injustice of the public and the jealousy of rivals."

The secret weakness of poor Vandoni was that he thought he was born for higher destinies and when he began to become acquainted with someone, he never failed to tell him of all the intrigues which went on behind the scenes and of which he regarded himself as a victim. Nor did he spare the count any of these stories during their walk together. Because Salvator encouraged him out of kindness and submitted to this appalling boredom in order to allow Karol and Lucrezia a little time to be together, Vandoni seized the opportunity to unfold to him all the setbacks of his theatrical life and could not even resist the desire to recite out loud, on the beach, fragments of Alfieri and Goldoni, so as to show him how well he could have acquitted himself in leading parts.

While Salvator was undergoing this ordeal, Karol, sitting in a corner of the drawing room, was maintaining an absolute silence and Lucrezia was attempting to start a conversation which would lead them to pour out their mutual feelings. She had not yet penetrated the depths of his heart on the matter of jealousy, and she refused to believe Vandoni's warning. As it was no part of her natural frankness to beat about the bush in a matter which concerned her, she rose, approached the prince and taking his hand firmly, said: "You are mortally sad this evening. I wish to know the reason. You are trembling! You are ill or suffering from a secret grief. Karol, your silence hurts me. Speak! I order you to in the name of love and I beg you on my knees. Answer me! Is it my persistence in refusing to unite my fate with yours that affects you thus and will you never resign yourself to it? Well, Karol, if that is so I will yield. I only ask you for a year in which you may reflect."

"You have been very well advised by your friend, Signor Vandoni," replied the prince, "and I owe him a great debt for his intervention. But you will allow me not to submit myself to the conditions that you deign to lay down for me on his behalf. I ask your permission to retire. I am a little fatigued after the declamations I have heard this evening. Perhaps I shall grow accustomed to them if your friends again become constant visitors at your house. But as yet I am *not* accustomed to them

198 / Lucrezia Floriani

and my head aches. As for the persecutions I have made you suffer and of which you yourself must be weary, I implore you to forget them and to believe that I shall henceforth respect your peace of mind sufficiently not to renew them."

Speaking thus in an icy tone, Karol rose and bowing very low to Lucrezia he went and locked himself in his room.

27.

Of all angers, of all vengeances, the darkest, the most atrocious and the most agonising is the one which remains cold and polite. When you will see a person master himself to that degree, say if you wish that he is great and strong, but never say that he is tender and good. I prefer the coarseness of the jealous peasant who beats his wife to the dignity of the prince who rends his mistress' heart without turning a hair. I prefer the child who scratches and bites to the one who sulks in silence. By all means let us lose our tempers, be violent, ill bred, let us insult one another, break mirrors and clocks! It would be absurd, but it would not prove that we hate one another. Whereas, if we turn our backs on one another very politely as we part, uttering a bitter and contemptuous word, we are doomed, and no matter what we do to be reconciled we will become more and more alienated.

Such were the thoughts of Lucrezia when she was left alone and in a state of utter dismay. Although usually mild-tempered she had had great outbursts of indignation in her life. At such times she had abandoned herself to the violence of her distress, she had cursed, she had broken things, she may even have used coarse language – I could not vouch for that; she was a fisherman's daughter and came from a country where at every turn oaths by the body of Bacchus and that of the Madonna, by the blood of Diana and that of Christ make the Christian and pagan heaven intervene in the agitations of domestic life. But what is certain is that she had never been able to repulse and drive away from her heart, absolutely and suddenly, the beings whom she loved sufficiently to be irritated with them. Consequently she was utterly unable to understand those cold and pale furies which signify an antihuman detachment, a hateful stoicism, an eternal relinquishment. For more than a quarter of an hour she sat motionless, crushed by the outrageous words of her lover.

At last she stood up and walked to the drawing room, wondering if she had just had a frightful dream and if it was indeed Karol, the man who this very morning had wept at her feet with love and seemed to be consumed in divine ecstasy, who only a moment ago had spoken the language of spite and affectation, worthy of the puerile tricks of drama, but surely unworthy of real affection and deeply felt passion.

Incapable of enduring anxiety of this kind for long without understanding it, she went up to the prince's room, first knocked discreetly, then with authority, and finally, seeing that there was no reply and the door resisted, she forced the bolt and entered.

Karol was sitting on the edge of his bed, his averted face sunk in the pillows which were reduced to tatters. His cuffs and his handkerchief had been torn to shreds by the nails of his fingers which were hooked and quivering like the claws of a tiger; the pallor of his face was terrifying, his eyes were bloodshot; his beauty had disappeared as if by hellish magic.

With him, extreme suffering turned to a fury all the more difficult to contain as he did not know he possessed this deplorable faculty and never having been thwarted he did not know how to fight against himself.

Lucrezia set down her candlestick beside him. She removed his feverish hands from his face and looked at him dumbfounded. She was not surprised to see a jealous man in the throes of a fit of fury. It was not a sight which was new to her and she also knew that one does not die of it. But to see this angelic being reduced to the same excesses of violence and weakness as Tealdo Soavi or any other man of his stamp was so unreal and made so little sense that she could not believe her eyes.

"You wish to humiliate and degrade me right to the end,"

cried Karol, repulsing her. "You wished to see how far below myself you could make me sink. Are you satisfied now? With which of your lovers are you going to compare me?"

"These are very bitter words," answered Lucrezia, gently and sadly. "I shall not be offended by them because I see that you are certainly not yourself at this moment. I expected to find you cold and disdainful as you were just now, and I was coming, in the name of love and truth, to ask you to explain your scorn. I am distressed to find you as enraged as you are and I do not think that the triumph you attribute to me is very flattering to my pride. What language is this between us, Karol? Oh God, what has happened that you should doubt the dreadful pain I endure when I see you suffer so? But if I am the unwitting cause of it I must possess the power to bring it to an end. Tell me what I can do. If you need my life, my reason, my dignity, my conscience, I shall put them all at your feet if I can only cure you and calm you. Speak to me, explain yourself, make me understand you, that is all I ask. To remain in doubt and let you endure these torments without attempting to alleviate them, that is impossible for me, that you will never get me to do. So open that bruised sick heart to me and if in order to help me to read into it you must overwhelm me with reproaches and insults, do not restrain yourself. I prefer that to silence. Nothing will offend me, I shall justify myself gently and humbly, I will even beg your forgiveness if needs be, although I am entirely ignorant of my crimes. But they must be very grave if they hurt you so much. Answer, upon my knees I beg you."

In order to show so much patience and resignation Lucrezia must have been overwhelmed by an immense love such as she had never believed she could experience after so many storms of the same nature, after so many disappointments, so many fatigues of heart and mind, so many humiliations and rebuffs. She had never lied, had always been devoted and ready for self-sacrifice, yet had never debased or compromised herself even for the sake of personal interest. All this was dictated by a real and sensitive pride and to descend to justifying herself had always appeared to her to be beyond her powers, and suspicion was a mortal insult to her.

However she humiliated herself for a long time with infinite meekness before this unhappy child who did not wish to speak because he could not.

What could he have said, to be sure? The chaos into which his reason had sunk was too painful to be deliberate. To follow Lucrezia's advice, insult her, reproach her bitterly, would doubtless have relieved him, but he did not have the faculty of involving others in his sufferings because he did not have the egoism which wants others to share them. And besides, how could he insult his mistress? He would have preferred to kill her – and kill himself with her, and carry his passion into the grave. But desecrate her with words? It seemed to him that if he could have resolved to do so, he would have condemned her before God and God would have parted them for all eternity. To be reduced to such a state he would have to love her no more, and the more he suffered through her the more he felt himself the slave of passion.

She could only guess at what was happening within him, for he only revealed himself by indirect replies and painful non-disclosures. She appeared to be defending herself feebly, but actually her restraint was perfect and it was impossible for the name of Vandoni to come to her lips.

"Come now," she said when she had reached the end of her patience and had exhausted all the strength of her love in dragging out of him a few vague words terrifying in their depth or obscurity. "Come, my poor angel, are you jealous and don't want to admit it? You, jealous? Ah, how bitter it is for me to have to say it, for me whom you have accustomed to soar above all human woes on the wings of sublime love! How you are hurting me and how far I was from believing that *you* could have done so! Ah! Let me only answer you with painful and frank reproaches. You do not wish to reproach me. I would prefer it because then I could clear myself, whereas now I am reduced to finding something to defend myself with. But before I talk reason to you – since I must – let me grieve, let me weep! This is the last cry of our unhappy love which is vanishing towards the heaven from which it had descended and where it will now return forever. Let me tell you that this day you have committed a great crime against me, against yourself and against God who had blessed our infinite trust in one another. Alas! Through suspicion you have sullied the purest, most perfect, most exquisite passion of my life. I had never loved, never been happy. Why do you tear my joy and delight from me so soon? You swept me up to heaven and now you hurl me brutally down to earth. Oh God, dear God, I did not deserve it. I was floating with you in the empyrean. I believed in the eternity of our bliss. Everything of this earth appeared to be no more than dreams and ghosts to me; except for my children whom I bore in my arms towards this higher world, I cared for nothing... And now I must descend, I must walk on human paths, tear myself against the thorns, bruise myself against the rocks...

"See, you wished it thus. So let me speak of those things, of Vandoni, of my past and of the duties, perplexities and troubles which the future can hold in store for me. I was hoping to traverse them alone, leaving you calm and indifferent to these miseries which are alien to our love. The burden of the work and duties of this earth would have been light to me if I had been able to preserve you from coming into contact with them. You would not have even noticed them, if you had remained yourself and if you had retained the high trust which made us so strong and so pure! You have lost it, you have taken away from me the talisman which would have made me invulnerable to pain and anxiety. I am now going to tell you what obligations weigh upon my real life, what considerations I must retain, what duties my conscience traces out for me. But in order for you to understand them, you must take the trouble to reason a little, to know my past, to judge it and draw a serious conclusion from it, once and for all! Vandoni..."

"Ah," cried Karol, trembling like a child, "don't pronounce that name again and spare me everything you wish to tell me. I haven't nor will I perhaps ever have the strength to hear it. I hate this Vandoni, I hate everything in your life which is not yourself. What does it matter? It is not part of your duties to reconcile me to what hurts and revolts me around you. Let me, seeing that it is possible to me – and only to me – let me see in you two distinct beings: the one whom I have not known and do not wish to know; the other whom I know, whom I possess and whom I do not wish to see involved in things which I detest. Yes, yes, Lucrezia, you have said it; it would be descending and again falling into the mire of human paths. Come to my heart, let us forget the atrocious sufferings of this day and let us return to God. What does it matter to you what has happened within me? That concerns me and I have the strength to endure it, since I have the strength of loving you as much as if nothing had perturbed me. No, no, no explanations, no narrations, no confidences, no arguments. Take me in your arms and transport me far from this cursed world where I only see dimly, where I do not breathe, where I am condemned to crawl even lower than the rest of men if I am to live without your love and without your ecstasy."

Lucrezia contented herself with this false reconciliation and for the sake of peace she pretended to be satisfied with it. But in this she was fatally wrong and through her own fault was plunged into the depths of pain and distress. From that day Karol grew accustomed to believing that jealousy is not an offence and that the woman one loves can and must always forgive it.

Towards midnight she encountered Salvator who had just taken leave of Vandoni and had the delicacy not to tell her how ridiculous and boring he had found this worthy fellow. She had not the courage to admit to him the extent to which the prince had been irritated by the presence of her former lover, but she could not refrain from thinking how admirable friendship is, how much more indulgent, helpful and generous it is than love. For he no longer concealed from himself Vandoni's weaknesses and she equally clearly saw that Salvator had sacrificed himself to rid her of him.

Lucrezia retired to her room and her children, resolved to forget the sorrows of this day and sleep in the hope of waking at daybreak like a watchful, active mother. But although in the course of her tragic life she had acquired more than anyone else the faculty of putting her troubles to rest, like a poor soldier on the field lying in the open with his hunger and his wounds, she spent a sleepless night, and all the bitter memories which had been lulled to silence in her breast awakened one by one to torture her relentlessly. Like so many mocking and menacing ghosts she saw her errors and disappointments, the ingrates she had created and the wicked she had been unable to convert. She struggled against the terrors of the past by seeking refuge in the present, but to no avail; the present offered her no security and the ancient griefs were only re-awakened thus because a new sorrow deeper than all the rest had come to rouse them.

When she rose, pale and broken, the bright morning sun, the flowers heavy with wet perfume, the nightingales drunk with their own song, did not restore calm and hope to her heart as on other days. She did not feel alive with the poetic sense of nature as she usually did. It seemed to her that henceforth between this fresh and smiling nature and her poor heart there was a secret enemy, a gnawing worm which prevented the sap of life from reaching it. However she refused to recognise the extent of her disaster.

Karol prostrated himself at her feet that day. He did not wish to make her forget his wrongs; he was unaware of them since, as was his habit, he had already forgotten them himself. But, after several days spent in tears and anger, he had need of tenderness, effusion and happiness. He was never more seductive and more adorable then when the paroxysm of his bitterness and spite had rid him of his suffering. Lucrezia still had to fight against his plan of marriage, but this time she resisted courageously. The happenings of the previous day had enlightened her and she was not in a mood to place herself in a position where he could withdraw his proposal a second time. If the offer of his name was, on his part, a great homage rendered to the love which she deserved, the fact of withdrawing his offer in a moment of jealous suspicion was an outrage whose force proud Lucrezia felt more than he did. Without telling him what new strength she had summoned against him in this situation, she deprived him of all hope and this time he provisionally accepted her decree, without bitterness, acknowledging that he deserved the punishment of being submitted to some long trial.

But two days did not go by without the return of fresh storms. A travelling salesman succeeded in entering the house in order to recommend the purchase of certain hunting weapons. Celio wanted a new gun and his mother first refused to let him have it. Then, wishing to give him a surprise, she took the traveller aside to bargain over and ultimately buy the object of this childish desire. The young salesman had a handsome face and a rather familiar and talkative manner. The beauty and fame of his latest client made him more eloquent than usual without however making him lose his head and preventing him from selling his goods at a fair profit. It was the eve of Celio's birthday and Lucrezia wanted to put the sporting gun, which was elegant and light in weight, under the boy's bolster, so that he should find it at night when he went to bed. The salesman hastened after her into the bedroom without expressly asking for permission, merely to hide the gun personally and receive the price agreed upon. Karol who had been to take a siesta entered at that very moment and found Lucrezia alone in a bedroom with a handsome youth who was speaking to her in an animated manner, looking at her with bold eyes and straightening the counterpane on the bed, while she (thinking of Celio's delight when he found his surprise) was smiling at him happily!

This was more than enough for Karol's imagination to leap into fatal action, swift as it was to be insulted, and always grasping the apparent fact without understanding and explaining it. Outside the door of Lucrezia's bedroom he muttered a strong offensive word and fled like a man who has just witnessed his dishonour. He required all that remained of the day to regain his calm and the clarity of his mind. And Lucrezia was required to descend to an explanation degrading to both her and him. This time she treated him like a sick person who must be persuaded and cured without his hallucinations being taken seriously. But what happens to all the rapture and the love when he who is the object of it behaves like a raving madman?

On another occasion a messenger came to tell Lucrezia that Mangiafoco, the fisherman who had once sought her in marriage and had caused her so much terror and aversion, was on the point of death and was asking to see her. This man had never dared to appear before her since she had returned home and it was not without repugnance that she consented to go to him. But it was a duty of piety and mercy, and without hesitation she left for the far side of the lake with her father and Biffi. She found a dying man who begged her forgiveness for the suffering and fear he had once caused her and implored her to pray for him, that his soul might find peace. She comforted him with kind words and her generous compassion brought solace to the last moments of this man, an old soldier, a brutal, lawless bandit, yet gifted with a certain intelligence and a few patriotic and romantic instincts.

Having witnessed his last agonised dying breath, Lucrezia returned home somewhat distressed. Karol was present when, in simple words, she told Salvator what had happened and the words, alternately absurd and profound that this man had said to her as he was fighting for his life. Salvator was of the opinion that his dear Lucrezia had acted admirably in thus following the voice of duty, but Karol said nothing. He had been uneasy about this sudden departure and absence which had lasted from sunset until midnight. He could not conceive that one could have so much interest in a wretch who had so ill deserved it. And how had he had the audacity to summon to his deathbed a woman to whom he had made himself so hateful? He must have had faith in her kindness and her ability to forget insults . . .

He spoke these reflections in a rather strange tone. Lucrezia who had not yet learned to expect his jealousy at every turn and who had not dreamed that her good deed might appear criminal to the prince, looked at him in surprise and saw that he was angry. His eyes were red and he was cracking the joints of his fingers; it was a kind of nervous mannerism which betrayed his resentment and which she was beginning to recognise.

She could not refrain from shrugging her shoulders. Karol did not observe it and continued:

"How old was this Mangiafoco?"

"Sixty at least," she replied coldly and severely.

"And without doubt,' Karol resumed after a moment, "he had a bold face, a bristly beard and picturesque rags? And he was a bandit out of a play or novel? A theatrical bandit whom one could not look at without shuddering, I suppose? The imagination of women takes pleasure in such exteriors and they are always flattered at heart if they have chained a wild animal. Doubtless as he died he looked like a wounded tiger who casts on the dove a last glance of covetousness and regret."

"Karol," said Lucrezia sighing, "do you regard a dying man as a very pleasant thing to depict? You should go and see him now that he is dead. That would make your irony fall away immediately and would cut short your poetic metaphors. But you will not go, you who speak so well. You will not have the courage; his cottage is dirty."

"How easily offended she is to-night," thought Karol. "Who knows what took place between her and that wretch?"

28.

On another occasion Karol was jealous of the priest who came on a charitable errand. Then he was jealous of a beggar whom he took for a gallant in disguise. Next, he was jealous of a servant who being very spoilt like all the rest of the servants in that house spoke with a boldness which struck him as unnatural. Then it was a pedlar, then the doctor, then a big simpleton of a cousin, half townsman, half yokel, who came to bring some game to Lucrezia and to whom she very naturally behaved like a kind of relative instead of sending him to the servants' hall. Matters reached such a stage that she was no longer allowed to glance at the face of a passer-by, comment on the skill of a poacher or the neck and withers of a horse. Karol was even jealous of the children. Did I say even? I should have said especially.

Indeed they were the only rivals he had, the only beings to whom Lucrezia devoted her thoughts as much as she did to him. He was not aware of the feeling he experienced on seeing them devour their mother with caresses. But as, second to the imagination of a religious bigot, there is none more outrageous than that of a jealous person, he soon began to dislike, if not detest the children. He finally noticed that they were spoilt, noisy, headstrong and temperamental and he imagined that no other children were like them. He grew weary of seeing them almost always between their mother and him. He found that she yielded to them too much, that she made herself their slave. On the other hand he was horrified when she punished them.

This system of maternal control, so simple and so clearly indicated by nature, which consists primarily of adoring one's children, being continually occupied with them, giving them everything which can make them happy, yet censuring them and checking them when they go too far, scolding them roundly and even heatedly at times, only to reward them tenderly when they deserve it – all this was the opposite of his way of seeing things. According to him one should not be too familiar with them, for then one would have less difficulty in making oneself feared, if the necessity arose. They should not be caressed and addressed familiarly,* but should be held at a distance and young though they are be made into little men and little women who are very good, very polite, very dutiful and very calm in temperament. Quite early in life they should be taught many things which they are unable to believe or understand at the time, in order to accustom them to respect established rule, usage and religion without questioning the utility and excellence of the principles of which these practices and rules are nothing but the consequence. Finally, one must forget that they are children, one must deprive them of the charm, pleasures and freedom of this early existence which is theirs by divine right, make their memories work in order to stretch their imaginations, develop the habit of form, and delay the explanation of the substance; in a word do the exact opposite of what Lucrezia did or planned to do.

In all fairness it must be said that this mania for contradicting and this wearisome fault-finding, were not continual and absolute with him. When jealousy was not possessing him, that is in his lucid moments, he said and thought entirely the contrary. He adored the children and he admired them in all things – even when there was nothing to admire. He spoiled them more than did Lucrezia and made himself their slave without the slightest idea of his own inconsistency. It was because at that time he was happy and showed the angelic and ideal side of his nature. The outbursts of rapture which punctuated his love for Lucrezia were the thermometer which indicated the highest point of his

---

*i.e. use "tu" when speaking to them. [Translator's note].

sweetness, goodness and tenderness. What a seraph, what an archangel he would have been had he been able to remain so always! During such moments which could last at times for hours and even whole days he was the embodiment of kindliness, mercy and devotion to all beings who approached him. He stepped off the path so as not to tread on an insect; he would have thrown himself into the lake to save the house dog. He would have transformed himself into the dog if only to hear the shrieks of laughter of little Salvator; he would have changed into a hare or a partridge to give Celio the pleasure of shooting at him. His tenderness and effusiveness were so great as to be excessive and even absurd. At such times he became one of those sublime ecstatics who must be locked away as madmen or adored as gods.

But then what a fall, what an appalling cataclysm throughout his whole being when the outburst of joy and tenderness was followed by one of pain, suspicion and resentment! Now the whole of nature changed its face. The sunshine of Iseo was armed with poisoned arrows, the mist on the lake was pestilential, the divine Lucrezia was a Pasiphae, the children little monsters; Celio would end up on the scaffold, Laertes had rabies, Salvator Albani was the traitor Iago and old Menapace was Shylock the Jew. Dark clouds piled up on the horizon, full of Vandonis, Boccaferris, Mangiafocos, rivals disguised as beggars, travelling salesmen, priests, lackeys, pedlars and monks, these clouds then burst and showered on to the villa a host of former friends and former lovers (for him they both belonged to the same race of vipers) and Madame Floriani, sullied with hideous embraces, beckoned him with infernal laughter to witness this fantastic orgy!

Please do not believe that his imagination, deprived as it was of all restraint and continually excited by his natural disposition and mad passion, did not reach the extravagance of the above picture. It would be impossible for me to follow his imagination and make *you* follow it in all the frenzied storms it traversed. Never did Dante dream of tortures similar to those which this hapless being created for himself. They were serious because they were so absurd, and no matter how

212 / Lucrezia Floriani

grotesque the apparition, it still terrifies children, the sick and those who are jealous.

But as he was above all polite and reserved no one ever had the slightest suspicion of what was happening inside him. The more exasperated he was the colder he appeared and one could only judge of the degree of his fury by that of his icy courtesy. It was then that he was truly intolerable because he insisted on arguing and submitting the realities of life, of which he knew nothing, to principles which he could not define. And then he brought wit into play, false, brittle wit, in order to torture those whom he loved. He was bantering, artificial, precious, utterly disgusted with everything. He seemed to be biting very gently, for sheer pleasure, and the wound he was making went deeper and deeper into one's soul. Alternatively, if he had not the courage to contradict and mock, he withdrew into a scornful silence, a fit of sulks which rent his victim's heart. Everything seemed alien and indifferent to him. He stood aside from all things, all people, all opinions and all ideas. The words he used were "I don't understand that" and when he gave this reply to the kindly conversational attempts to distract him, one could be sure that he thoroughly despised everything one had said and one could possibly say.

Lucrezia was afraid that her family and Count Albani might happen to sense this jealousy which she herself had at last guessed at and by which she felt mortally humiliated. She therefore carefully concealed its wretched cause and strove to minimise its deplorable effects. At the beginning she had worried greatly about Karol's health and life, but later she was able to verify that he never felt better in health than he did when he had given way to an inner agitation and an anger which would have killed anyone else. There are constitutions which draw on their sufferings alone for their strength and seem to be renewed by consuming themselves, like the phoenix. So her alarm was abated, but she began to suffer strangely from an intimacy which can only be compared with the inferno of the poets. In the hands of this terrible lover she had become the rock which Sisyphus rolls endlessly to the top of the mountain and lets fall into the depths of the abyss; a miserable rock which never shatters.

She tried everything: gentleness, anger, prayers, silence, reproaches. Everything failed. If she pretended to be calm and gay so as to prevent others from penetrating her unhappiness, the prince, utterly ignorant of that kind of strength of will which he did not possess, was irritated to see her brave and magnanimous. At such moments he hated what he mentally called her fund of bohemian casualness, a certain toughness due to her common stock. Far from feeling any alarm for the hurt he was inflicting on her, he told himself that she felt nothing, that out of kindness she had certain moments of solicitude, but that in general nothing could touch a nature so resistant, so robust and so easy to distract and console. It seemed that at such times he was even jealous of her health which was apparently so excellent and he reproached God for the calmness with which He had endowed her. If she smelled a flower, picked up a pebble, caught a butterfly for Celio's collection, taught Beatrice a fable, stroked the dog or plucked a fruit for little Salvator, he would say to himself "What an astonishing nature! Everything pleases her, everything amuses her, everything enraptures her. She finds beauty, perfume, grace, utility and pleasure in the smallest details of creation. She admires everything, she loves everything! Therefore she does not love me, for I admire, cherish and understand nothing but her in the whole world! An abyss separates us."

This was fundamentally true: a nature which is rich through exuberance and one which is rich through exclusiveness cannot fuse. One of the two must consume the other and leave nothing but its ashes. And this is what happened.

If by chance Lucrezia, overcome with fatigue and sorrow, did not succeed in hiding her sufferings, Karol, seized by a sudden return of his old tenderness for her forgot his ill humour and became excessively anxious. He ministered to her on his knees, he adored her at such times even more than he had done at the height of their love. Why could she not have pretended all the time or allow her courage and strength to collapse completely? If she had always appeared before him downcast and listless or if she had been able to assume a perpetual air of gloom and dissatisfaction she might have cured him of his morbid temperament. For her sake, he would have forgotten himself, for this fierce egoist was the most devoted and tender of men when he saw a friend suffer. But as in such a situation he himself also suffered deeply and sincerely, Lucrezia in her nobility blushed at having yielded to momentary weakness. She hastened to shake off her languor and appear calm and strong once more. As for pretending to resentment, she was utterly incapable of it. She rarely felt angry with him, but when she was angry she did not restrain herself but rebuked him violently. She had never disguised anything, never pretended, and as most often she only felt sorrow and compassion when she was the victim of the injustice of others, she also usually suffered without being angry and above all without sulking. She despised such feminine wiles and, in her own interests, she was wrong to do so. She was given plenty of proof of it! There is something in human nature which makes one continually abuse and offend when one is always sure to be forgiven, even when one has not the grace to apologise.

Salvator Albani had always known that his friend was inconsistent and temperamental, both excessively demanding and excessively unselfish, but in the old days the good moods used to be the most frequent and the most durable. Now on the contrary since his return to the Villa Floriani, Salvator saw the prince lose more and more of his hours of serenity each day and sink into a habit of strange sullenness; his character was becoming visibly more bitter. At the beginning it was one bad hour a week, then one bad hour a day. Gradually he had only one good hour a day and finally one good hour a week. However tolerant and good-humoured the count was, he ultimately found Karol's behaviour intolerable. He said so first to his friend, then to Lucrezia, then to both of them together. Finally he felt that his own character would become bitter and deteriorate if he persisted in living in their company.

He resolved to leave them both. Lucrezia was aghast at the idea of remaining alone with this lover whom two months earlier, she would have liked to carry off to the ends of the earth and live with him in the desert. By his sweet gaiety, his bright, philosophical way of looking at all domestic troubles, Salvator was of immense help to her. His presence still restrained the prince and compelled him to discipline himself, at least in front of the children. What was to become of her? Above all, what was to become of Karol when their good companion would no longer be there between them to preserve them from one another?

As she implored him not to go, her panic and her grief betrayed themselves; her secret escaped from her lips and she burst into tears. Dismayed, Albani saw that she was deeply unhappy and that if he did not succeed in taking Karol away with him, at least for some time, she and he were doomed.

This time he no longer hesitated. He felt neither pity nor weakness for his friend. He spared none of Karol's susceptibilities. He braved his wrath and his despair. He did not conceal from him his intention to do his very utmost to detach Lucrezia from him if he did not do so himself by leaving her. "Whether it is for six months or forever is immaterial," he told him as he concluded his harsh exhortation. "I cannot foretell the future, I do not know whether you will forget Madame Floriani, which would be very fortunate for you, or whether she will be unfaithful to you, which would be very sensible of her. But I know that now she is broken, ill and desperate and she needs rest. She has four children. It is her duty as a mother to preserve herself for them and to rid herself of intolerable suffering. You and I will leave together or fight, for I see quite clearly that the more I warn you, the more you shut your eyes, and the more I wish to drag you away, the more you cling to this poor woman. Whether through persuasion or force I shall take you with me, Karol. I have vowed it solemnly on the heads of Celio and his brother. It is I who brought you here, it is I who made you stay here. I ruined you when I thought I was saving you. But there is still a remedy and now that I see things clearly I shall save you despite yourself. We are leaving to-night, do you hear? The horses are at the gate."

Karol was deathly pale. He had great difficulty in unclenching his teeth. At last he uttered this laconic and decisive reply:

"Very well. You will take me to Venice and you will leave me there and return to receive the prize for your exploit. This was arranged between you two. I have been waiting for this dénouement for a long time."

"Karol," cried Salvator, swept by the first real fury he had ever experienced in his life, "you are indeed fortunate to be weak, for if you were a man I would crush you with my fist. But I tell you that this thought is characteristic of an evil being and such words belong to a cowardly, ungrateful person. You fill me with horror and from this moment I abjure all the friendship I have had for you so long. Farewell, henceforth I shun you. I never wish to see you again, for I would become a coward and wretch like you."

"Good," retorted the prince who having reached the highest pitch of fury was correspondingly bitter, cold and contemptuous. "Go on, insult me, strike me, let us fight so that I may die or depart. That is the plan, I know it. How sweet the night of pleasure will be when you will be rewarded for your chivalrous conduct."

For one moment Salvator was on the point of flinging himself at Karol. He seized a chair in both hands, uncertain as to what he would do. He felt he was going mad, he trembled like an hysterical woman, yet he knew that at that instant he would have had the strength to bring the house down on his own head.

For one moment there was a horrible silence during which one could hear rising in the calm evening air the sweet voice of a child saying: "Listen, Mother, I know my French lesson and I am going to tell it you before I go to sleep:

"Deux coqs vivaient en paix, une poule survint,
Et voilà la guerre allumée!
Amour, tu perdis Troie!"

The window was closed and Stella's voice was lost. Salvator gave a bitter laugh, broke the chair as he set it down again and rushed out of Karol's room, slamming the door behind him.

He went and knocked at Lucrezia's room and said to her, "Lucrezia, leave your children for a while. Call the maid. I wish to speak to you immediately."

He took her far into the park. "Listen," he began, "Karol is either vile or ill-starred, the most cowardly or the most insane of your lovers, but what is certain is that he is the most dangerous of them and the one who will kill you with pin pricks if you do not leave him at once. He is jealous of everything, he is jealous of his own shadow. It is a disease. But he is jealous of me and that is infamy. He will never make up his mind to leave you. He does not wish to depart, nor will he. It is for you to flee from your own house. There is not a moment to lose. Jump into a boat. Catch the next stage coach, go to Rome, Milan, the end of the world – or hide, hide in some cottage. Perhaps I am raving. I am so furious I cannot think clearly, but we must find a way . . . I have it. It is painful but certain. Let us fly together. We would only go two leagues from here and we would only stay two hours. That will be enough. He will think that he guessed correctly, that I am your lover. He is proud, and will accept the inevitable without hesitation. And you will be free of him forever."

"You are insane yourself, my poor friend," replied Lucrezia, "or else you wish him to go insane. And as for me, it is enough for me to suffer because he is suspicious of me. I shall not bring myself to become the object of his scorn."

"Unhappy woman, don't you see that to be suspected is the same as being scorned! Do you still value the esteem of a man whom you can no longer take seriously? What madness! Come, go with me. What do you fear? That I should take advantage of your prostration and against your wishes justify the charming opinion Karol has of my character? I am no coward and if you require further reassurance allow me to tell you that I am no longer in love with you. No, no, Heaven preserve me from it! You are too weak, too gullible, too absurd. You are not the strong woman I once believed you to be; you are nothing but a child without brains or pride. I swear to you that your passion for Karol has cured me completely of the love I might have conceived for you. Come, time presses. If at this moment he came to implore you, you would open your arms to him and you would vow never to leave him. I know you. Let us fly then. Let us save him and let us transform his phantom into a reality. Let him believe that you are a liar and a wanton. Let him hate you and leave you with a curse, shaking the dust of this place off his feet. What do you fear? The opinion of a madman? He will not indict you before the court of the world:

he will maintain eternal silence about his disaster. Moreover if you wish, you will justify yourself later. But now we must cut the disease off at its root. We must fly."

"You forget only one thing, Salvator," replied Lucrezia, "and that is whether he is guilty or unfortunate, I love him now and always. I would give my blood to relieve his suffering, yet you think that I could rend his heart in order to regain my peace. That would indeed be a strange method!"

"In that case you too are a coward," cried the count, "and I abandon you. Remember what I tell you here. You are lost."

"I know that," she replied. "But before you leave you will make your peace with him!"

"Don't drive me to it! I am capable of killing him. I am leaving immediately. That is safest. Farewell, Lucrezia!"

"Farewell, Salvator," she said to him and flung herself into his arms. "We may never meet again!"

She burst into tears but she let him depart.

29.

The day following Salvator's departure Lucrezia left the house before the prince had come from his room. She had thrown herself into a boat and recovering the vigour of her youth she made her own way to the other side of the lake. Opposite the villa, on the far bank, there was a little wood of olive trees which brought back to her memories of love and youth. It was there that fifteen years earlier she had often met her first lover, Memmo Ranieri. It was there that she told him for the first time that she loved him and it was there that she had later planned her flight with him. It was there too that she had hidden so often to avoid her father's watchful eye or the attentions of Mangiafoco.

Since her return she had never wished to go back to this grove which her first lover in his youthful enthusiasm had called her *sacred wood*. One could see it from the window of the villa. At times in the early days of her return Lucrezia's eyes had rested on it inadvertently; but not wishing to awaken her own memories she had looked away as soon as she became aware of her thoughts. Since she had loved Karol she had often looked at the wood and admired the way the trees had grown and had never even thought of Memmo and the ecstasy of her first love. Yet, out of instinctive delicacy, she had never directed her new lover's walks here.

When she had left the house a few hours after Albani's departure and had ventured blindly on to the lake she had not conceived the plan of going to visit the *sacred wood*. She was in pain, she was feverish, and she felt the need to be steeped in the morning air and restore her faltering soul by physical movement. It was an instinct unreasoned but irresistible which drove her to send her skiff gliding into that sheltered little creek. She left it there among the undergrowth and jumping on to the bank she plunged into the mysterious depths of the wood.

The olive trees had grown tall, the brambles had spread, the paths were narrower and darker than in the past. Several of them had become overgrown with vegetation. Lucrezia had difficulty in finding her bearings and striking the paths where once she could have walked blindfold. For long she sought a stout tree under which her lover often met her and which still bore her initials carved by him with a knife. The letters were very difficult to recognise and she guessed rather than read them. At last she sat down on the grass at the foot of this tree and sank into thought. In her mind she repeated the story of her first passion in all its details and compared them with those of her latest love, not to establish a parallel between two men whom it would never have occurred to her to judge dispassionately, but to ask her heart what passion it could still feel and what suffering it could still endure. Very slowly, coherently and lucidly she unfolded for herself the whole story of her life, all her efforts at devotion, all her dreams of happiness, all her disappointments and all her bitterness. This recital of her own existence terrified her and she wondered if it was indeed she who could have deceived herself so many times and realised it without dying or going mad.

There are few moments in life when a woman of such a character is able to see so clearly into herself and estimate herself honestly.

People without egoism and pride do not have a very clear vision of themselves. Because they are capable of everything they do not know precisely of what they are capable. Always full of love for others and constantly concerned to serve their well-being, they end by not merely forgetting but not knowing themselves. Lucrezia had had occasion to examine and define herself less than three times in her life, but never had she done so as completely as now and with such absolute certainty. This too was the last time she did so, for all the remainder of her life was the foreseen and accepted consequence of what she was able to verify at this solemn moment.

"Let us see," she said to herself. "Is my latest love as passionate as the first? It was more so once, but it no longer is. Karol has destroyed the illusions of happiness almost as quickly as Memmo did.

"But is this latest love which is now hopeless, any less profound and less durable? For me it is still so tender, so devoted and so maternal that it is impossible for me to see it end and it is in this that it differs from the first love. For I told myself then that if Memmo deceived me I would stop loving him, whereas to-day I feel disillusioned and yet I cannot convince myself that I shall ever be able to recover from this love. It is true that I forgave Memmo much and for a long time, but each time I was aware of a perceptible diminution in my affection, whereas to-day the affection persists and is not diminished by reason of my suffering.

"How does that happen? Was it Memmo's or my fault if, being younger and stronger then, I broke away from him more easily than I can do to-day from Karol? Perhaps it was partly Memmo's fault, but I think it was more mine.

"It was above all the fault of youth. At that time our love was bound within us to a desire and need for happiness. I thought myself blindly devoted and in my every action I sacrificed myself, but if my love did not refuse to make such excessive and too often repeated sacrifices, it must be because, without my knowledge, I had a resourceful personality. Isn't that one of the facts and rights of youth? Of course it aspires to happiness, it feels that it has the strength to go in search of it and believes it will have sufficient to retain it. It would not be the age of energy, restlessness and great effort if it were not driven by the ambition to win great victories and the appetite for great happiness.

"What remains to me to-day from my successive illusions? The certainty that they could not and were not to be fulfilled. Such is reason, the sad triumph of experience! But as it is no easier to drive reason out when it comes to dwell in us than it is to summon it when we are not strong enough to receive it, it would perhaps be futile and wrong to curse its cold benefit and harsh council. Come, the day is at hand when I salute you and accept you, oh wisdom without pity, judgement without appeal!

"What do you want with me? Speak, clarify. Must I forgo love? Here you send me back to my instinct: am I still capable of love? Yes, more than ever, since it is the essence of my life and I feel that I live intensely through pain; if I could no longer love, I could no longer suffer. I do suffer, therefore I love and exist.

"Well then, what must I renounce? The hope of happiness? Probably. It seems to me that I can no longer hope. And yet hope is desire, and not to desire happiness is contrary to the instincts and rights of humanity. Reason cannot prescribe anything which is outside the laws of nature."

At this point Lucrezia was at a loss. For a long time she mused, straying into apparent digressions and memories which seemed to have nothing in common with her arduous investigation. But to upright and candid souls everything acts as a clue. She found herself back in the centre of the maze and thus resumed her argument. Let the reader be patient; if he is still young the argument may be of use applied to himself.

"The fact is," she thought, "that one would have to define happiness. There are several kinds, one for each age. Childhood thinks only of itself, youth thinks of completing itself by a being associated with its own joys; maturity must realise that whether well or badly lived its personal life will sooner or later end and it must think exclusively of the happiness of others. I had said this before I had reached that age, I had felt it, but not as completely as I can and must believe and feel it to-day. I will no longer derive my happiness from the satisfactions which will have myself as object. Do I love my children because of the pleasure I have in seeing them and caressing them? Does my love for them diminish when they hurt me? It's when I see them happy that I am happy myself... No indeed. At a certain age there is no other happiness save that which one gives. To seek any other kind is madness. It is attempting to violate the divine law which no longer allows us to triumph through beauty, charm and innocence.

"I shall therefore try more than ever to make those I love happy without worrying or even concerning myself with the suffering they will cause me. By this resolution I shall obey the need for loving which I still experience and the instincts of happiness which I can still satisfy. I shall no longer ask for the ideal on earth, for trust and passion from love, for justice and reason from human nature. I shall accept errors and faults, no longer in the hope of correcting them and rejoicing in my victory, but with the desire of reducing them and through my affection making up for the harm they do to others. This will be the logical conclusion of the whole of my life. At last I have disentangled this clear solution from the cloud of confusion in which I sought it."

Before leaving the olive grove Lucrezia mused again in order to rest a while after thinking. She saw before her mind's eye the recent illusion of her happiness with Karol and the happiness she thought she could give him. She told herself that she was wrong to have cherished such a beautiful dream after so many disappointments and mistakes and she asked herself if she should humiliate herself before God for it or complain to Him for submitting her to so fiery an ordeal.

This short phase of her last intoxication had been so vivid, so sweet! It was the purest, the most perfect, and it was already ended for ever! She felt sure that it would be useless to try and find a similar one with another lover because there was not a second nature on earth which was as exclusive and passionate as Karol's, a soul as rich in outbursts of emotion, or as strong in ecstasy and adoration.

"Well, isn't he the same still?" she said to herself. "When the demon which torments him is asleep doesn't he again become as he was once? Doesn't it seem, on the contrary, that he is more ardent and more intoxicated than in the early days? Why should I not grow accustomed to suffering days and weeks and then forget everything in those hours of divine rapture?"

But then she was halted in her fancy by the fatal light which had been kindled in her. She felt that her mind, which was fairer and more logical than Karol's, had not the faculty to forget its own anguish in the space of a single moment. As she lay in his arms, remembering the insult which his jealousy had just inflicted on her, she could not understand the strange and terrible gift which some people have of despising what they adore and adoring what they despise. She could no longer believe in happiness, she no longer felt it. She had lost the power of feeling it.

"Oh God," she cried in her heart, "forgive me for expressing one last regret for the perfect joy You allowed me to know so late and which You have withdrawn from me so quickly! I shall not blaspheme against Your kindness, I shall not say that You made game of me. You wished to shatter my reason, I did not defend myself. As always I yielded naïvely to rapture and now, in my distress, I do not forget that this madness was happiness. Blessed be the name of God then, and with Him the hand which caresses and strikes down."

Then Lucrezia was seized with immense grief as she bade an eternal farewell to her dear illusions. She fell to the ground and writhed there, her eyes brimming with tears. Stifled cries oppressed her heart and she sobbed aloud. She wished to give vent to a weakness which she felt must be her last and to tears which would never flow again.

When she was calmed by overwhelming fatigue she said farewell to the old olive tree, the witness of her first joys and her last struggles. She left the wood and never returned there, but it was her constant wish that she should utter her last breath beneath its guardian shade; and every time she felt herself weakening, she looked at the *sacred wood* from the windows of her villa, thinking of the cup of bitterness she had drained there and finding in the memory of this last crisis an instinctive strength which would defend her from both hope and despair.

30.

And now I have reached the goal which I had intended and the rest will be no more than a kindly act on my part for the benefit of those who insist on some dénouement or other.

The sensible reader will, I am sure, be of my opinion and find dénouements quite unnecessary. If I could follow my own convictions and fancy, no novel would come to a definite end, because then it would resemble real life more closely. For what love between a man and a woman ever stopped with absolute finality through a parting or a prosaic union, through infidelity or the sacrament? What events are there which fix our existence in never changing conditions? I agree that there is nothing prettier imaginable than the ancient concluding formula "And they lived happily ever after." That was said in prehistoric literature, in fabled times – happy times, if one believed in such innocent lies.

But nowadays we no longer believe in anything and we laugh when we read this charming refrain.

A novel is never anything but an episode in life. I have just related to you events which offer unity of time and place in the loves of the Prince de Roswald and the actress Lucrezia Floriani. Now, do you wish to know the rest? Couldn't you tell it me yourselves? Can't you see even better than I can where the characters of my protagonists are leading? Are you anxious to know the facts?

If you insist on it I shall not take long and I shall cause you no surprise, since I have always promised not to. They loved each other a long time and lived very unhappily ever after. Their love was a desperate struggle as to which would consume the other. The only difference between them was that Lucrezia would have liked to modify the character and calm the spirit of Karol so as to make him as happy as anyone else, whereas he would have wished to recreate the being he adored in order to assimilate her to himself so that she should enjoy with him an impossible happiness.

To be sure, if one wished to follow and analyse everything, it would require ten more volumes, one for every year they endured attached to the same chains. These ten volumes could be instructive but would risk becoming even more monotonous than this one. In short, Lucrezia suffered all the injustices of her lover with unbelievable perseverance, and Karol failed to recognise the devotion of his mistress with incredible obstinacy. Nothing could cure him of his jealousy, because it was not in the nature of his passion to enlighten itself and grow mellow. Never was a woman more ardently loved and at the same time more slandered and vilified in the heart of her lover.

She had always asked God to make her meet a soul exclusively devoted to love, like hers was. Her wish was only too well fulfilled; Karol's love poured over her inexhaustible torrents of love and gall.

What Salvator had predicted for them came true in certain respects. The world discovered Madame Floriani's retreat and came to greet her there. Her former friends came flocking to her; there were all kinds of them. Boccaferri had his turn and, incidentally, it turned out that Boccaferri was seventy years old. None of them gave the slightest cause for jealousy to Karol, yet all were the object of his mortal jealousy and his irreconcilable aversion. Lucrezia fought bravely to preserve the dignity of those who deserved her consideration; some, with a laugh, she abandoned to Karol's lashing tongue and others she avoided as best she could. However she did not wish to be cowardly and, in order to humour him, drove away unhappy beings who were worthy of interest or pity. He regarded such things as unpardonable crimes on her part and ten years later when their names came back in conversation he exclaimed with a conviction which would have been comical if it had not been deplorable: "I'll never forget the harm that that man did me!" And all the harm he had done was not to have been shown the door by Lucrezia.

She tried to distract him, make him travel, even leave him for a few brief hours in the year. He trailed his jealousy everywhere, he loathed postilions and innkeepers and never slept a wink when he was travelling for fear that someone was forever about to steal his treasure from him. He threw money about in handfuls, but in love he was miserly to the point of madness. When he was away from Lucrezia for some weeks, devoured by anxiety he fell ill because he did not wish to confide it to anyone and was unable to make its bitterness fall on the one who was innocently causing it. She was compelled to call him back. He regained his health and life as soon as he could make her suffer.

He loved her so much, he was so faithful, so absorbed, so fettered, enchained, he spoke of her with so much respect that it would have been a glory for a vain woman. But Lucrezia did not hate anyone sufficiently to wish him or her that kind of happiness.

He ended by triumphing, as always happens to a will bent on a single goal. He brought Lucrezia back to the villa which was still the most secluded place they could find and there he succeeded in isolating her so effectively that people thought she was dead long before she actually was.

She was extinguished like a flame deprived of air. Her torture was slow and without respite. It requires years to destroy with pinpricks a being physically and morally robust. She grew accustomed to everything. No one knew better than she how to renounce the satisfactions of life. She always yielded, even while she appeared to be defending herself; the only thing she would have resisted was caprices which would have made her children unhappy. But Karol, in spite of what he suffered from this division of affection never tried to alienate them for a single moment from their mother. He employed all the self-control he possessed never to let them see that she was the victim and that he assumed over her the right of absolute ownership.

The play was so well acted and Lucrezia was so calm and resigned that nobody suspected her unhappiness. The children had ultimately learned to love the prince, that is, all except Celio, who was polite to him, but avoided speech with him.

Lucrezia, thus reduced to solitary confinement, did not regret the world and her friends. She had left them once to please herself and now she was leaving them again to please another, but still without bitterness. She loved retreat, hard work and country life, devoted herself exclusively to the education of her children and taught Celio dramatic art for which he showed a passionate vocation.

But Karol, finally deprived of subjects for jealousy, now turned his attack to Lucrezia's ideas, studies and opinions.

He persecuted her politely and gracefully in all things; he did not share her taste or opinion on any subject. Inaction devoured him. Having dedicated all his will power and every moment of his existence to the possession of one woman, he was morally the most ruthless despot, just as physically he was the most vigilant jailer. Poor Lucrezia saw her last consolation poisoned when the spirit of contradiction and the bitterness of childish, irritating controversy pursued her into the purest and most innocent sanctuary of her life.

"She was wrong to consent that Celio should be an actor, it was an infamous occupation. She was wrong to teach Beatrice singing and Stella painting; women should not be too artistic. She was wrong to let old Menapace amass money..." In short, she was wrong not to oppose the vocation and instincts of all her family – not to mention that she was wrong to love animals, be fond of scabious, prefer blue to white, etc, etc; whatever she did she was always wrong.

And suddenly Lucrezia Floriani was forty. She was no longer beautiful. Despite the fact that she was condemned to an inaction which was inimical to her need for activity, she lost her fullness of figure. Her complexion had become sallow and if not for her beautiful eyes, her distinction and grace and her open and frank smile, she would have been painful to behold – she who had been the most beautiful woman in Italy. As for the prince, the older and uglier he made her, the more seductive did he find her and the more dangerous to other men. He was as much in love with her as on the first day; he could not persuade himself that young men would not fall madly in love with her if by some misfortune they set eyes on her.

Lucrezia suddenly felt weary of being overtaken by the sufferings and infirmities of a premature old age without gathering its fruits, without inspiring confidence in her lover, without winning his esteem, without ceasing to be loved by him like a mistress and not as a friend. She sighed as she told herself that she had striven in vain in her youth to inspire love and in her mature age respect. Yet she felt that at these different ages she had deserved what she was looking for. She embraced her children one night and said to them in a tone which startled them in the midst of their habitual serenity: "You are everything to me and if I wish to live a few more years it is for you alone."

Indeed, she no longer loved Karol. He had filled the measure to overflowing, doubtless with a single drop of water, but the cup was brimming over, the vase that is too full and is compressed must break. Lucrezia remained silent even with Salvator who had finally come to see her without however reconciling himself too cordially with the prince. She felt that she was breaking, but she was brave and refused to believe death imminent. She at least wanted to see Stella married and Celio started on his stage career. The day before she died she made the most beautiful plans imaginable for them; but alas! love was her whole life. In ceasing to love she was to cease to live.

In the morning she went to sit in her father's cottage. Celio had accompanied her. She appeared better in health because her face had become fuller. She uttered no complaint for fear of worrying her children. She teased Biffi on his Sunday suit. On hearing the lunch bell she got up. All at once she gave a cry, clutched Celio's shoulder and fell back smiling, on to the same chair where as a little peasant girl she had sat so often with her distaff, spinning flax.

Celio, who by now was twenty-two, had grown into a tall, handsome, strong young man. He lifted his mother in his arms, thinking that she had fainted. In this way he walked towards the park, but as he was about to go through the iron gates he found himself face to face with Karol and Salvator Albani who had just been looking for Lucrezia. Karol did not understand and stood like a statue. But Salvator understood immediately, and coldly, without pity, for he knew that Lucrezia's death was the result of Karol's relentless doing, he said in a low voice, pushing him back: "Run to the other children. Take them away. It would kill them. Their mother is dead."

This last word struck Celio to the heart. He looked at his mother's face and saw that she was indeed dead although her eyes were still open and calm and her mouth was smiling. With the corpse still in his arms he fell in a faint.

Karol saw nothing of what was happening. An hour later he was alone, still standing before the iron gate petrified and dazed. His eyes were staring at a stone which happened to be immediately in front of him and he was reading a verse written on it which time and rain had been unable to erase:

Lasciate ogni speranza, voi ch'entrate!

He re-read it and tried to remember in what circumstances he had already seen it. He had lost the power of feeling any grief.

Did he die or did he go mad? It would be too easy to dispose of him thus; I shall say no more about it ... unless I am minded to start another novel in which Celio, Stella, the two Salvators, Beatrice, Menapace, Biffi, Tealdo Soavi, Vandoni and even Boccaferri will play their parts around Prince Karol. It is quite enough to kill the principal character, without being compelled to reward, punish or sacrifice all the others, one by one.